The Woman Who Always Wore Black

PETER A STANKOVIC

Also by Peter A Stankovic

Murder in Chatswood
www.amazon.com/gp/product/B085HMSJDY

Mail Order Bride
www.amazon.com/gp/product/B07DTXCBHK

The Lost Hours: A Futuristic Thriller
www.amazon.com/gp/product/B075TG7M1W

Stranger
www.amazon.com/gp/product/B01N25RO5I

Crooks and Losers
www.amazon.com/gp/product/B019DIWAIO

Cheaters
www.amazon.com/gp/product/B00RFI6QDK

Lack of Ambition
www.amazon.com/gp/product/B0792NXKQF

The Heirs

ONE:

Friday (January)

I'M GUILTY.

I know that but nobody else does. And I'm not about to tell anyone. After all there is something called self-interest. I hear sirens. I scramble out of my three-bedroom apartment which I share, rather shared, with Adrian and Jeremy. It's my apartment but with two dead bodies sprawled on the floor, I no longer want to be there. Blood is spilled all over the floor and some is spattered up the living room wall. Red on green, not a fashionable colour scheme.

The shock of what I see makes me conjure up weird thoughts. Maybe it's my survival mechanism, thinking such nonsense as colour schemes. Adrian, always cheerful, is now dead with two bullet holes in his stout body, one in his chest and one in his neck. Blood must have gushed out of his chest and neck like a torrent, considering the mess around him. I almost cry at the sight of poor innocent lanky Jeremy, shot in the head, spoiling his pale and slightly freckled face with a vast splash of red, like a rissole with too much ketchup sprayed atop it.

Outside the flat, in the hallway, I stand still, pausing to look about. My neighbour's door is shut. My stomach feels queasy, but I don't have time to feel sick. Nor is this the right time to contemplate what might have happened or why.

I take the staircase. Ground level is seven floors down, but I'm fit. I don't want to risk the elevator in case it gets stuck or I run into a resident. The lifts have also been unreliable of late. They need to be serviced but I can't imagine the scungy building management people doing the right thing. If you want something fixed in this block, one needs to complete a myriad of forms. Again, my mind has wandered. Footsteps from above bring me back to the present.

This is not the time to allow irrelevant matters to intrude. Right now, I need to flee.

On ground level, I look around to assess which of the two exits I should take. A couple using the front entrance have just come in from outside. They look frozen. The woman has arms wrapped around herself and is shivering, despite the multiple layers of clothes she's encased in. The man is wearing a heavy black greatcoat but still appears to be grateful he has entered the warm lobby of the tower.

As I walk towards the front door of the high-rise apartment complex, two uniformed cops are making their way up the stairs outside. I walk out the entrance and survey the falling snow which makes visibility poor. On my way down the icy steps to the footpath, the cops, a man and a woman, pass by me. They don't take any notice of me, probably too intent on checking their steps so they don't slip on the snow covered exterior. I wonder who called them. Perhaps the shots that killed my flatmates were loud, alerting my neighbour, an elderly woman. I don't know, I wasn't there. I didn't kill them, but I feel guilty, nevertheless. As I feel I may have prevented the murders, a fog of sadness envelops me. I advertised for them to share the flat with me and now they are dead.

I walk along the frozen street, trying to remain upright in shoes not designed for this weather. I slip when I cross the street but, luckily, I keep upright.

It's cold. Snow lies on the ground. White mounds of the stuff cover every surface. London rarely gets snow so when it does get a downfall, it's bad for travelling. But on this occasion, with the snowfall extreme, going anywhere is chaotic. The weather over the last week has been horrific. The worst snowfall in anyone's memory. The television news, internet accounts and radio reports all say this particular Arctic blast is serious with people perishing, schools shut, business offices closed and transport a nightmare. It would be great to escape these conditions to warmer climes. No way could I get a flight out, conditions what they are, back to Australia where the temperature usually doesn't include a minus.

I walk on. Vehicular traffic is stalled. Not many pedestrians are about though. It seems people are staying indoors unless they must get somewhere urgently. I have the hood of my jacket over my head. The cold stings my face but I don't mind. It'll keep me focussed. I head into the Underground station. Soon the cops will realise I live in the flat which now has two dead young men in it. If I'd stayed to explain my version of events, I know the police would take me in for questioning. That's an inconvenience I'd like to avoid. I doubt they'd believe what I would tell them, particularly when I don't have an alibi for the last few hours. I had been at the movies and I'd tossed the ticket stub away.

I need to find a place to stay. At this stage I don't know who to contact. Then it dawns on me. A friend not too far away. I'd have to make a call but knowing that my mobile phone could be tracked, I can't afford to use it. I text a message before stomping on the device in the sodden footpath until it smashes. After examining the destruction, I pick the pieces up and discard them in a refuse bin.

I descend the stairs at Camden Town station and catch the tube to Leicester Square. On the tube I get a seat. It's a Friday but not peak hour and I guess tourists are staying in their cosy hotel rooms. Everyone is wrapped up in winter gear, to combat the unusually extreme cold.

As the train slips through the tunnel, I sit and, after a moment, close my eyes. I avoid staring at anyone as nobody, in my experience, is friendly on these rides. I try to work out what has happened to my flatmates, Adrian, and Jeremy.

The three of us are Australians living in London for a few years, at least until today, to get work experience and to travel within Europe from a useful base. I arrived first, almost two years ago, and as a scientist, I managed to obtain a research job in the GlaxoSmithKline headquarters in Brentford, West London. Adrian, an accountant, transferred to London with one of the large accounting firms six months ago. Jeremy, until his untimely demise, was still looking for work, but he arrived merely two months ago. This morning, we were all at home because of the frightful weather conditions. Adrian's employers as well as mine had advised us not to travel due to the freak snow deposits. However, around noon, I did venture out to see a film but then I'm relatively foolish and take risks.

So why were we targeted? I wonder as the tube suddenly comes to a stuttered halt.

The tube stops at Warren Street. I stare at the word Warren. There's something about that word but I can't place it. As the train moves off, I shake my head as the connection eludes me. I watch as a young woman, wrapped up in jumpers and a bulky coat, takes off her gloves so she can text on her phone.

At Leicester Square, I switch to the Piccadilly line and ride the tube west to Gloucester Road. When I emerge from the entrance at Gloucester Road, I see snow everywhere. I pull up my hood, put my hands in my pockets and wander down the road. It's freezing, and I wonder when there'll be a break in the weather. I miss Sydney. Over the past months, I was getting used to the winter darkness and cold of London, but this is ridiculous.

Gloucester Road is an upmarket area. I've been here before but even the snow doesn't hide the apparent wealth of the residents. I hurry past shops and turn into Cromwell Road, checking that I haven't been followed. Apartment blocks line one side of the road and I dash across the street alongside them. Snow is still falling and I'm keen to get inside a warm flat.

I don't have to go far to enter a building where Richard, my best friend, lives. I had texted him to say I needed to see him. As an actor for stage and film, he was glad for some company. I knock on his front door and he opens almost immediately. We shake hands and he ushers me in.

'Nice to see you,' he says.

'Same here,' I say.

'Wicked weather,' he says, 'I'm glad there are no rehearsals on today. What's up?'

As he's an old mate, I grin at him, thinking about how much I ought to disclose. Richard is a lean man with thick brown hair and a prominent full moustache, and he wears a T-shirt and jeans. The central heating is on, full blast. I take my black fleece-lined jacket off but keep the dark sweater on until I've warmed up. Richard takes the jacket and drapes it over a chair. I sit on an armchair in the cosy living room.

Richard and I attended film school together. We became friends during the night course, finding we had similar interests. Since then we've been hanging out every second Friday at a pub up the road. 'I was wondering whether I could sleep on your couch for a few days.'

'What's wrong with your place?'

'My flat is a crime scene.'

'Are you kidding me?' Richard is looking at me to assess whether I'm pulling his leg. His brown eyes hold mine.

'I wish it were a joke,' I say.

'Really, what happened?'

I tell Richard that I arrived home to find my flatmates on the living room floor, shot dead, blood everywhere. The place was in disarray with furniture pushed around, drawers opened, papers scattered. In short, the flat had been turned upside down. He waits until I'd finished my story before talking. Richard, in my experience, is one of those rare people who don't interrupt while somebody else is speaking. Another attribute, on top of his sense of humour, I like about him. I don't tell him that I have wondered whether I was meant to be killed as well because I don't understand what's happened. 'There you have it.' I stand and stretch my arms, starting to feel human again. The cold is disappearing slowly.

'Why do you think your place was targeted?'

'I have a formula for a revolutionary product but to kill innocent people doesn't make sense,' I say.

'Wow. Let me get you a hot drink. You can stay as long as you like. And you can use the second bedroom too. I've broken up with Sharon, so I won't be having anyone over for a while.'

'That's good of you,' I say, relieved he hasn't freaked. 'What happened with Sharon?'

'I think the relationship had run its course. She and I had little to say to each other lately. The sex had also dried up.'

'Well that's a problem. You'll find somebody else, I'm sure,' I say, trying to cheer him up.

'I'm not looking. The single life isn't so bad. Make yourself comfortable.'

I don't respond. It's not like I can give good relationship advice. I sit on a sofa which has seen better times.

He heads for the kitchen while I view the prints of actors and actresses he's hung on the wall. I only recognise Hugh Grant and Glenda Jackson.

'Won't the police find out who you are from your flat, name and work-place and so on?' Richard asks as he returns with two cups of tea.

'They'll find out my name but not where I work. I've not revealed that information to anyone as I work in a special unit doing secret experiments for military purposes.'

'What about your picture?'

'I have no photos of myself at home. And I don't post to social media. They'll only have my name from emails on my laptop, and they'll no doubt ask questions of the landlord.' I could kick myself for forgetting to bring my laptop, but I was too frazzled to retrieve it from under my bed where I'd stored it the night before after use. I don't even know if it's still there.

'Sounds like you're some kind of secret agent.'

I laugh. 'Near enough. May I borrow your phone?'

'Sure.' He hands me his Samsung phone.

I'm grateful Richard has been so accommodating and I don't know when it would be possible to return to my place, if at all. I just hope I haven't put him in danger too. The deaths of Adrian and Jeremy are a mystery. I can't imagine either of them involved in drugs or gun running or anything which would invite a hit. Logically then, I would have been the target, and no doubt because of my formula. But I just can't hide away. I need to act, to plan a strategy. But first I need to cancel some plans.

I call Liz, a woman I've dated twice. We were meant to meet tonight.

'Hi Liz,' I say when she picks up, 'how are you?'

'Cold. I'm at work but we only have a skeleton staff. Anyone living outside inner London were told to stay home. The snow and the freezing conditions have made it impossible for many of them to get in.'

'We were going to go out tonight, if you recall. Should we call it off?' I ask, hoping the icy conditions will make her realise how foolhardy it is to tempt the elements by going outside.

'Oh. I was looking forward to seeing you. Are you sure? The restaurant should be open.'

'Really?' I'm surprised she's so keen. For a start, I've just experienced a devastating shock and my stomach is still churning. But I can't tell her anything about this, so I won't protest. I add, hoping this is a way out, 'You're sure the place will still be operating?'

'I'll check later but it'll be a shame if you can't make it. If there are any changes, I'll let you know.'

'Okay. Can you use this number as I've lost my other phone?'

'No problem. Warren and Anne are going to join us.

Warren! The name rings a bell, but it doesn't mean anything to me. Or does it?

TWO:

Friday

~

ON THE WAY out of Richard's place, later that night, I thank him for giving me a key to the flat. I'd asked him to join Liz and myself at the pub, but he declined, saying he'd rather curl up with a good book. First, he said, he is going to watch the next episode of a detective series on Netflix then pop into bed to read. Outside, the weather has not relented. This year will go down as a horror year, weatherwise. It is worse than ever and I'm still wearing the same clothes I arrived in. Getting ready for the night seemed strange. But I'd taken a shower and Richard let me use his deodorant. I'll have to buy new clothes tomorrow.

Looking out for cops and people who look suspicious, I make my way to the Underground, wondering if the trains are running. The snow has piled up and I imagine it must be like this in Norway or Russia in winter.

Standing on the platform, I worry. Have the police found a photo of me yet? How actively are they searching for me? I keep my hood over my head so that cameras can't pick up my face properly, but I'll have to change my appearance in due course. The tube arrives and I get in. Nobody is paying attention to me. Everyone is too busy rugged up, probably keen to get home after a day at work. When I get inside the tube, this time standing, I contemplate the proposed get together with Liz and her friends. Why is Liz keen to have another couple join us? When we arranged the date a week back, it was supposed to be just the two of us. I guess I'll find out, but it still feels odd. Anne and Warren.

Then it hit me. Warren. Of course. Weeks ago, I had been chatting to Warren about my plan to stop work at GlaxoSmithKline as I'd developed a breakthrough to turn back ageing, working overtime on my own project. It was something I'd started in Sydney, working privately. And I didn't want any large pharmaceutical company to get hold of the formula and restrict marketing the product. Any significantly-sized organisation might realise many of their products would have little value once my invention were approved. After all, if ageing were halted or reversed, imagine all the pills people could stop taking.

Then I recalled that evening more clearly. It was two weeks ago, in a pub somewhere in the West End. Warren was with Anne and I was with Liz. Did I talk too much? Now I can't remember the content of the chat and I wonder whether anyone blabbed to someone who didn't want this discovery to occur. Maybe I was being crazy, but I can't think why else someone would come to my apartment with murder in mind. But my flat had been ransacked when my mates were killed. Was someone already after the recorded formula? Well if they were, it was too bad. I didn't keep it at home. Some of it was written down and kept in a safety deposit box at my London bank and some of it was in my head.

Somehow, I had to get to the bottom of this. Apart from the police searching for me, believing that I was responsible for the deaths of my flatmates, other people might also be after me. To kill me. And I need to find out whether Warren or the two women present that night, Liz and Anne, had somehow, deliberately, or unwittingly, betrayed me.

It's 7:10 p.m. when I enter the Indian restaurant the place is buzzing. Almost full, despite the snow outside. The patrons appear to be young with nobody over forty, as far as I can judge. I'm thirty-nine, probably amongst the oldest diners. The British are a hardy lot though and bleak weather is something they're probably used to. Then I see Liz towards the back of the restaurant and she's chatting with a couple who are, no doubt, Warren and Anne.

When I arrive at the table I smile. 'Hi.'

Liz stands and gives me a peck on the cheek. 'You remember Warren and Anne, don't you?' she says.

I recall that Warren is some kind of broker, but I can't remember what kind. He is broad shouldered, carries weight around his middle and is aged in his mid-thirties to forty, I guess. His thick black hair is swept back, without a part, and with his round shaven face, he looks very much the corporate animal. He looks up and extends his hand. I shake it. He has the pallor of someone who's not seen much sun.

Anne nods hello but doesn't stand. She is slim and dark-haired. Liz on the other hand is blonde and more substantial, curvy, in fact, compared to Anne. I remember when we were last together that Liz was also almost a head taller than Anne who is twig-like, if truth be told. But I have no bias. My girlfriends have come in all shapes and sizes. What's important to me is that I can get along with a woman, both physically and spiritually, someone who has a sense of humour, doesn't take themselves too seriously and likes me.

I sit down next to Liz and ask whether they've ordered food or drink.

'We've arranged for pappadums to come but we were waiting for you before ordering,' Liz explains. 'Would you like some wine? Warren brought a bottle of Chardonnay.'

I nod, and Warren pours some of the 2016 unoaked Chardonnay into a glass. I'm not keen on this type of wine but then I can't complain. I should have brought a bottle of wine myself. Liz hadn't mentioned anything about tonight but then I don't know Liz well and she may have thought it forward to ask me to bring wine.

'Dreadful weather,' says Anne, 'The taxi driver had all sorts of bother getting here.'

I hope the weather isn't going to dominate the conversation. I'm also trying to work out how I might steer the discussion to the previous occasion when we were all together, to find out whether I'd mentioned the anti-ageing work I'd done. And to figure out what I did say, exactly. I hope I hadn't mentioned that I'm rushing to get my drug tested. The University of New South Wales have carried out research and have also come across a discovery which could lead to a revolutionary drug that actually reverses ageing, improves DNA repair, and could help NASA get astronauts to Mars. So, the race is on. This drug, if successful, could be worth billions. But I'm drifting off in my fantasy world and I need to focus on the present.

'How did you get here, Liz?' I ask.

'I came by tube, straight from work,' says Liz. After a moment, she adds, 'Let's look at the menu.'

'I know what I want,' says Warren. 'So, how's work going with you, Ethan?' Warren is looking directly at me.

Was he the person interested in the drug, I wonder? 'Slowly,' I say, 'The company has me working on a new medication for bowel cancer. And you?'

'The markets are haywire currently but I'm getting more clients,' says Warren, looking across at Liz.

'How do you get your clients?' asks Liz.

'Recommendations are the best. But we also use surveys which we've paid for to call likely candidates.' Warren raises his hand to alert a waiter. 'Have you all decided what you want? I'm starving. I've come straight from the office and didn't have lunch.'

A man wearing a turban comes over to take our order. Anne suggests ordering a variety of lamb, seafood and vegetarian dishes to share. Warren agrees and he orders for all of us. I don't like his pushy approach but it's not something I'm going to make a fuss about.

We eat and drink and I'm careful not to drink too much. The conversation is no longer about work and I listen to the other three rather than contributing a lot myself. My mind is still on my murdered flatmates and whether my formula is at the heart of the matter. Finished, I call for the bill and place a credit card in the leather sleeve provided. Liz brings out her purse, but I tell her I'm paying for her. Once the bill has been settled, we agree it's not a night to go to a nightclub. The conditions outside are simply unpleasant.

Outside near the entrance, Liz and I say goodbye to Warren and Anne who wander off, looking for a taxi. The cold is biting, and I put my arm around Liz. 'I can't invite you back,' I say but I don't t explain why. I'm not about to reveal the murders to anyone except Richard. Luckily, there are no photos of me at my flat and all my key documents, like passport and visas, are in the bank's safety deposit box. I want to go to Richard's to figure out how I should go about the next phase of my fugitive existence. But Liz surprises me.

'That's okay. Come to my place,' she says.

'Where's that?' I probably should decline but that doesn't make sense. If I don't go with her now, I'll have to make an arrangement later to be intimate with her and later might be too late. I like her and I don't want to turn down such an invitation, despite my concerns about the police.

'Not far by tube,' she responds.

'Okay,' I say. I'm not too thrilled to go along as I'm still in danger but I need to talk to her about our evening out two weeks ago. The tube is relatively empty when we board, the cold keeping all but the stupid and foolhardy indoors.

We shuffle, more than walk, along the snow-covered road to Liz's flat near the Notting Hill Gate underground. The cold chills my cheeks, so intense is it, and I put my arm around Liz's shoulders, hugging her close. She wears a perfume with a lovely fruity fragrance, but I couldn't name the brand if my life depended on it. At her front door, she shivers while searching for the housekey. We go inside and it's warm, the central heating being on. I guess Liz is not worried about the cost. And who can blame her? But it says something about her character. She's not a cheapskate like Adrian was.

In high heels, Liz comes up to just below my ears in height. However, at the restaurant, Liz switched her six-inch black heels for sneakers, a sensible option travelling in these Artic-like conditions. The more I analyse her, the more I like her. We hadn't been to bed yet and I wonder whether tonight might change that. But I'm not here to enjoy her physical charms, rather to pump her for information. And if this requires making love to her, so be it.

Once she's dumped her handbag onto a table near the entrance and taken off the outer layers of clothes, Liz asks if I'd like a cup of tea.

'Coffee if you have it,' I say. I haven't got to like tea like the English do. To them it seems an obsession.

'Make yourself comfortable,' she says.

Liz's one bedroom flat, a fact she mentioned on the way over, has peach-coloured walls in the living room as well as a white sofa. I walk around to look at the books in the bookcase – mostly romance novels and one autobiography by Sarah Knight called You Do You. I pick up the non-fiction book and read what's below the title which says: "*How to be who you are and to use what you've got to get what you want*". Interesting, I think. Liz may well be ambitious. It's still too early to tell whether this points to her character or whether she's just keen to read the advice.

Instead of sitting down as requested, I wander into the kitchen/dining room. Here the walls and appliances are white which gives the appearance of modernity and sterility. The place looks exceptionally clean. It's also tidy, with no dishes or food standing loose.

'Need some help?' I ask.

'No, silly. I'm quite capable of making tea and coffee. But I appreciate the company. I don't really like living by myself. I've been here nine months now and I still haven't got used to it.'

'Where were you before?'

'At home, with my parents.'

'Where's home?'

'West Acton for the last dozen years and before that, Manchester.'

'Oh,' I say, wondering whether Liz is too young for me. This doesn't bother me, but she might not react well if she knew she was dating a much older man.

'Yes, I know, it's odd for a thirty-year-old woman to be living with her parents. But that's just how life has panned out. Do you know how expensive it is to get a property or even rent a small flat in London?'

'I have some idea,' I say. This reminds me that my landlord will be seeking his usual rental payment at the beginning of next month which is in two weeks' time.

I sit on a stool at the white island in the kitchen. Liz has taken her sneakers off and now wears slip-ons. The sneakers have been put away somewhere because I can't see them. I wonder whether she'll use a hot cloth to wipe me down after we have sex.

Liz finishes making the hot beverages, places cups on the island and sits opposite me. 'We may as well have the drinks here. It'll save messing up the living room.'

This last remark startles me. She is a clean freak. This isn't the most objectionable trait a person can have but I may not be the right person for her. I'm clean but not very tidy, happy to leave clothes lying on chairs or on benches, if I haven't the time to put them away. I change the topic. 'How long have you known Warren?'

'Not long. Anne's my best friend and I only know him through her.'

'Do you like him?' I sip some coffee. It's instant coffee but I don't complain. Whereas Liz has this fascination with tidiness, I'm very particular about my coffee, generally visiting places I know make quality coffee, using premium coffee beans. Much the same as Jerry Seinfeld loves coffee, and cars. His show *"Comedians in cars getting coffee"* I've always found amusing and highly entertaining.

'He's alright. Don't you like him?'

'I don't know the guy. Tonight, was only the second time I've met him. And I don't remember much about the first time. Do you recall that night?'

'Sort of. I think you and Warren had too much to drink. You played some drinking game and Anne and I were sensible enough not to get involved.'

I wonder how much I can learn. This is the conversation I wanted to have. 'What were we talking about? My mind is a blank about that night.'

'Oh, I don't know. Let me think. Drinking, believe it or not. Politics. Work. That's all I remember.'

'Right,' I say.

'You were blotto.' Liz laughed.

'And what did I say about work?'

Liz peers into the distance then closes her eyes.

'Can't recall?' I sip the coffee.

'That's right. Something Anne and I found funny. Anti-ageing.'

THREE:
Saturday

'A NTI-AGEING,' I REPEAT, 'that's an odd topic.' Leaving a little coffee in the cup, I push it away. I'm sure Liz will scrub it thoroughly before she retires to bed.

'Yes. Weird. But I think you started it. You said something like, I'm working on it when Warren said the idea was fanciful.'

'Really. Surely I was kidding.' I say, watching Liz closely. I notice how nicely scrubbed her skin looks. She probably uses lotions and other feminine products to keep her skin glowing and clean. In a way, her fastidiousness with being clean is admirable. "Did I mention I had a formula on the anti-ageing drug?'

'Not that I can recall but then I didn't hear all of the conversation, only bits. I don't know who would take the idea of ageing being controlled seriously.' Liz sips her tea.

'You're right, it's daft. Okay, look, I have to get going,' I say, knowing a little more about that night two weeks ago.

'You're crazy. You can't go home in this weather. Stay here,' Liz says with some intensity.

'Are you sure?'

'Of course. You pop into the shower while I clean up.'

I place my clothes on a chair just outside the ensuite bathroom, hoping this is acceptable. The bathroom is light blue and looks immaculate and I admire the well laid-out towels and the neat arrangement of soaps, toothbrushes and all items in here. I turn on the taps and get the water going to reach a comfortable temperature before I stand under the stream. Just as I step into the shower stall, Liz joins me. She is naked. I have no control of my body and I cannot hide my erection.

Liz does what comes naturally. She applies soap all over my body. I wait, allowing the ritual to play itself out. But before she finishes, I cannot restrain myself, and kiss her. Soon our bodies crush together.

Later, in bed, after the highly erotic cleaning session and very satisfactory sex, I hold her. She has her back to me. As I drift off to sleep, I recall an earlier episode of my life.

It's summer, in Sydney. The day was overcast with the occasional burst of light rain. I'd just graduated from the University of New South Wales and I celebrated with other Science graduates. We're at a popular student pub near the university in Randwick and I met Angela. She gave me her phone number before she headed off home. I stayed at the venue with dozens of students and I got wasted.

Angela and I met up again. And again. We shared a love of film and we had the same sense of dark humour. After twelve months of enjoying life together, our relationship seemed headed for something serious. I had an interesting job, an adequate salary and a woman I loved. Life couldn't have been better. But when I suggested that Angela and I live together, trouble began. She revealed she was ten years older than I was. I dismissed age as a reason to break up. But Angela couldn't get past it. She claimed she could not waste more time having fun. She wants a family. Arguments ensued and we parted.

The next few months were bad. I brooded, became withdrawn. My attitude to everything changed. Performances at work declined. I lost my job. To make ends meet I found uninspiring casual work. I still thought of Angela daily. I drank excessively and avoided social contact. This moping had to stop. It was not good for my health or my future.

One day, I was having coffee at a local café. I picked up a newspaper and read that a scientist was working on a solution to ageing. The article struck me as idiotic. But it changed my life. I became obsessed with the idea and I got back into the workforce to earn money. In my spare time, I built a lab and started to develop a formula for anti-ageing.

Two years later I was in London.

Now, I'm still here in this cold city. When I wake at seven o'clock, I see a naked woman wandering around, opening drawers and taking out clothes. Am I dreaming? I close my eyes and open them again. I'm not dreaming. Then I recall the previous night. It's Liz. 'Good morning,' I say.

Liz comes over. Her massive breasts are hanging free and I touch them. She slaps my hands away then kisses me on the cheek. 'Morning, Ethan. I'm about to make breakfast. You just have time to clean your teeth and have a shower.'

'Right,' I say, watching her get dressed. If we were ever to be in a living-together arrangement, I know I'd certainly always be clean. I do as she tells me and get to the kitchen to find a plate of bacon, eggs, tomato and toast waiting for me. A cup of coffee follows. She sits down opposite me and begins to devour her food.

As much as I would like to spend the day with her, I can't as I need to buy clothes and food as well as go back to my flat. So, I enjoy my breakfast as best I can, given the questions whirring inside my head. Questions about the murders and murderers. Questions about how far the police have progressed and whether I'm being actively sought. After all, my neighbours in the tower block don't know me. I've never even seen them. Breakfast done, I say, 'Thanks for everything, Liz, but I have to go.'

'Sure. I need to buy groceries for the week too. Will you call me?'

'Yes,' I say, not knowing if I'll be around next weekend, or even alive. And if I don't call, she'll put it down to men being unreliable or mean. Besides, she can't call me because I've destroyed my phone. I ask for paper and pen and I jot her number down, saying I've lost my phone.

We kiss goodbye then I hasten to the Underground. The weather has relented somewhat, light snow falling but the air is still chilly, my face the only part of me exposed to the minus degrees' temperature. I'm pleased I bought leather gloves. They save my fingers falling off.

THE MAN IN the black trench coat seems to be taking an interest in me. At least that's what I think. He keeps peering at me and I certainly don't know him. I've walked back to my building and I'm across the road from it. I need to get things from my flat. I realise it's dangerous. There may be police posted outside or even working inside.

The man in the trench coat is just inside the tower. I've been out here in the blistering cold for ten minutes and I need to get inside or keep moving. I walk on, away from the building and pop into a café. I order coffee and find a table at the rear of the large establishment. I watch the door. Nothing happens for a moment and I breathe a sigh of relief. Perhaps I'm being paranoid, scared of shadows.

The coffee is deposited in front of me. As the waitress turns away, I see Trench Coat enter the café. He is tall and well built, around forty years old and he seems to be searching the place. Does he have a weapon? Was he the killer of my flatmates? And he's figured I'm stupid enough to return. I have no weapon, the forks and knives on the table of little practical use against a pistol and a determined assassin. I'm a sitting duck. Will he kill me here, in front of all these witnesses? There is no back exit. Going to the toilet won't help. I'm stuck. I wait. He might try talking. He could threaten me with his gun and insist I go outside. My only strategy then is to toss hot coffee into his face and punch him in the throat. I've seen this done in a film. I'd need to hit the right spot, of course. Probably not viable without some practice. I realise I'm not prepared for anything so dramatic.

He walks towards me and I take a deep breath. I don't want to die. Not right now, anyway. But, surprisingly, Trench Coat takes a seat at a table to my left. He sits down and begins a conversation with the man who was already there.

I finish my coffee and walk past Trench Coat who takes no notice of me. He is busy gasbagging to his mate. Outside I shiver, probably more from fear than the icy conditions. I trudge along snow-laden footpaths to my building. I creep up the stairs, careful to check that nobody else is taking this way to ascend or descend. On the level where my flat resides, I open the fire door carefully, trying not to make any sound. I peer along the hall. There are four flats on this level, two on either side of the hallway. I don't see anyone, cops or otherwise.

There is police tape stretched across my door. I take keys from my pocket and insert the appropriate one into the lock on the door. I turn it and the door opens, pleased the locks haven't been changed. I duck under the tape and enter, closing the door quietly behind me. Then it strikes me that the door is intact. The killers hadn't broken in; they were allowed in. I rack my brain to work out who the guys might have known to allow them entry. Then again, a knock on the door might have been answered. There was no reason for my flatmates to think there was any danger from a visitor to our place.

I see that the mess made by the intruder or intruders has not been cleared. The police and forensics people may have more work to do. I move to my room. I step through the pile of papers, clothes, books and CDs on the floor, making sure I don't disturb things. I grab a carry bag, fill it with clothes and shoes, zip it shut and wander through the rest of the flat to see if there is anything else I need for a short stay elsewhere. Although it would be great if the police caught the actual killers, I'm not optimistic. Life is never that simple.

On my way back to Richard's place, I stop off at my work. In a secret compartment in my desk, there are several experimental anti-ageing pills that I'd developed in my spare time. Most have failed. All except one have been tested on white mice, using a minute portion of powder crushed into their food. There is one untested pill in a pill box. I was going to test this one during the coming week. But I don't have time to worry about that now. I place the pillbox in my case and leave.

I will test this pill on myself. Although it takes a reasonable time to adequately test new drugs, I will take the risk. After all, I'm facing plenty of other risks.

FOUR:
Sunday

~

I WAKE EARLY. THE bed in Richard's spare room was not as comfortable as the one in my flat but, hell, I'm alive and not in custody. What more can I ask for under the circumstances? I haven't taken the pill, the one I'd stored at work, awaiting an opportunity to test it on mice. I ponder the implications of trying it on myself while in the shower.

As people age, their blood vessels lose the capacity to deliver oxygen and nutrients to muscles, resulting in loss of endurance, I'd read in a study of genetics at the Harvard Medical School.

In the report, published recently in the journal Cell, the researchers said mice treated with a naturally occurring compound had shown signs of blood vessel growth. The compound, called nicotinamide mononucleotide, or NMN, strengthens metabolism, cardiovascular functions, and cell maintenance.

The research is part of a fast-growing field of study aimed at finding ways to combat age-related frailty as well as physical and mental diseases.

NMN, according to one expert, could not only restore energy and vitality in humans but also increase their life expectancy and improve health in later years.

This is interesting research, but I'm not interested in increasing lifespan. My efforts are related to reversing the ageing process by attacking cells and making them do more than regenerate. I want to introduce chemicals to the system to effectively re-create a body from any age to a chosen age. Hence, I want my thirty-nine-year-old body to turn into a twenty-six-year-old body. To reduce the age of key cells by a third, I used a technique mutating NMN.

I step out of the shower, use a large brown towel to dry off, thinking of the potential side-effects of my drug. To date, nothing untoward has happened to the mice who digested the crushed pills. Should I take the risk? What have I got to lose?

In the kitchen, I pour water into the kettle and switch the power on. Richard walks in, hair shaggy, expression unreadable.

'Tea?' I ask.

'Coffee's good at this time of day. Why are you up so early?'

'I had too much on my mind and tossed and turned in the early hours,' I say.

'Check the news channel. See if you're wanted,' Richard says.

I do as he suggests, and we sit in front of the television, sipping coffee. There is no further mention of the killings in my tower. But that doesn't mean the cops aren't looking for me. The only time the tragedy made the news was on the morning news after the event.

'Nothing to worry about,' says Richard.

'Should I hand myself in and proclaim my innocence?' I ask. I'd thought of doing this before, but I dismissed the idea, realising I would be held and questioned for the time I should be spending questioning the people I'd spoken with two weeks ago. And I don't want to reveal the anti-ageing business to the police. If I made up a story other than the truth, they'd see through it, I figure.

'I'm suspicious of authority,' says Richard.

'I am too,' I agree, happy with Richard's response.

'Besides, you don't know whether they are looking for you. They may be focussed on forensic evidence left by the real killers.'

~

I WANDER OUTSIDE in the afternoon, having spent time reading the Sunday papers. Snow has stopped falling and it's easier to walk on the footpaths with icy conditions absent. More people are around too, no doubt enjoying the respite in the weather.

I haven't taken the anti-ageing experimental pill yet. It's in my pocket. I'm still tossing up whether testing the substance on a human is wise. And if I'm going to test it on a human, it's only right that I be the guinea pig. Unlike other experiments, my formula also attacks the brain. This is the major divergence from current thinking on anti-ageing which only seeks to alter body chemistry.

Walking down the road, thinking about when I should try the drug, I'm unaware of a vehicle which slides next to me. The next thing I know, a huge man grabs my arms and pulls me into the back of a van. I resist but he's caught me by surprise and the momentum he has plus his power forces me inside. The back door is closed and a few seconds later, the vehicle moves off.

'Hey,' I shout, 'let me out.' I bang on the walls but to no avail. I wonder whether anybody has seen the abduction and whether it will be reported. But I don't hold out much hope. Somebody may have seen the action, but it all happened so quickly that any person seeing it would have difficulty giving descriptions of the people involved. And what would they say? A man was pushed into the back of a van, details of which they probably couldn't describe accurately, then it drove off. It would raise more questions than answers and the police wouldn't be able to follow up. They'd need to wait for a dead body – mine.

I'm doomed. Will they take me somewhere to kill me? Or will these thugs torture me to find out about my formula? I'll find out soon enough. I swallow my pill so that they can't get their hands on it. I figure, like the Elvis Presley song, *"It's now or Never"*.

FIVE:
Sunday

~

WHEN I OPEN my eyes, I'm sitting on a hard chair in a large empty room save for another chair facing me. Nobody is here. I recall the back door of the van opening. Then two men manhandled me, pulling me down and I think I was injected with something. I must have blacked out because whatever happened next escapes me.

My wrists and ankles are restrained, tied to the chair with tough plastic cuffs. What now? Twenty easy questions, I want to ask. I have no option but to wait. Should I simply catch up on sleep or worry about what's in store for me? Remarkably, I feel relaxed and wonder whether the drug has induced this feeling or whether it's the pill I swallowed prior to the injection? There's nothing to look at in this hole. The grey walls are not inspirational. No prints or decorations here.

A door to the room opens suddenly and a barrel-chested bearded man walks in. He is accompanied by a shorter slim man whose face is almost fully covered by a dark beard. Are these the guys who grabbed me off the street? I think not as their physiques are different. But seeing these men as they approach seems like bad news. If they weren't going to kill me, they would use masks, wouldn't they? Now I'm terrified. Sweat pours down my back and my stomach is in knots.

The slim man sits on the seat. Barrel-chest stands beside me. Both men are dressed in black, head to toe. My overcoat is lying on the floor. It's not cold, a small blessing. Slim looks at me, waiting for something. Does he expect me to beg for my life?

'Mr Stone, we can do this the easy way or the hard way. The choice is yours,' says Slim, in an accent I can't place.

I've heard this said numerous times, in film or television, but always in the context of a criminal or cop wanting to extract information from their hapless victim. Maybe Slim watches too many crime shows. 'What do you want?'

'I think you know.'

'I can't read minds,' I say. I want Slim to tell me what he thinks he knows.

A hard slap jolts me. My right cheek stings. I strain against the cuffs, but I can't make them budge. Then comes a punch to my midsection. It feels like my guts are about to explode. I slump forward. The pain is excruciating. Barrel-chest stands rigid. He's probably enjoying this. Just another day at the office for him, no doubt.

'Tell me about the anti-ageing pills,' says Slim.

This is it. What I suspected. What can I say to avoid further punishment? If I share my secret, I'm dead. If I don't, they'll torture me until I spill the information. I can't win. This is not the way I want to die. I need to think fast. 'Okay,' I say, 'I'll tell you. First, can you tell me if you killed my flatmates?'

'We didn't kill anyone. Now talk,' Slim says.

I don't believe him. Not that it matters what I believe. And I have no faith that there is a higher being. Even, if I did believe in something, the consequences here on earth would be the same. 'Okay,' I say. 'It's true that I'm interested in anti-ageing. But I haven't got anywhere with it.'

Slim glares at me. I imagine, underneath the tough guy facade, he's wondering what to say next. After a moment which seems like an eternity, I expect another wallop. But it doesn't come.

Slim stands and he and his colleague walk towards the exit. Before Slim goes through the door, he turns and says, 'You think about it. I know you've done more than you say. When we return, you won't be treated so gently.' He exits the room.

I feel sick. What does he mean? It doesn't matter what he means. There's nothing I can do. Worrying won't help. These might be my last hours on earth. How am I going to spend them? I think about my life, all of my thirty-nine years. What were the highlights? I close my eyes.

My childhood was unspectacular. No firsts, no great sporting achievements. University too was less than exciting, until I met Angela. I can't recall anything else.

I hear a sound. I wake to boots marching towards me. I must have fallen asleep, going over my life which must have been boring, not even able to stay awake, let alone able to focus on a life not fully lived. I blink the sleep away. Then I see something terrifying.

The two men roll in a tray, a tray full of horrible implements. Knives.

SIX:

Sunday

~

SLIM AND BARREL-CHEST stop when they're closer to me. Slim appears stern while Barrel-chest remains casual, as before. Barrel-chest has rolled up his jumper and I can see tattoos creeping up his arms.

'Shit, who are you?' says Slim, his accent either Belgian or French.

"Fuck,' says Barrel-chest, 'He's changed his appearance.'

'Or this is somebody else,' says Slim, 'Someone who's substituted himself for Stone.'

'Not possible,' says Barrel -chest who comes over and hits me in the face with his right fist.

I barely feel the punch. But Barrel-chest's aggression angers me. I pull upwards and to my surprise the tight cuffs snap. I stand and break the ankle shackles. Then staring at the ugly head of Barrel-chest I strike him, my fist connecting solidly with his jaw. He falls like a bag of sand. I look at him and see that he's not moving. I don't think I hit him that hard.

Slim charges off.

I pick up my overcoat, shrug into it, walk over and stop at the tray of knives. I shudder when I see the array of dangerous sharp imple-ments. There are twelve knives, ranging from small to large, all razor sharp. I pick out one and, keeping it ready for battle, walk to the door. I open it and realise the room I had been in is a specially built basement. As I climb stairs to the next level, I come to another door that's locked. Damn. Are men outside, possibly with guns?

I wait and listen. I can't hear anything. I need to take a chance. Perhaps Slim hasn't organised his troops yet and I simply can't delay. I kick at the door and it splinters, the lock destroyed. As I walk out the huge guy who kidnapped me swings a baseball bat at me. I put my arm up defensively and the bat breaks into two. I can't believe it. I hardly feel the blow. I advance to the huge guy and realising I have strength I'd never had before, smash my fist into his side. He doubles up in pain as I hear ribs break. The driver then emerges from another room, fists raised, but when he sees the destruction, he flees, fast. Like he's seen a ghost.

I grab the big guy by the collar, pull him up, and order him to show me the exit. At the door, I push him back inside. I get my bearings then head for a tube station.

When I get back to Richard's place, I go straight to the bathroom. During my journey back from the South-east of London, via tube, I didn't feel the cold as much as when first I left the flat. I peer into the mirror and I'm stunned. I look like I've lost a good decade in age and my face has the kind of definition I've ever seen. Prominent cheek-bones and a firm jawline. The anti-ageing pill must have done the transformation within a relatively short time after I ingested it. Also, I feel fabulous, healthy, and strong, with all niggles I had previously gone. Wow. What have I created? Thinking back to the past hour when I snapped free of my restraints and managed to beat up large brutes, I realise the pill had given me super strength.

How?

Then it occurs to me that the drug had unknown properties, probably because I tinkered with both mind and body chemistry. I wonder if it has any side effects. I'll have to wait. Perhaps the downside will be just as devastating as the miracle I've engineered.

I walk through the flat and find that Richard has gone out. To wipe the sweat and other odours from my body, I take a hot shower, a long hot shower, not only for today but also for the previous day of incarceration. Whilst standing under the powerful stream of water, head back, I consider my next steps.

Dressed in fresh clothes, I call Liz with my new burner phone, one I purchased on the way here. I ask for Warren's phone number, but she doesn't have it. After some chat she gives me Anne's number and says Anne would have it.

~9

I KNOCK ON the door of a flat in a Greenwich apartment block. A brief moment later, the door opens. Anne looks startled. 'My God, you look so different,' she says, 'Young, incredibly young.'

'Do I?' I know I look younger, but I don't think it calls for her stunned expression.

'Come in,' she says walking inside.

'Nice of you to see me, Anne,' I say, following her.

'Please take a seat.'

Her flat is tiny. The kitchen and dining room and living room are all in one area, together. There's a bedroom and bathroom too but nothing else. There is no balcony and there is no view. I sit on the only sofa, a two-seater. Anne asks whether I'd like a drink. I say a coffee would be great. She sits in an armchair across from me, after placing a cup of coffee on the see-through glass coffee table in front of me. She puts her cup of tea on the other side of the table. I feel like I'm a detective, but I don't want to have her think I'm interrogating her.

'Sorry I wasn't around before which is why I texted you my address. I had a medical appointment, so I couldn't talk,' she says, 'but at least you're able to see my little abode.'

Like her flat, Anne is tiny. She's wearing a warm blue top and black leggings. 'Liz asked me to contact you,' I say.

'It must be important,' she says, picking her hot cup up and holding it between her hands.

'If I'm honest, I wanted to talk with Warren, but you told Liz he's abroad. Hence I thought I'd like to get your take on something.'

'Oh, what's that?'

'You remember our meeting at the pub a couple of weeks back?'

'Yes. You and Warren were off your faces.' Anne sips her tea. 'I had to hold Warren up while we waited for a taxi. It would have been funny, but it was absolutely freezing out.'

'And how did I get home?'

'You don't remember? You and Liz walked to the underground. One of the men in the only other group still drinking and kicked out of the pub with us helped you walk; you were so pissed.'

Some images come back to me. Four others were near us, drinking and having a good time. But I don't recall speaking with them.

'Can you remember much of the conversation that night?'

Anne puts her cup back on the coaster. 'Not really. Why? Is it important?'

I don't know how much to reveal to Anne. But then something comes to mind. 'I'm not supposed to talk about the work I do at GlaxoSmithKline and I'm keen to know if I did talk about work.'

'Why? Are you going to get fired?' Anne has a smirk on her face.

'Maybe. I'd just like to know, that's all. Mainly so I can defend myself if anything gets back to the company.' This is highly unlikely, but I want my need for information to seem plausible.

'You and Warren were talking about formulas, that's all I know. Liz and I were tuned out, chatting about other things.'

'I see,' I say. 'That's why I want to talk to Warren. When does he come back?'

'Wednesday, I think. He's gone to Brussels for a conference.'

'He's a broker, isn't he?'

'Yes.'

'What does he broke?' I ask, knowing I'm being silly.

Anne giggles. 'Very funny. He deals in equities and options and commodities, but I must confess, I don't take much notice when he talks about work. It seems boring to me.'

~

'MY GOD,' says Richard when he sees me later that night, 'What happened to you? You look like a twenty-year-old.'

I tell Richard about my adventure with the kidnappers and how I took the experimental pill so that they couldn't find it on me. The thugs hadn't bothered with my wallet.

'The pill certainly worked. And it's the only one you have?'

'Yes. I'll make another batch when I'm back at work tomorrow.'

'And no side effects?'

'Not so far, except for the exceptional strength.'

'That's not a bad thing,' he says, walking into the kitchen. 'Want something to eat?'

'Good idea. I don't want to go out again tonight.'

Richard takes ham, cheese and butter out of the fridge and places the items on a bench. He also puts four pieces of bread into the toaster. 'Grab a plate and help yourself,' he says.

I do as instructed. 'Thanks for this. I'll buy some groceries tomorrow.'

'Now that they know you're staying around here, they might come back with guns,' says Richard, scratching his head, making his unruly hair even more unruly.

'I'll keep a look out,' I say, knowing I should disappear again, but I have nowhere to go. 'If I catch anyone suspicious, with my new strength, I'll beat them to a pulp.' And I don't want to ask Liz because then I'll need to tell somebody else what's happening. Besides, she might freak when she sees me looking so young.

'Are you going to market this?'

'I don't know. I'll have to see what happens over a period of time, perhaps three to six months. Side effects might still arise. And the added strength might be attractive to the wrong type of people.'

'How so?'

'People may use the power to be destructive or hurt others.'

We sit down at the table with our toast and we eat in silence.

Richard makes tea. 'If you want coffee, you know where everything is. I must say I'm tempted to ask for a pill, but I might wait to see how it affects you over the next few weeks.' He grins.

'Thanks mate. I'm the guinea pig, is that it?'

'You got it.'

SEVEN:
Wednesday

~

I WAIT FOR THE next tube. The platform is crowded. People are rugged up with jumpers, coats and overcoats, some with all three on, it appears. I'm wearing new gear, purchased yesterday on my way back to Richard's. My new suit, business shirt and shoes fit perfectly on my six-foot two frame. Although I've still using my well-worn overcoat, I don't seem to feel the cold as I had before having taken the anti-ageing pill. I feel healthy and strong with no obvious adverse effects registering thus far. I've also manufactured a bottle of twenty pills. I did this late on Monday night when everyone had left my department. The bottle is in a drawer in Richard's spare room.

Conscious of being tracked, I observe everyone closely. The police have not shown any signs of being onto me yet, but I expect this to change. For the last two days, I haven't sighted men outside Richard's block of flats. I wonder whether they'd been frightened off by my sudden show of strength. But I won't be complacent. I've taken to wearing glasses and a cap when wandering around and I have these items in place on this occasion, just as I enter the underground.

The tube arrives and people rush the doors. I stroll on but find myself almost carried on by others behind me. Crushed by a sea of people, I hold onto a metal pole as the train rolls forward. I get off at Piccadilly Circus. The snow has disappeared, but it is still very cold, at least judging by the way people move, covered up. I walk to a restaurant, choose a table and settle, placing my briefcase on a seat next to me. I order a hamburger and a beer. Then I call Warren who's still at work in the city so I suggest meeting at a pub in the West End. He agrees.

I'm sitting at the rear of a tourist pub near Piccadilly Circus when Warren enters. He surveys the place, spots me and approaches. He shakes my hand then wriggles out of his overcoat which he places on a spare chair.

'Another lager?' he asks.

'Sure,' I say, 'Make it a half pint, would you?'

Warren returns with my half and his full pint minutes later. He takes up a seat opposite me.

'How was the conference?'

Warren takes a large mouthful of his ale. 'Great. But Brussels was fucking cold, worse than here.'

'I see.'

'You look different,' he says, 'although it's pretty dark in here.'

'Yeah, I've had that reaction from colleagues at work too.' He doesn't know the half of it. People in my department who see me regularly have been shocked and stunned by my new appearance. Some smart-arse types have said I'm not Ethan Stone and demanded proof. Others have just shaken their head. People from other areas in the organisation have done a double take but accepted my appearance, probably figuring they'd been mistaken previously.

'Anne said you visited her and asked about our conversation a couple of weeks ago. Is that why I'm here?'

I sip my second half-pint of lager. 'Yes. I wanted to make sure I didn't say anything out of place.'

'Like how?'

'Work stuff, you know.'

'Nothing comes to mind. Let me think.' Warren pushes his hand through his thick dark hair. 'You did say something about anti-ageing as I recall. I know because I scoffed at the idea and somebody next to us joined our conversation. He seemed pretty interested. But we debated the notion. Don't know that we came to any conclusion though.'

'Have you said anything to anyone else?'

Warren laughs. 'Me. Why would I? Daft idea.' He drank more of his ale.

'Well,' I say, 'you may have said something to someone you met, like a guy who was nuts and thought it was possible to reverse ageing.'

'I can't recall what I said but I tried to tell him it was nonsense.'

'You're probably right.'

Warren gulps the rest of his pint down. 'I needed that. Rough day at work.'

'How so?' I want to get off the topic of anti-ageing and I'm happy to listen to Warren's problems to do so.

'I have this client who's giving me hell because the trades I've put him in are losing money.'

'He must know trading shares or…'

'Options,' Warren corrects me.

I've still got half a glass of lager and I'm wondering whether Warren can wait another ten minutes for my shout. 'He's involved in risky instruments, isn't he?'

'Yes, but he believes we know what's going to happen in the market. We can only be guided by our analysts. Nobody really knows how the market will respond. Any event or announcement can move the market either up or down. But this Stanoski bloke thinks I can manipulate it. Idiot.' Warren peers at his empty glass.

I scoop up his glass. 'Same again?'

As I walk to the bar, I wonder who the hell would have taken an interest in my chat on anti-ageing. And it doesn't seem like Warren is lying. He is far too much ensconced in his broking concerns to worry about something even more dodgy than derivatives trading.

Somehow, I need to find the group of people who were also in the pub at midnight, two and a half weeks ago.

EIGHT:
Thursday/Friday

I REACH THE BAR and squeeze between a dark-skinned man and a bulky woman wearing a green cardigan. As I wait to be served, I hear a chair fall. I turn and witness a woman whose chair has fallen grab the hair of the woman beside her then pull her long straggly grey bits down. They struggle and fall over colliding with a man standing and spilling his drink. The man pushes the fighting women away. This causes the woman's partner to punch the man with the spilled drink. The punched man retaliates by smashing his glass into the puncher's face. Others join in and soon I see a full-scale brawl taking place. People pushing, punching, and kicking. One man tosses a chair at a group. He is then brought down by a rugby tackle from a large bloke. The entire pub, a dimly lit cavernous area, seems to be heaving with moving bodies in mere minutes after the original affray.

I find the scene amusing. I can't understand why people are attracted to fights and what makes them participate, given the slightest provocation. The booze might partly explain it, but I doubt that that's the full story. The sheer aggression repulses me. Since early times, humans have always been involved in battle, I know, from reading history. But, to imagine humans are still acting violently for any reason, almost, suggests to me that true civilisation is still far away.

I stay at the bar, hoping the unruly skirmish will abate soon. Warren has stood up and is watching with fascination. The man beside me leaves to join his friends. Green cardigan woman is still beside me. The bartender has vanished. I hope nobody challenges me or hits me as I might strike back. With my new strength, I could seriously injure someone, and I have no desire to do this.

Before the barroom brawl ends, the police arrive, no doubt curtesy of a call placed by the bartender. God, I'm trapped, I realise. The army of uniformed cops intervene, holding some ruffians who haven't stopped fighting after a warning whistle. They also direct some patrons outside, pushing the more aggressive into a police van. Teams of police then start talking to the innocent bystanders. I can't see an easy way to escape. If I try to leave now, I'll be stopped, and the attempt to go will alert the cops I have something to hide. Will they recognise me, I wonder?

'Name sir,' a short cop asks me. He has snuck up beside me as another cop questions Green Cardigan.

This is the test. Should I lie or tell the truth? I don't see that people have been asked for identification. 'Ethan Stock,' I say which is close enough to Ethan Stone and I could always argue Mr Short Cop misheard if I were called upon to explain the discrepancy.

'Did you see who started the brawl?'

'Not sure,' I say. 'It seemed to have started by people in one of the tables over there.' I point to the area where I had witnessed the first outbreak. Unless somebody died or was seriously injured, I doubt anything other than fines will be used as punishment.

'Can you describe the individuals from that table?'

I'm happy to co-operate as it seems I'm not going to be in custody. 'The lighting's pretty dim so I can't say for sure. But I did see two women pulling each other's hair. Then a guy began punching a man who'd pushed them away. One of the women had long blonde hair and the guy who fisted the other bloke had a bushy beard.'

'Nothing else?' Short cop asks.

'No.'

Short cop moves on. Nobody is drinking. I search for Warren, but he is gone. I leave as well.

~

WALKING DOWN THE corridor, amongst a group of a dozen men, I watch carefully. It's not safe. Suddenly, out of nowhere I'm set upon by four men. Two rush me, knocking me to the ground. Then all four kick me. I curl up into a ball to protect my groin and put my hands over my head, to keep my brain safe. The other prisoners laugh and call me names. They hate that I'm fifty but look as though I'm in my mid-twenties.

An alarm shrieks. I wake to find myself in bed. I silence the phone alarm. As I go about my morning ritual, I wonder whether the nightmare was a side-effect of the drug or whether it was a one off, like any usual nightmare triggered by something deep in the subconscious.

Dressed, I rush off to work. Richard has no work this week so he's sleeping in. It's Friday and the chill in the air hits me. Today I feel the cool air more than in the past few days. I wonder whether the pill is wearing off. Perhaps it's only good for a short time. Will I revert to my older self then? I guess I'll find out.

Before heading into the office, I buy a coffee and a bacon and egg roll at the on-site café. At my desk, I consume breakfast and review the formula which is in my head. I'm no longer comfortable adding further ideas to the notes on the formula I've already recorded. My guess is that there are people desperate to get their hands on my version of an anti-ageing drug. I still must assess its reliability over a period of time longer than a few days. How long is anybody's guess. A week. A month. At the least I need to have the experimental drug in my system for a few months. If I don't, and I try to market it, I might be criminally negligent.

Ralph McPhee approaches. 'Hi Ethan, are you coming to Gary's leaving party?'

I look up. McPhee is around five foot eight and stout with a wispy moustache, one I would have thought his friends would discourage as it doesn't look like it has the energy to grow to be a moustache of substance. 'When is it?'

'Tonight.'

'Sorry, I'm busy,' I say. Although I've had drinks, on rare occasions, with my closest colleagues, I've not socialised much with the bulk of department employees and they'll think me rude for declining the invitation but I need to carry on with my investigation into the deaths of my flat mates.

'Too bad. Your loss,' says McPhee who walks on to the next cubicle.

During the day, I continue with the project I've been assigned, but my mind returns to my precarious situation every few hours. I can't shake the feeling that something dreadful is going to happen. I don't know where the danger will come from. Or how many people are after me. It's hardly a recipe for going to a party to enjoy myself.

Close to five o'clock, Liz calls. I've given her my work number as I want to keep my burner phone available for calls I need to make. 'Hello Ethan, she says, 'I've been waiting for you to call.'

'Sorry,' I say, 'I've been busy, and I may not be able to meet up this weekend.'

'Work?'

'That's right. Let's get together next weekend.'

'Alright but I'll expect you to call me.'

'Of course.' She breaks the connection and I hang up.

~

I'M AT THE pub where I got drunk in the company of Liz, Anne and Warren. My watch tells me it's eight o'clock and I order a lager. No spirits tonight. I take my drink and sit in the corner, away from the majority of Friday night revellers. I'm hoping the environment will bring back images from that previous time. I may see others from that night, but I don't hold out much hope. Being a pub a little out of the way of the tourist area, there may be a few regulars who come in for their usual Friday night drink.

I sit and watch. For thirty or forty minutes, nothing of interest happens. Patrons come in, order drinks, and find a seat or stand near a dart board, watching players compete. There's no one I recognise. I finish my beer. I debate whether I should simply leave and come back tomorrow night, a Saturday. But I order another half-pint of lager.

Halfway through my second drink, I see a familiar body. She's dark-haired with a slim yet curvy figure and from the back, her gait looks exactly like someone I've seen before. She's followed by a man who I think was the same guy who spoke to me that fateful Saturday night. They order their drinks and look around for a spot.

As I consider how I should approach them, I see them threading their way in my direction. Suddenly the woman pokes her partner's arm and he looks towards me. They walk over, smiling.

'Hey,' the man says, 'Ethan, right?'

'That's right. Sorry, I've forgotten your name.'

'Matt. And this is Kate,' he says, 'Where's the gang?'

'I'm by myself tonight.'

'Can we join you?'

'Of course.'

Matt is slim, too, as though he's not had enough to eat. He's wearing black jeans, a blue-collared shirt underneath a leather jacket. He's also carrying an overcoat. 'You look different, somehow. Don't you think, Kate?'

'Yes. Like you're younger. Which is impossible,' Kate says.

I'm glad the lighting is dim in my corner. Still, they can see a change which is disconcerting if I want to play it low-key. 'Trick of the lighting. So, how have you been?'

Matt and Kate make themselves comfortable at the table. Matt's overcoat and Kate's handbag and coat are set beside me. They sit across from me, drinks on coasters in front of them. 'Nice to be here. Our flat is freezing,' Kate says.

'Don't you have central heating?'

'Mine's stuffed,' says Matt.

Kate looks at her partner. 'You did get in touch with the repair man, didn't you?'

'Not yet,' says Matt.

'Jesus,' says Kate, 'you need to be more responsible. Grow up. I can't oversee everything.'

'Don't worry darlin',' Matt says, 'Not your problem. Just look after your own flat.'

I watch the dynamics of this couple and wonder how long they are going to stay together. I see Matt ignore her comments as he takes a long pull of his pint. He looks at me. 'Imagine if that fantasy of being able to get younger were possible, I'd never grow up, would I?' He laughs, slapping his hand on his thigh.

'Did you hear us talking about it?' I ask.

'Well, yeah,' says Matt, 'you guys were pretty loud the other night.'

'That's all it was though, a discussion.' I want to establish whether Matt and his group took it as anything other than a debate.

'I thought it was a hoot,' says Kate, 'So much so that I mentioned it to a friend who believes in science fiction.'

'Who was that?' asks Matt.

'Gina.'

'Who's Gina?'

'You've met her,' Kate explains, 'She's one of my cousins. She's the one who always wears black.'

'Oh yeah, I remember. A real weirdo,' says Matt.

As I listen to this couple bicker and argue, I wonder what the hell I said that night. Surely no one would take me seriously. Was I so confident I told Warren I was developing a solution to ageing? That's not me. I rarely talk about what I'm doing. I usually announce results once everything has proved successful. So why did I spill my guts? More likely, I may have said I was experimenting with mice and to date, nothing has happened and that I didn't expect anything would. After all, I had no idea any formula would actually work. If anything, I had some concept of how body chemistry would react under different conditions with the introduction of other chemicals. 'Would this cousin take whatever you said seriously?' I ask, hoping to explore further. I mean, somebody did take whatever I said as being possible, and now I'm being hunted.

'She's a nutter,' says Matt, dismissively.

'No, she's not,' says Kate, 'she has a different view of the world to you. That's all.'

'If she's into sci-fi, I wouldn't mind meeting her,' I say.

'That can be arranged,' says Kate. She rummages in her bag, takes out her phone, asks me for my number and transfers Gina's details onto it. 'Just call her Sunday. I'll let Gina know about you when I meet her tomorrow.'

'Thanks,' I say, 'What are you guys drinking?' They tell me, and I head to the bar. It appears I have to carry out the investigation even further afield.

As I bring back drinks, I wonder whether the woman in black will tell me whether she passed on information or whether she'd lie, being responsible for having hired killers hunt me.

NINE:
Saturday

~

AT BREAKFAST, AFTER having gone out to buy bakery items for the two of us, I sit on the wooden chair in the dining room, contemplating my next move. Richard joins me and looks pleased that I've made coffee and set a croissant and peach Danish on a plate for him.

'What's the occasion?' he asks.

'Just great to be alive,' I say.

'That's a positive outlook, I must say. I know I'd find it difficult to be sanguine if I had your troubles,' Richard says, sipping his coffee.

At that moment I hear sirens in the distance. And the sirens appear to be coming closer. Richard ignores them and bites into his Danish. I have some coffee, but I keep my ear tuned to the now ever closer sounding noise. The sirens stop suddenly, and I breathe more freely. A minute later I hear footsteps outside. There's a knock on the door.

My mind flashes back to a time when I was eight years old. My mother had been annoyed with me for playing soccer in the back yard and kicking the ball through a window. She threatened that my father would be told unless I cleaned up the mess I'd made. But I didn't take her seriously. At five o'clock an hour before my father was due, there was a knock on the door. I waited in our small kitchen while my mother opened the door. Thinking it was a friend of the family, I snuck an apple filled pancake mother had made for desert into my mouth. Then I heard her call me. I walked down the hall and saw our neighbour, a woman in her twenties smile at me. My mother said, 'You know Jenny, don't you Ethan, she is going to take you to Bible studies.'

Fearing something worse than Bible studies, I waited. But nothing bad happened. Jenny who was plump with a friendly face took my hand and guided me next door where she told me stories from the Bible which, she said, were lessons in life. I sneered. Out of nowhere Jenny slapped my face, a stinging rebuke. She eyed me to suggest I need to be respectful.

The second knock startles me, my body tight with expectation. I can't run. Richard pushes up from his chair and ambles to the door, twirling his moustache. He opens the door and I can see from my chair that there stand two cops. I wonder whether I would use my new-found strength if they come in to arrest me. Of course, they might use weapons to subdue me. A taser or a pistol. I sit back, adrenaline coursing through my system, not knowing how I'd react if they come in.

'Yes?' says Richard nonchalantly. His act is perfect. Totally innocent. No hint he might be harbouring a wanted criminal.

'Is this David Morrow's place?'

'Sorry, he's on the floor above.'

'Thank you, sir.' The police move on and Richard shuts the door.

'Wonder what that poor sod's done,' says Richard as he sits down again.

I shrug, pleased that I didn't need to act.

～૭

It's nine o'clock and I decide to call Gina, the strange woman in black Kate talked about. I know I was meant to call on Sunday but if Kate were going to tell her about me today, she probably would have done it by now. And if Kate hadn't called by now, she probably wouldn't call at all. I'm impatient, always have been, and I figure I can introduce myself anyway.

My day today, after the initial scare with the police visit, went unspectacularly. I went for a walk, noting how cold everybody was. People were wearing trench coats, bulky jumpers, hoodies, even Australian Ugg boots and multiple layers of clothing. I wore jeans and a black leather jacket and felt fine. I was watchful on my wanderings, but I didn't see anyone who I felt was suspicious. Being Saturday, there were crowds everywhere, people shopping or going out for a meal or to the underground station. It would be difficult for someone to mount an attack on me, particularly as it was daylight.

I spent some of the day watching television as Richard had gone out. And I read and researched news and music on the internet. I also checked out the process for patents for my invention. So now, at nine o'clock, after enjoying a baked dinner which Richard had served up, I am in my room and I find Gina's number. I hesitate for a moment, working out the best way to word my call.

I stab numbers on my phone. Three rings go by then a soft voice answers. 'Hello.'

'Gina?' I ask.

'Yes, who's this?'

'My name's Ethan Stone, and Kate suggested I call…'

'Oh yes, you're the anti-ageing scientist, aren't you?'

'That's right,' I say, relieved that she sounded positive. 'I was wondering whether we could meet up.'

'When?'

'Tomorrow,' I say.

'I'm out most of the day. Come 'round at six. I'll give you my address. Got a pen?'

TEN:
Sunday

I ARRIVE OUTSIDE A set of terraces in a dinghy street in Camberwell, South London. There is little illumination as most of the street-lights aren't working. From the pavement, the block of flats looks unappealing. I check the address I've written down. Yes, this is the place. It could use painting and repair as it seems to be about five hundred years old. There are stairs leading up to a green door and a set of steps going down to a basement flat. This one has a dark yellow door. The filthy looking door is set flush against a concrete wall on the left with a large window to the right of it. A lace curtain prevents a view inside.

A motor bike roars past. I examine the residential street and note that there are two West Indian boys playing ball at the end of the street. Nobody else is out in the cold crisp air. Snow has turned to sludge which lies along the gutter.

I put the piece of paper with the address and phone number of Gina York written on it into the pocket of my trench coat. I descend the stairs to the basement as instructed and knock on the door. Up close the wooden door looks more lemon than yellow with stripes of flaking paint ready to be ripped off. I consider my situation. I've come to a place, not knowing anything about the occupant or occupants. It could be an ambush. Or it may be perfectly innocent. Perhaps I'm being paranoid. I knock on the door again. Two sharp raps with my right-hand knuckle.

After an agonising minute or two, the door creaks open to reveal a woman dressed completely in black. Head to toe. She has a pale white face with long raven black hair drifting below her shoulders. The paleness suggests she hasn't seen any sun in years. She's probably Vitamin D deficient. Her long black dress flows to the ground. It's not obvious if she has shoes or is barefoot. She also wears a black coat.

'Gina?' I ask.

'Yes, and you're Ethan?'

I nod.

'Come in,' she says, and she leads me down a short hallway to a living room separated from a kitchen by an island bench.

The flat is small, and it looks like it only has one bedroom, a bathroom, and this large room. She puts the kettle on and gestures for me to sit in one of the chairs in the kitchen. The rectangular kitchen island bench accommodates four chairs. When she's poured tea for both of us, she sits opposite me. Up close, I see she wears black lipstick and black eyeliner. She looks scary. A woman in total black.

'You're a science fiction fan, I understand,' I say to open proceedings.

'Yes, I am. So as a scientist, I imagine you're not,' she says.

'How do you know I'm a scientist?'

'Word gets out. I'm curious about the anti-ageing science.'

Gina appears to be in her thirties so I'm not quite sure why she has an interest in anti-ageing science. For me it is different. At least it was. Angela was my inspiration but I'm sure she is married now, and she probably has children. Angela and I won't get together again but the science has since intrigued me. I still think of Angela, with her luscious brunette hair, sometimes brooding expressions, and her wide childbearing hips. She thought I was only out to have fun. Little did she know I wanted her, for her sake, not purely to have a good time.

But she couldn't be persuaded. She assumed I would leave her when she was older and that I would seek a younger companion. That's what happened in her family. Her father left her and her mother for his young secretary when Angela was thirteen. Her mother was forty at the time and Angela thought this fate would befall her too. Irrational perhaps, but how does one fight against beliefs.

I sip my tea. I'm not fond of tea but I can drink it. 'Why are you interested? You're still young.'

'My boyfriend is old,' she says.

I'm surprised by the way she says 'old', rather than 'older'. Surely, it's common for women to have older male partners. 'How old?'

'Come, I'll show you,' she says. She stands and walks to the front door. I follow. We go outside, and I'm surprised that Gina hasn't put on an overcoat. Then she ascends the stairs to the flat upstairs. I can see she lifts her skirt, revealing low-heeled black shoes and shapely legs. She takes a key from her pocket and opens the door. She looks back to see that I'm following. We walk inside. We walk along a carpeted hallway. Gina's basement flat hallway is linoleum.

At the end of the hallway is a lounge room with two sofas, a flat screen television, two chairs, a drinks cabinet and a fireplace. On the left-hand side is a spiral staircase which runs to another level.

Gina calls out, 'Derek, it's me.'

I look around, wondering from where Derek will spring. There were two rooms to the right of the hallway, both doors closed. But Derek slowly makes his way down from upstairs. He has a cane and looks like he's at least eighty years old. He has pale skin, even paler than Gina's, some wheat coloured hair around the sides of his head and he wears a white-collared shirt, and beige trousers. I can't believe this is Gina's boyfriend. He looks more like her grandfather. But I can see why she's interested in anti-ageing science now. This guy is close to saying goodbye to the planet.

Derek reaches the bottom of the stairs and hobbles over to us, extending his hand. I shake it. He says, 'Hello.'

'Derek, this is Ethan, the man who is working on an anti-ageing formula,' Gina says.

'Hi Derek,' I say, 'I wouldn't get your hopes up. I've discussed the topic with friends, but the science is still elusive.' I'm not going to offer him one of my pills. It might finish him off, I feel, watching the frail old man fiddle with his cane.

'Please sit down,' he says pointing to the sofas.

Gina and I sit on one well-used sofa while Derek eases into a chair with loads of cushions. He places his cane against his thigh. Gina turns to me and says, 'So you don't have a formula?'

'No,' I say.

'But you're working on one?' Derek says this whilst moving in his chair with some discomfort.

'Not really,' I say, wondering whether Gina had convinced him that a breakthrough in this area of scientific research had happened.

'My friend was adamant that you were close to coming up with a solution,' Gina says.

'Well…'

'If you need money, I'll get it. My sister is married to a rich man who would also be interested.'

'It's not a question of funds.' I fold my arms across my chest, uncomfortable with this line of enquiry.

Gina excuses herself and walks up the staircase, leaving me with Derek who peers at me, waiting for my response.

'We're looking into it,' I say. I don't want to tell him that's it's my personal project as he may then expect something I can't or don't want to deliver.

'I see. Gina seemed more upbeat about it. Said she thought it was a real possibility.'

'Right,' I say, not knowing what to say. This guy could use something to render him less feeble. Vitamins or something perhaps. I simply can't get my head around the fact that he and Gina are more than friends. But then I don't really know their situation. She seems quite familiar with his place, so I assume she's been here many times before. She did say he was the boyfriend, but it doesn't seem possible. I imagined she said this to make me sympathetic to his condition. 'Can't help what Gina believes.'

At that moment, Gina returns. He hovers in front of me, hesitant, her prominent bosom staring me in the face. Eventually, having not spoken whilst standing, she sits next to me and asks whether I can see something being developed in the near future.

'That might be a possibility. There are scientists doing experiments on white mice,' I say.

'Have they had any success?'

'I believe they are working to stall ageing, not to reverse it.'

'What a bummer,' she says.

To change the subject, which is beginning to bore me, I look at Gina's black nail polish and ask, 'Are you both Goths or just you?'

'I guess I am although I don't belong to any group. Just love the look.' She laughs. 'Derek definitely isn't.'

A knock on the door interrupts proceedings. Gina jumps up to answer. My back is to the door so when Gina returns, she looks at me and says, 'This is Ethan Stone.'

I turn to find two policemen with guns trained on me. And one with no gun who speaks.

'Mr Stone, you are under arrest.'

ELEVEN:
Sunday/Monday

THE CELL IS small and rectangular. The bunk is hard. There are no windows. The walls are painted an awful grey, so pale it barely qualifies as a grey. Their interior decorators have done a poor job. The toilet is a metallic grey receptacle and stands in the opposite corner to where I'm sitting. I've been placed in this cell because I've answered all questions with a 'No comment' response. I've asked for a lawyer and I was told a Duty Solicitor will be contacted on my behalf.

As I sit here, I relive the past few hours. Gina, I now realise, called the authorities when she went upstairs. As I couldn't help her ancient boyfriend become younger, she had no further use for me and decided to punish me. She must have seen my picture displayed in the media. After watching the news with no story about me, Richard and I didn't bother checking the television each day. The cops handcuffed me and led me away. Then they put me into an interview room at Camberwell Police Station after a two-minute drive from Gina's slum dwelling. I was read my rights after being formally arrested on suspicion of murder.

Not sure how long I'll be waiting, I lie on the hard bunk and close my eyes. What has made Gina call the cops? And what is it that's so important for her to want her lame and ancient boyfriend to become young again. I just don't get it. A clang at the door makes me open my eyes. In walks a woman dressed in a charcoal grey suit. She is about forty. She is tall and slim. She isn't beautiful, her face lived in. Her eyes are dark and searching.

I get up and stand, leaving my hands by my side.

'I'm Shirley Masters,' she says extending her hand 'I'm the duty solicitor'.

I shake her hand. 'Ethan Stone,' I say.

The door closes leaving the two of us alone. She sits on the bunk and I sit beside her. She pulls out a silver biro and a pad from her slim leather case. She looks at me. 'Tell me your version of events, Ethan. You've been charged with murder, so I need to know whatever you can remember.'

'I'm not guilty of any murder or murders,' I say, explaining my arrival at my shared flat and fears for my safety. I claim I ran because I did not expect anyone to believe my flatmates and I had no argument or disagreements. I don't tell her about the men who are after me or the anti-ageing experiment.

'Where were you when the murders took place?'

'I was in a cinema.'

'Did you keep the ticket stub?'

I shake my head.

'Would anyone have seen you? I mean somebody who can vouch for where you were?'

'Not that I can think of.'

Masters sighs. 'Ok. Let's tell the story as you've explained. The tricky bit is you running away. But we'll deal with that as best we can.'

Lazily, I stand up again not knowing what else to say.

'You should have called the police,' Masters says turning back at the cell door, 'you know that, don't you?'

I nod and watch her worn face crinkle into a smile. The door opens and she disappears.

THE INTERVIEW ROOM is grey and claustrophobic. Just as well I don't have any problem with small enclosed spaces. With four bodies in the room, it feels crowded. Facing Shirley and myself are DI James Fisher and DS Kirstie Ainsworth. Fisher begins the talk once Ainsworth has set up the recording devices. He states his name then asks for others present to do the same.

'Mr Stone,' says DI Fisher, 'why did you murder your flatmates? Didn't get on? An argument?'

'I didn't kill anyone,' I say.

'Don't mess with us. You killed them then ran. Why else wouldn't you be at your flat to explain? Or at least call us?'

'I knew it would look bad, so I wanted to be pro-active. I wanted to find whoever did this.'

DI Fisher grinned. 'You're no detective. Why did you think you could do a better job than the police?'

No matter what I say, I won't be believed. 'I didn't think. My flatmates were regular guys who didn't harm anyone, and they didn't deal drugs. I was incensed. My decision was impulsive and stupid, I now know but at the time, it seemed right.' I can't let on that I believe the killers were after me for a formula which could make a huge difference to the human population.

'You have no alibi either, do you?'

'I was watching a movie.'

'You went out in that freezing weather to watch a film?'

'Crazy as it seems, yes.'

'What was the film you saw?'

'*Avengers: Infinity War*'. I tell him about the movie. He frowns. Fisher persists with wanting to know details of what time I left the flat, what time I returned to the flat, what I did during that time and what I did when I found the bodies.

I outline my precise movements then he questions me about the same details a different way. He's trying to catch me in a lie, but I have no need to lie.

Finally, Shirley Masters speaks. 'He's told you this repeatedly. You have no evidence. It's all speculation.'

'His answers are not plausible,' Fisher says. 'Now, tell us about the movie. What happened bit by bit?'

I tell the detectives about the movie, the plot, who was in it and where it was shot. As it was a film premiering on that day, there is no way I could have seen it previously.

'DS Ainsworth will check it out. In the meantime, you will stay here.'

I slump in the chair, my spirits deflated.

'Who were the key stars?' DS Ainsworth asks.

'As I said, Robert Downey Jr and Chris Hemsworth.'

'Yes, I know. Are they the only ones you remember?'

'Scarlett Johansson plays the Black Widow,' I say looking directly at DS Ainsworth. She has flawless white skin, not unlike Gina, my friend in total black.

'That's unacceptable, keeping him in lockup without any evidence,' Masters breaks in, 'You have nothing to hold my client on.'

'We can hold him a while longer, without reason,' responds DI Fisher.

Arguments over, I'm escorted back to my cell. I wait until the door closes before lying on my bunk and closing my eyes. I'll get some sleep while I wait for DS Ainsworth to view the movie. Of course, the cops could check it out on IMDB, but they might not believe the detailed plot when simply summarised on the popular movie site.

Monday

I wake when a tray is shoved into the cell. Looks like I slept on the hard bunk overnight. The single blanket is on top of me, probably an unconscious action of mine at some stage during the night. The offerings on the plastic tray are not to my taste. Horrible shit really, if truth be known. I'm hungry but I only take the coffee in the Styrofoam cup and drink it. Same with the water, a moment later, but I decide not to even try the greasy sausages and toast. I will survive.

I wait. My mind wanders. I should call work but what am I going to say? That I'm in jail on murder charges?

Sometime later, the cell door opens and Shirley Masters walks in.

'How did you sleep?' she asks.

'My joints are sore. Not used to a hard surface, I guess. But it seems I slept through the night okay.'

'I have some good news. You're released but you can't leave London for the time being. You must hand in your passport to DS Ainsworth who will accompany you when you leave here.'

'Great. Thanks, Shirley. Are the police looking at other people for the murders or am I the only suspect?' I ask, relieved that I can walk around freely again.

'They've almost finished analysing the forensics on your flat. You could move back in a couple of days, if you wish. You have to be contactable though, so you'll have to get a new phone since you said you've destroyed yours, and give the police your number.'

'Okay.' I don't like it, but I have no choice.

I thank Shirley who gives me her business card. She explains she does pro bono work, but she usually works at a London law firm and that I can call her if I have other legal issues to resolve. I meet DS Ainsworth who escorts me out of the building.

'Where are we going?' she asks.

DS Ainsworth is stocky. Dark short hair, dark eyes, solid features with her curvy butt her most prominent feature. She looks like she suffers no fools. I tell her where my bank is located, and she drives there in silence. She waits for me outside. I hand her the passport once I've retrieved it from my safety deposit box. She opens the passport and examines my picture to confirm it's me, then asks whether she can drop me off somewhere.

'Thanks, detective but I'll be fine here. I'll get the tube.'

'Alright, take care.' The detective climbs into her police car without further ado.

As I turn, a man is running towards me. Flat out. Running like his life depended on it. Then I see another man coming around the same corner shouting, 'Stop him.'

I don't know what gets into me but as the first man is almost abreast of me, I ready myself. Then I tackle him around the chest like a seasoned rugby player as he tries to avoid me. He struggles but I'm too strong and I hold onto him, placing him in a headlock. DS Ainsworth gets out of the police vehicle and looks at both of us. We wait for the second man who is out of breath to come alongside.

'What's this all about?' asks DS Ainsworth, holding up her warrant card.

The unfit chaser says, 'He came into my store and stole two phones.'

'You can let him go,' says DS Ainsworth, staring at me. She looks at the first man and says, 'Did you take these items from this man's shop?'

He hesitates. I glare at him conveying with my look that I'm prepared to hurt him. Then he nods.

As the shop owner waits for the outcome, DS Ainsworth asks whether he wants to press charges.

The overweight shop owner shakes his head.

DS Ainsworth tells the thief to return the phones, then cautions him and lets him walk away. The shop owner thanks us and heads back in the direction from which he came.

'You're extraordinarily strong,' says DS Ainsworth.

'The gym, Detective Sergeant Ainsworth.'

'Call me Kirstie,' she says. Her eyes meet mine but this time they tell me she's attracted to me.

'Okay Kirstie. How long will you keep my passport?'

Kirstie Ainsworth smiles. 'Perhaps we can discuss that over dinner.'

Was my show of strength such a turn on or does she want to wrestle with me to find out how strong I really am? She is a solid looking woman and one most men wouldn't want to tangle with. But I'm up for a challenge. 'Why not?'

She hands me a business card and gets back into her vehicle.

I walk towards an underground station. I wonder if Kirstie Ainsworth is serious about getting together. From my understanding, her meeting me outside of her work would be a conflict of interest. But who am I to judge?

TWELVE:
Friday

~

DS Kirstie Ainsworth does not look like a police officer now. She stands at the door, arms akimbo. She is wearing a sheer black lace halter-neck skirt over contour cup pads and black knickers. Her see-through lace-top black stockings cover legs with thighs thick enough to strangle a crocodile. Her hips are wide, and her body is large but curvy. I'm turned on by the sight of this magnificent amazon. I wonder how I will react with my enhanced strength. Perhaps my performance won't be any different now compared to my pre-pill times, but I need to test it out, and Kirstie will be a wonderful guinea pig. But this will be more than scientific research. Her smile melts any resistance or doubts I may have had. I want her.

She saunters towards me, hips swaying side to side. Her slow and deliberate advance is mesmerizing. I'm naked apart from my underdaks, torturously tight. I'm spreadeagled on a large bed in Kirstie's one bedroom flat in Peckham, covers pulled aside. My head is supported by multiple pillows which allows me to watch the spectacle before me. I recall the previous few hours.

Kirstie had called around midday to invite me out for a drink. I was surprised particularly as I hadn't thought much about her comment earlier in the week about getting together socially. I agreed to the date, and we met at a cosy South London bar. Was this meeting some kind of official follow up, carried out in a casual manner to put me at ease? But Kirstie didn't raise any questions relating to the murders. After a couple of drinks, I asked about the conflict of interest issue she may have been concerned about. I, on the other hand, had no quibble with it.

She explained. 'Yes, I know, it's wrong but I couldn't care less. I'm thinking of leaving the job anyway, whether I quit, or I'm sacked. Being a cop is not satisfying and it's bloody dangerous. On top of that, I get nasty comments. I'm called pig and fat and all sorts of horrible names. And not only from the crims.'

'What are you going to do?'

'My big sis wants me to help in the business she started two years ago. Apparently, the orders have gone up a lot since last year and she could use me.'

'To keep things in the family?'

'That's right.'

'What sort of business?'

'A women's fashion store in the 'burbs.'

'Why did you join the police force in the first place?'

'My dad. He was a cop. As he had two daughters and no sons, he tried to influence us to carry on the family tradition. My older sister, Trish, got a commerce degree so she wasn't interested. I, on the other hand, had no qualifications and I didn't know what I wanted to do with my life. The police force seemed like a sound career choice at the time, so I went to police college. But after years in the job, I came to hate it.'

'Is Trish bigger than you?' I'm curious about this, envisaging a larger woman than Kirstie.

'Nah. Not anymore. I got bigger at twelve. Trish is an average size woman. Why?'

'No reason,' I said.

'You're lying. Don't try to fool an experienced detective.' Kirstie finished the pint of warm beer.

My lager was only half gone. 'I have a thing for large ladies,' I admitted.

She smiled. Told me to finish my drink. When I did finish, she took my hand and led me out of the pub.

Comforted by the fact I didn't need to be wary of her motives for being with me, I accepted her invitation to go to her place. Not in a police cruiser but in her own vehicle, a blue Mini Minor.

Now, I watch as Kirstie gets to the edge of the bed. She sheds one piece of clothing then another and another in a slow teasing fashion making the uncontrollable part of my flesh rock hard, almost sending my underdaks into outer space. Then she slides into bed next to me and removes the cloth barrier between us with some difficulty. We kiss. To my surprise I feel unusually strong and my mind whirls with anticipation. Our hands explore each other's bodies and the sensation transports my senses into a form of ecstasy, a high I've never reached with alcohol or drugs. This stage of our intimacy is only exceeded by the next development as she moves up and over me, pushing a rubber adhesive to the erection which is now almost more powerful than anything I've experienced. When she rides me, I don't seem to notice that she outweighs me by many kilograms. I feel like Superman.

My staying power has also improved and we're able to experiment with a variety of positions. I don't think about anything as I'm in the moment, appreciating the sheer joy of being. Sometime later we both experiences climaxes together. Such an ending may well be a cliché in romance novels, but this is the first time I've experienced such mutual pleasure with a woman. In the past, I've generally had difficulty holding on, often coming first, then having the obligation of working a second shift. But not tonight. It must be my invention. I can see sky-high dollars in this pill if marketed properly. Men will not worry so much about the anti-ageing property, except for the vain or those in advanced years, but most will jump at the chance to avoid premature ejaculation permanently.

Breathless, Kirstie says, 'Wow. I've never had a sexual experience like that.'

'It was great,' I say, trying to sound nonchalant. Naturally, I am overwhelmed by how the whole experience played out. I had no idea my pill could deliver such bonuses. Reversing age would have been good enough. Extra strength and increased virility are pure gifts. My God, if nothing goes wrong with this after a month or two, I'll have to reconsider my asking price. I had intended on selling the formula, once tested and approved, but now I'm wondering whether to develop the product and market it myself.

Kirstie slips out of bed and pads out of the bedroom. For a large woman, she is almost ballerina like in her movements. Two minutes later, she returns and hands me a beer. She has one too. What a woman. Enjoys sex and beer. Should I propose marriage right now? Of course, I'm being flippant.

We sit upright in bed, just savouring the moment.

'I'm pleased you've not brought up the subject of the murders,' I say.

'I'm fairly sure you're in the clear. We found a gun which we believe is the murder weapon and your prints aren't on it.'

'When did this happen?' I remember having my DNA and fingerprints taken but this is news.

'On Wednesday. We were going to let you know as soon as it's conclusive.'

'Did you find any prints?'

'Only a partial. And it wasn't yours.'

'That's a relief. Do you have any suspects?'

Kirstie sips some beer from her bottle of Peroni. 'No. Let's not worry about that. I think you've tired me out and that's a first. Must be your youth.'

'How old do you think I am?'

'Twenty-four or twenty-five. I'm forty-one so way older.'

I digest this news. I'm also wondering whether I'm decreasing in age as Benjamin Button did in the movie of a man going backwards in age. I'll need to check that out. 'I'm not as young as you think but I'll accept the compliment.'

We finish our beer, just chatting. We seem to be comfortable in each other's company, but I wonder whether she's keen to see me again. The sex was spectacular, but I doubt I could date a cop for long, her hours at work being anti-social and the danger ever present. But if she's serious about quitting the job, I would be interested in getting into a relationship with her.

'I have to work this weekend,' Kirstie says, 'but I'd like to see you again.'

'Alright. That would be wonderful,' I say. 'Should I call you or will you call me?'

'Probably best if I call,' she says.

When I leave, after giving Kirstie a passionate kiss, I feel excited. I've never been chased by a woman before. What a marvellous feeling.

Saturday/Sunday

The weekend is busy. After obtaining permission from the police to go back to my flat, I retrieve all my belongings and settle into another flat in Belsize Park. The process is agonizing but necessary. I can't live in a place which has had not only people, but friends, murdered. I wasn't close to my flatmates, but I'd gotten to know them, and they were regular guys.

Richard helps me move. At the end of the day, late on Sunday, we seek out a nearby pub. After a brief walk, we find The Washington, in England's Lane. It looks good and feels comfortable. It's a wood-panelled Victorian pub with mirrors and an embossed red ceiling. With our beers, we order burgers and chips.

'Nice place you found. Can you afford it?' Richard asks.

'My salary will cover it. I wanted to share initially because I was new in London. But that experience with Adrian and Jeremy has worn thin.'

Rickard strokes his moustache. 'You'll be able to invite female company over without worrying about flatmates.'

'Good point. You'll be happy I'm moving out, I imagine, so I won't cramp your style.'

Richard laughs. "Sure, but to tell you the truth, after my break-up with Cynthia, I'm not rushing to get involved with another woman.'

The meals arrive. My burger looks so huge I'll need to crush it down to get my mouth around it. Richard uses a knife and fork and we devour the food silently. The only thing missing in this burger is beetroot which I've only found in Australian burgers. I finish before Richard, finding my fingers are sticky from the sauce. I excuse myself and wash my hands and face in the bathroom.

When I return to our table, I find Richard talking to a young woman. Richard says, 'Brenda, this is my friend Ethan.'

'Hi Ethan,' says Brenda, 'Are you an actor too?'

'No. I met Richard at a film class but I'm a behind the camera guy.'

'Really. You're good looking so I don't understand why you don't want to perform. I'll do anything to get a juicy part.'

'I'll keep that in mind when I produce my next short film,' I say.

'Great,' says Brenda, 'I'll leave you two boys continue your drinking. See you Rich.' She walks off.

'Old friend?' I ask Richard.

'She had a small part in my last production, and we hit it off.'

'Shakespeare?'

'No, just a local play.'

After a few more beers, we head out. I invite Richard over, but he wants to get back to his flat. Entering my new abode, I look about. Still lots to do – unboxing belongings and rearranging furniture. But right now, I don't have the energy or the inclination.

When I slide into bed, teeth brushed and day clothes discarded, my mind summons up an image of Brenda. Her smile was radiant, and it seemed she liked Richard yet he didn't appear interested. I remembered his ex-girlfriend, Cynthia who was tall and slim. Brenda on the other hand was shorter than Cynthia and more rounded. Perhaps Richard had a type and his women needed to be thin. I'd not thought about it before and I never figured I had a type but now I wonder. Both Liz and Kirstie have meat on their bones. Is that my type? Thinking these thoughts, I soon fall asleep.

THIRTEEN:
Monday

ONDAY MID-MORNING, I'M at my desk at work, surveying chemical analysis data on the screen. My stomach is grumbling. I'm also bored. I get up and walk over to Heidi's workstation.

'Fancy a coffee?' I ask.

'From the kitchen?'

'No, let's go outside.'

Heidi is new to my section, not the company, and I want to get her perspective on something. She is in her thirties and has had experience at the company for twelve years. We find a small café and order.

'How do you like our group?' I ask.

'Still getting to know everyone. You've been the most elusive.'

'Sorry about that. I'm not a great people person.'

'I get that. I'm not too keen on pubs and small talk, like most of my colleagues in my previous sections. But I try to fit in.'

'Are you suggesting I don't try to fit in?'

Heidi smiles. The coffees are delivered. She puts a spoonful of sugar in her flat white. 'You don't seem to care about fitting in. Am I right?'

I taste my cappuccino. 'You're not wrong. I get absorbed in my work.' I don't tell her I'm more focused on my private experiments. 'Tell me something. If you could have a wish, to stay the age you are for the next fifty years or to become a decade younger, what would you choose?'

'What sort of question is that? What a choice.' Heidi runs a hand through her short brunette hair. 'Why?'

'Just choose.'

'Become a decade younger, I guess. I wouldn't want to be like Dorian Gray. Looking twenty while I'm eighty. Then turning old suddenly. Yuk.' Heidi shivers, the picture of such an instant crystalizing in her mind.

My phone rings.

Heidi mouths, in silence, that she needs to get back to work, leaving me to answer it. 'Hello,' I say, the iPhone screen telling me it's a 'No Caller ID' number.

'Ethan, it's Warren. How have you been?'

'Fine,' I say, waving to Heidi as she exits the cafe. It's odd for Warren to call. I wait for more.

'And the anti-ageing thing? Is that going well?'

'I didn't think you believed in that,' I say, standing up then walking outside. I don't want other people to overhear me.

'No, I don't. Just wondering why an intelligent fellow like you is wasting his time.'

I get suspicious when someone calls me intelligent. They're setting me up for something. 'Maybe I like challenges.'

'Good. I have a proposition for you,' he says.

I'm outside now and the weather is still cold, but it has become warmer over the last few days and a hell of a lot better than last week. People are still rugged up though. I'm not feeling the cold as badly as others, given I'm only wearing a shirt and jacket, having left my overcoat at work. 'Oh yeah,' I say.

'Would you like to make some money?'

'I'm working so I'm being paid,' I say, wondering where this is going.

'Yes, I know. But I can make you some real money.'

'Don't waste your breath,' I say, wondering whether Warren is a scam artist.

'As you know, I'm a broker and you've met me, so you know I'm an okay guy, right?'

I don't know anything of the sort, but I play along. 'I guess,' I say. What I do know now is that Warren likes to blow his own trumpet.

'Well, we deal in equities, options, commodities, FX, what have you. There's a move up on oil and I can get you in at a good start and you'll see a good jump in only a month or two.'

'Really, and what will this cost me?' I ask, knowing I should shut him down now.

'Only ten thousand,' he says as though this is pocket change that I have sitting under the mattress.

'Ten thousand pounds?' I laugh.

'If you don't have the money, you could borrow. You have a job and…'

'Let me stop you there,' I say walking along the footpath towards the huge GlaxoSmithKline building, 'Even if I had that sort of money lying around, I wouldn't be interested.'

'Why not? Doesn't everybody like to make money?'

'Perhaps but I'm not into that kind of risk,' I say.

'I don't understand,' he persists, 'Let me show you some charts and you'll see it's a no brainer.'

'Thanks, but no thanks,' I say firmly. If he doesn't stop, I'll have to become rude.

'Your loss,' says Warren. 'Are you and Liz still going out?'

'We're not exclusive but we may get together again. Look, I have to go.'

'Okay. See you around.' Warren clicks off.

As I arrive at my cubicle, I sit and stare at the screen. I check my email then lean back and contemplate what's just happened. Why did Warren try to sell me on trading? Is this what brokers do? Meet people then try to make them a client? I shake my head then return to my work.

I OPEN THE door and there is Liz with a bottle of wine and a pot plant. She smiles when she sees me.

'My Lord,' she says, 'you look so young.'

'Come in,' I say relieving her of the bottle and pot plant, 'A gift wasn't necessary.'

'Of course, it is. New home. Lovely place. So clean. I love the white walls and cabinets.'

'I'll take you for a tour soon,' I say, 'Coffee or tea?'

'Tea please. I know I've arrived out of the blue but when you told me you'd moved into this area, I couldn't resist.'

I 'm still getting used to this flat which is expensive. It's such a change from my previous flat which felt cramped, having flat mates and their gear inside. I boil water, grab two cups, spoon coffee in one cup and place a teabag in the other. I turn and sit at an angle to Liz at the coffee table in the lounge which contains a black L-shaped sofa. I notice her staring at me.

'Nice of you to pop 'round,' I say, not having invited her and somewhat surprised at her showing up. 'I was going to have a house-warming the weekend after next to give me time to unpack.'

'I can't get over how young you look. You can't tell me you haven't taken something, some chemical aid, surely. Or did you have surgery?'

I didn't want to explain myself, but Liz and Richard are the only people who knew me before the experiment. Reluctantly I say, 'I'm trialling a chemical formula. I need to understand how it works and what side effects it may have. I guess the reversing process has worked, at least in the short term.'

'You bet. Now I feel like an old hag being with someone so young.'

I move next to Liz and take her hand. 'Don't be silly. You never know; the side-effects may be fatal. But if the anti-ageing process sticks, I can offer it to others. Are you interested? And what would you rather, staying the age you're at now or becoming, I mean looking, significantly younger'

Liz grins. 'I'm not sure. A drastic change like you've undertaken will scare my family and close friends, so I'd have to think about it.'

I go back to the kitchen, finish making the tea and coffee then bring both cups to the living room.

I sit down and search Liz's eyes. 'Have you thought about it?'

'I'd choose staying the age I am. I don't know why but suddenly looking a decade or more younger seems scary.'

'Okay, good to get some feedback. I'll need to tinker with my formula to achieve what you're suggesting. Currently, my formula is geared to the reversal process.'

'Yeah, well you do look fantastic, I must say.'

I watch Liz drink some tea. 'Please don't talk to anyone about this,' I say.

'Why? It's a fabulous invention. You'll make millions.'

'Maybe so but until I'm sure it's safe, I can't risk others wanting it.'

'I understand. Don't worry I'll keep your secret.' Liz stretches her legs.

Looking at Liz's firm thighs, I recall that fateful Saturday night when she and I met Warren and Ann. 'Don't tell Anne either.'

Liz laughs. 'Why would I tell her?'

'She's your best friend, isn't she? And don't women tell their best friends everything, including sexual experiences?'

Liz blushes. 'Maybe. However, as you've asked me not to tell anyone about your new-found youth, I won't breathe a word.'

I take her hand and we both stand. 'Let me show you the rest of the flat.'

In the bedroom, Liz says, 'What a lovely room? Has it been christened yet?'

I push her on top of the doona. 'You're going to be the first.'

We kiss but then Liz undoes my grasp. 'I didn't come over for this.'

'Okay,' I say, sitting up.

'You're not going to sulk, are you?'

'No. Let's go back to the living room and enjoy that bottle you brought.'

Back on the sofa, wine glasses half-filled, we talk about movies. 'I saw The Leisure Seeker with Helen Mirren last night. I went with Anne.'

'Was Warren with you?'

'No. Why do you ask?'

'Do you know he called me to get me to invest in something?'

Liz put her glass back on the coaster on the coffee table. 'Really. What sort of investment?'

'I don't know. He wanted ten grand.'

'Well, he is a broker.'

I dropped the subject. We finished the bottle and I called a taxi. Liz kissed me at the door and said I should call her. I think she didn't want sex because I hadn't specifically invited her over. Perhaps she thought visiting a man's home without an invitation for sex would make her appear a slut. I don't think like that, but I wasn't going to push it. I'm not sure about my feelings for Liz or Kirstie yet. Both are great company and excellent bed partners.

I check the time. It's 9:30 p.m. Too early for bed. I think of calling Kirstie but decide against it. She may be on duty and I have nothing much to say.

FOURTEEN:
Saturday/Sunday

~

IT'S THREE O'CLOCK on a gloriously cold winter's day. The sun is out today, a rare treat for Londoners who are walking about, still rugged up with overcoats, boots, jumpers and scarves. I have a black trench coat on, mainly to fit in, and I feel pleasantly warm. Kirstie, walking beside me, is shivering and keen to get to our destination, so that central heating can do its work.

We walk across the Tower Bridge, a famous British icon, built in the late nineteenth century. It is a combined bascule and suspension bridge and one which I'd photographed when I first arrived in London. The bridge is raised and lowered at various times, but I've never witnessed the process. During my first six months in London, travelling by public transport or walking, I saw many of the famous buildings and tourist attractions. After that I fell into the usual native Londoner's routine of commuting from home to work and back again without noticing my surroundings.

Today, I'm pleased to be again exploring the hidden treasures the city has to offer. Kirstie and I agreed to go to a café nearby, one she had previously discovered during her rounds as a cop. Today she is off duty.

'It's not much further,' she says. Her hands are wrapped in wool gloves and also tucked into the pockets of her overcoat.

As we descend steps on the left-hand side at the end of the bridge travelling towards Butlers Wharf, I note a laneway which I presume takes us to the cafes and restaurants I viewed from the centre of the bridge. At the bottom, I wait for Kirstie, then side by side we wander down the darkened laneway, the sun hidden by the tall buildings.

As we walk along, content to look about and not speak, I'm surprised when I see a man who, coming from the opposite direction, is almost upon us. He has a medium build, uncombed straggly fair hair, and an overcoat with deep pockets. He stops and looks closely at us.

'Bitch,' he says, drawing a pistol from his coat pocket.

Startled, Kirstie says, 'Jacko, when did they release you?'

'Been out a week,' he replies then aims his gun at her.

I rush him, knocking him over, but the pistol has gone off and I black out.

A woman dressed in white peers at me. My eyelids flutter and after a few seconds, they open. The woman is a nurse. She is slight with wavy black hair. The name tag says "Emily". The room smells of antiseptic. Not a fragrance of my liking.

'Mr Stone, can you hear me?'

I have a tube in my mouth so I can't talk. I nod.

'Good. You're very lucky. A bullet grazed your skull, but it didn't penetrate. I'm going to check your vitals. Just stay calm and relax.'

There's not much I can do except lie here and relax. Apart from the tube in my mouth, I have a cannula attached to my right arm. There's no point panicking. At least I'm alive but my head is throbbing.

I recall the incident near London Tower Bridge. When I realised Kirstie was in danger, I launched myself at the guy with the gun and barrelled into him chest first. As the gun was pointed at Kirstie and not directed at me, I was able to knock him down. Otherwise had he aimed for me, the damage would have been worse, if not fatal. I wonder whether Kirstie is okay, but I can't speak to ask.

The nurse finishes her job and tells me she'll return with some water. She removes the tube from my mouth, and I feel the dryness of my lips. I move my head a little but it's painful. I lie down again. It's been a relatively peaceful week except for Saturday. I have no idea what day it is but figure that's the least of my problems. The room I'm in is windowless so I don't even know whether it's day or night.

The nurse returns and she hands me a bottle of water. I take it, open the top and drink greedily. I'm hungry. 'Emily, what's happened to my companion?'

'Are you talking about the woman who was here before?'

'Yes.' Kirstie had called me the night before, the Friday, and said she'd resigned from the force and wanted to take me to a nice place as I'd inspired her to leave the police to pursue other interests. I can't recall what I said which might qualify for inspiration. Perhaps it was her talking about it. It may have crystallised something at the back of her mind. I don't know. All I know is that she was happy when she talked about it Friday night, after her shift ended at eleven o'clock.

'She's downstairs and has been told you're conscious. She'll be up in a moment or two.'

"Thanks. I'd like something to eat,' I say.

'A doctor will be here shortly. Once he's examined you, we'll get you something.' Emily walks out of the room.

Kirstie strides into the room a moment later. She comes over and holds my hand. "Thank God you're okay.'

"Did you get shot?'

"Thanks to you I didn't. After you fell on top of Jacko, I heard the gun go off. I rushed over and kicked the pistol away. I grabbed it and trained it on Jacko, Maurice Jackson being his name, and told him I would shoot if he didn't do exactly as I instructed. I saw the blood and called backup and an ambulance. It all happened so quickly. The bastard is back where he belongs. I don't know why they released the scumbag in the first place. This time he's going down for an awfully long time.'

'A friend of yours?'

'Oh yeah. I've arrested him several times, but we've always found it hard to get anything to stick. He was in prison for drug dealing recently but we know he's also involved in murder and other crimes.'

Kirstie pulls a chair over and continues to hold my hand. 'I'm just so grateful you're alive. I've never had anyone put their life on the line for me before, or even stand up for me. You're wonderful. And so brave.'

What could I say? I acted instinctively. The anti-ageing pill must have influenced my actions. In the old days, before I'd experienced the strength-enhancing drug, I would have simply stood there, bewildered. 'I'm not brave. Just stupid.'

Kirstie comes closer and brushes my cheek with her lips, painted dark red. 'Nonsense. Once you're well, I'm going to make it up to you.'

The doctor arrives, and Kirstie stands up. She waves "goodbye", says she'll call, and exits the room.

Thursday

I'm back at home, in the bathroom. When I peer into the mirror, I'm shocked. My skin is no longer as smooth as it was last Saturday, and I note a few grey hairs have returned on both sides of my head. It looks like I've aged a decade, to be exactly as I was before I took the experimental anti-ageing pill. Why had it worn off? Was it due to the bullet grazing the side of my skull? Or was it due to the shock my system received as a result of being shot? Which would suggest that once the body receives any serious shock, such an incident could rewind the entire anti-ageing reversal process. Finally, I wonder whether the pill has an expiration date. But a few weeks doesn't seem right. This is one part of the experimental process I need to add to my notes on the entire experience of using the pill.

I walk out of the bathroom and to the large window in the living room. From here, I observe the trees, some without leaves, and the vista beyond. The view is comforting. Nature has a way of calming one, making you realise how insignificant each individual is.

There's no reason to worry. If the drug didn't work as I wanted, I've lost nothing but time. This is normal with any new product. Trial and error until the right combination forms. I need to assess the formula again, after another go with the pills I still have. I've been recording daily changes to my body since I've taken the drug. Heart rate, weight, blood pressure and any physical changes. And naturally, any side-effects. The only two side-effects so far are: extra strength and reversal of the process once the body is traumatised.

I see a bird fluttering from one tree to another. I turn back and sit on the sofa, thinking about the last few days. The doctor had insisted I stay in hospital until it was clear I wasn't going to suffer any trauma. He was astounded that I'd recovered so quickly. Kirstie came to see me a couple of times, but she still had to work through the notice period, two weeks. I hadn't called anyone except Richard who popped in once. When he learned what had happened, he grinned. Told me not to rush at someone pointing a gun.

I take a bottle of Heineken from the fridge and sit down again. I call work to say I'll be in next Monday. I'd called work from the hospital last Monday to say I was ill. Telling my boss I'd been shot would open up too many questions, so I didn't elaborate. I'm well covered as I hadn't taken sick days before.

Now, I must decide what to do about my formula. It's tempting to say I've tried one version and it didn't work out. But I feel committed. It worked for a brief time and I still believe I can contribute to humanity so I should carry on, trying the same batch of pills before making adjustments. What happened with the gun episode was a setback. I grab my laptop and surf the internet, just to still my mind.

FIFTEEN:
Saturday (One Week Later)

~

DRIZZLE MAKES MANY of the pedestrians walking along Brompton Road carry umbrellas. I did not bother with one, allowing the rain to flow over my trench coat and my uncovered head. This was London's default climate, I felt, having been here for a couple of years now. The period of my presence in the UK didn't make me an expert but I knew from others that the cold and rain were always a possibility in this city. I arrive outside Harrods, brush water off the top of my head and enter.

The week has flown by. A busy week, catching up on work which I'd had to postpone because of my hospital visit and five-day recuperation stay. The effects of the shooting have worn off, both physically and psychologically. I'd also taken another anti-ageing pill. After spending a few days at home after returning from the hospital, I brooded and questioned how I should proceed with experimenting further on the anti-ageing formula. So far, no obvious improvements or alterations have come to me. The previous weekend was dull. I'd stayed indoors, making my flat as habitable as possible. When I realised my strength had deteriorated, I simply swallowed another anti-ageing pill. Of course, I had no idea that it would work again. But it did. The medication restored my youthful appearance and my strength. I took another photo of before and after and compared the results with my previous before and after photos. They were remarkably similar. This was encouraging, proving that the results from the same batch were reliable.

Liz was unavailable last weekend as she told me she was travelling to Spain with some girlfriends. Apparently, she'd been invited to a wedding in Barcelona and then agreed to extend the time away to go to Majorca. Left alone, as Kirstie had to follow up on a case up north, I watched television and read a novel as well as completing the unpacking of the last boxes.

I find the café which is located in Harrods. I see it's called Café Godiva. Kirstie is waiting for me but she isn't on a horse, naked, despite the place she's chosen. As I approach her, she smiles. A cup is in front of her on a table for two. I kiss her on the cheek. She stands and gives me a hug.

'Glad you could make it,' she says, 'I've missed you.'

We sit down. 'Good to see you too,' I say, 'how was the trip.'

'Fine. Too long but it's done now. I have one week left on the job. Also, I have some good news.'

'Let me get you another drink,' I say, standing.

'A latte please.'

At the counter I order coffees and ponder my good fortune. An invention which seems to work and a wonderful and loving woman. Looking at a display in the café, I wonder whether I could make the pill chocolate-flavoured. I also order two croissants then return to my chair. 'Now, what's the good news?'

'We traced the gun used in the murder of your flatmates. It was stolen, which is no surprise, really. But we now think from the partial print that an assassin was hired to carry out the job. Someone we've known about for some time.'

'Can you arrest him?'

'Doubtful, as he has no known address. In fact, he's probably no longer in the country. We believe this man is French and is an international gun for hire.'

'Wow, sounds like whoever organised the hit meant business.'

'Yes. And you can't think why anyone would target your flatmates?'

'I can't.'

Kirstie leans back as another coffee cup is placed on the table before her. I also receive a cup. 'Would somebody be after you?' She searches my eyes.

'I don't know,' I say.

'I don't think you're telling me the truth, and this isn't an official enquiry. I can sense when somebody isn't being truthful and all I want is to make sure you're okay.'

I've never trusted cops, nor, if I think about it, anyone in authority. I also don't trust people in general. So, it's difficult for me to reveal much about myself or what I'm doing. Which is why it was so devastating to me to learn I had talked too much when I was drunk and in the company of Liz, Anne and Warren. But that's history and now I'm suffering the consequences. 'I've been attacked before,' I say.

'What?' Kirstie looks genuinely shocked. 'When, how?'

I explain about the kidnapping but don't mention my enhanced strength by taking my pill. I simply say I was lucky to sneak off. 'It makes me think I was the target,' I say.

'Bloody right it does,' she says. 'Why didn't you tell us this when you were being questioned at the station?'

'Because the reason for me being a target is unbelievable. And hence I would be locked up in a mental institution if I mentioned it.'

'Can you tell me?'

'All I can say is that it's related to work I'm carrying out. Something personal, not related to company business. An invention I began in Sydney but until I've tested it properly, I'd rather not say.'

'Why the secrecy?'

'My invention sounds implausible and is more in the realm of sci-fi than realistic, although other scientists have considered doing a similar thing. And because it has nothing to do with the company I'm working for, I've had to be careful talking about it.'

'I see.' Kirstie drinks from her cup and gives me a strange look. 'What?'

'You're not a sharing person, are you? And you don't trust me enough with your secret.'

I gaze at her, drinking in the details, wondering whether I can really trust her. I like the denim jacket she's wearing. It goes well with her black shirt, tight blue jeans and knee-length black boots. 'Other people have died because of this secret, and I don't want to put you in danger should you slip and make mention of it to someone else.'

'Alright, I won't press you now, but will you tell me eventually?'

'Sure.'

'Perhaps I can help. If I knew what you are into, I, or my colleagues, might be able to be on alert for any further attacks.'

'But if the hitman has fled, further attacks should not happen,' I say, uncertainty making my insides roil. I smell coffee as a waiter walks past with two cups in hand.

'Who knows? It depends who set it up and whether a one-time payment has been made and the contract terminated.'

'Are you suggesting that the man who ordered the killing may engage somebody else? Or worse still capture and torture me for the information?'

Kirstie places her right hand over my left hand. 'I'm not trying to scare you, but you never know. I mean, if the reason for the hit was worthwhile before, it may still be needed if the job hasn't been carried out.'

'I understand. You do see things differently to most, me included. Probably your police training.' I place my other hand over the one she has placed on mine. 'Let's finish here and go somewhere with no people around. Then I'll tell you.'

SIXTEEN:
Saturday

~

HUDDLED TOGETHER, KIRSTIE and I find our way to Hyde Park. The cold keeps crowds away so there are only a few people wandering around. The grass is a luscious green and I look out at the vastness of the park. We find a bench and sit, side by side, our bodies touching to ward off the cold. I turn to Kirstie.

'You're working all weekend, you said?'

'Yes. From this afternoon, most of tonight and all day tomorrow. After that I'm available for you any time. Now, what were you going to tell me?'

The drizzle has stopped. The sky looks metallic, in contrast to a light grey an Australian overcast day might exhibit. For some, the ongoing cloud and darkness in this country, day after day, might cause depression. I am not so inclined. Warm climes are for holiday makers. Cold, grim-looking days focus the mind on work. Certainly, it does for me.

I said, 'I'm a scientist, as you know, and I know I haven't told you much about my work so it might not have registered. Well, be that as it may, I want to tell you something about my activities now. I've developed something, a drug, which competitors might want and want enough to kill me.'

'Are you a drug dealer?'

'Very funny. No, I'm not a drug dealer, rather a drug creator,' I say.

'Can you tell me?'

I gaze at the lush green surroundings. There are few people about. A tall young man walks beside a young woman of indeterminate age. They seem to be in deep discussion. I consider my answer. 'I'm working on an anti-ageing pill.'

'Is that why you're looking so different today? In hospital you looked like you'd aged a decade, but I wasn't going to comment.' She laughs, as though she doesn't believe it.

I smile at her. She looks closely at me and puts her hand over her mouth. 'Oh my God, you're experimenting with it. You look as good as you did before you got shot.'

'Well, being shot doesn't agree with the formula,' I say.

'Perhaps you should avoid people with guns. But seriously, you've taken a pill, haven't you?'

'Yes,' I say, observing a bird on the ground, pecking at something on the wet grass.

'So how old are you?'

'Thirty-nine.'

'That's good. I won't feel like I've stolen from the cradle now. You're almost my age.' She puts her arm around me and pulls me closer. She kisses me.

'You don't like young men?'

'I do, but they're not likely to stick around. I thought we might have a fun time, and eventually you'd move on. Know what I mean?'

'Ha ha. Life is full of surprises,' I say, standing. 'Let's walk. You're cold, aren't you?'

'I am.' Kirstie gets up, takes my hand, and we wander across the park to the nearest tube station. Before she leaves me, we hug.

THAT EVENING, AFTER having a drink with Richard at the pub, I go home alone. First, I and arrange another time for a beer with Richard. Done we shake hands goodbye. At 8:30 p.m., I'm sitting on the sofa, admiring my new flat. I've done a few things to make the place comfortable and in tune with my preferences. There are prints on the walls now. Bold, abstract, portraits. There are two portraits I enjoy. One is black and white and shows the face of a beautiful woman. She has a radiant smile and bright eyes. The photo reminds me of the woman in Sydney, Angela, my first love, the one who felt she was too old for me. Like Kirstie, she thought I'd grow tired of her and leave. But it was she who left me before she'd invested too much time with me by getting to know me and having a good time.

I hear a sound outside. Then my front door is smashed. Wood splinters as men push my door aside.

I stand but then I see a semi-automatic gun pointed at me. It looks, to my untrained eye, to be a Winchester Magnum. I remember researching it after seeing the same type in an action movie.

'Sit down,' instructs a tall man in a black balaclava, followed by two other men, similarly attired. In addition, they all sport blue jeans, black shirts, black jackets and heavy dark brown work boots.

I sit. 'How can I be of service?' I know this is not the way to speak but I can't help it. It's my nature to be a smart-arse. It's gotten me into trouble before. I know I shouldn't get shot and I wonder what it is they want. I can guess but I'll wait for a response.

The leader, slightly taller than his two companions, says, 'Shut up.' He motions for his men to search the place. I wait.

A few minutes later, one of the dark-clad men, says, 'Nothing.'

'Where is the formula?' says the leader.

'What formula?'

One of the henchmen strikes me in the face with an open palm. I hardly feel it.

'Did you kill my flatmates?' This is daring of me and I expect another hit, but it is not forthcoming.

'They were useless and, unless you tell me what I want to know, I will kill you as well.'

'How do I know you won't kill me once I give you what you want?' I'm buying time. If I can get the gun out of the leader's hand, I have a chance. The other two have lowered their guns, feeling confident one will be sufficient to keep me constrained.

'You don't.'

'Shoot me, but you won't get the formula which is currently in the hands of another person.'

'Who?'

'Why would I tell you?'

The leader is frozen. He looks like a statue and I'm picturing his brain whirring. I think he must be a hired gun, probably hired by the same person who ordered the initial attack. He doesn't sound French, so I assume he's a different hired killer from the hitman Kirstie told me about. And I wonder whether it's the same gang which kidnapped me. If not, then they don't know about my strength. Finally, he utters, 'AJ, keep an eye on him. I have to make a call.'

The leader disappears. AJ raises his gun.

'Be careful. If you accidentally shoot me, you'll never get the formula.' Even if I gave them the formula, it will be of no use. The changes I've made to the written version are in my head.

'Shut the fuck up,' says AJ in a Northern English accent.

The leader returns. AJ lowers his gun, a common revolver. The leader says, 'He's coming with us.'

'Look, I can give you the formula, but you'll need to test it on yourselves. The pill is quick acting. Look at me. It works.'

'What do you mean?'

'There's a recent photo of me on my phone. You'll see I'm much older looking in the photo than I look here, in person.'

'So what?'

I smile. 'I see. You don't even know what you're after. Your employer hasn't told you much, has he? You guys are simply hired muscle with no brains.'

The leader takes a step forward as though he's going to smash my face in, but he stops. 'What are you talking about?'

'The anti-ageing pills. That's the formula your boss is after.'

'Show me your photo,' he commands.

I take the phone off the coffee table which sits to the side of the sofa and open the photos session and show images of myself to him. He examines it and looks at me. He says, 'Wow, what a difference. You have the formula here?'

'No,' I say.

'I'd like to have some of these myself. Where is this formula?'

'It's at work,' I lie.

'Okay. You'll come with us. It's night so nobody will be there, right.'

'Right.'

We're on the road to GlaxoSmithKline. Even inside the cabin, the temperature is cold judging by the driver who has turned up the heating in the vehicle, a Toyota Rav4 SUV. The leader sits in the front passenger seat, next to AJ who is driving. The third man, who hasn't spoken yet, sits in the back seat beside me, his pistol trained on me. I sit behind AJ, the mad driver who thinks he's a Formula 1 racing star weaving in and out of traffic as he passes other vehicles. I wonder if he needs to catch a flight later in the evening. Nobody speaks, AJ using the sat-nav system to find the way to the company's address which I wrote down for him on a scrap of paper. As we drive along, I see street-lights and illumination from some high-rise buildings. I wonder who knew my address. Richard, Kirstie and Liz are the only people I've told. But I can't believe any of them are behind this incident. Once we reach my work, there's nothing there which I can give this gang.

I need to think fast.

We stop at traffic lights and I try to guess how far we've come, but I can't make out any landmarks to give me a clue. Either way, these assassins will kill me. I know too much. The vehicle, although it may be stolen, is seriously mistreated. Knowing details of the SUV won't help me. I suspect the vehicle will be discarded once the job is done. Probably burnt so that forensic evidence is destroyed. The voices of the leader and AJ are clear. The leader's accent is unmistakeably Irish, AJ's English but no-speak has not revealed himself yet. Again, knowing this will be of little use. The gang won't take a risk and let me live. It seems killing me is the only solution for the person orchestrating this plan.

Then, as we turn a corner at speed, I grab the wrist of the guy holding the gun and twist it away from me. We jostle for supremacy but I'm too strong for him. In the struggle the gun fires. A bullet pierces AJ's head and he slumps forward; the car loses control. The leader grabs the steering wheel and tries to right the car before it veers onto the footpath.

I smash my elbow into the gunman's head and take the gun from him.

'Stop the car,' I say, pointing the gun at the leader.

He complies, putting his foot on the brake whilst pushing AJ aside. I order the two surviving men out after taking their weapons. I also get them to take AJ's body out. Then I remove their balaclavas and snap their faces with my phone camera.

Standing outside the vehicle, on the footpath, I say to the leader, 'Who's your boss?'

He shakes his head.

'Speak,' I say, pointing the gun directly at him.

'I don't know. We get our instructions through a middleman.'

'And he is?'

'No idea.'

'Take your clothes off,' I say, raising my voice.

'What? It's freezing,' they both protest in unison.

'You heard.'

They get undressed and I toss their clothes into the vehicle as I keep the gun aimed at them. 'Now, if I ever see you again, I'll kill you. You will also have the police looking for you, so I suggest you leave the country.' Before they can respond I hit them unconscious. The cold conditions will not do their health any favours.

I get into the car and drive off.

SEVENTEEN:
Sunday

I'M BACK AT Richard's flat.

My front door is broken and, after driving back to my apartment, I secured it as best I could. On Monday I'll get it repaired.

Richard walks out of the bathroom with a towel around his midsection. His chest, dotted with straggly bits of hair, is bare. 'Breakfast in or out?' he asks.

'Let's wander down the road and get something at that café you like, you know the one?'

'Sure. But are you going to be safe?' asks Richard, stroking his moustache.

'I'll be fine. It's broad daylight and there are plenty of people about now that the weather's improved.'

Richard goes to his bedroom to dress. Last night, when I explained what happened, he said he couldn't believe the drama. He said he'd not told anyone about my new address. I can't live in fear and I won't. I now possess three guns, courtesy of my recent visitors, which I've hidden in my flat. Next time someone barges into my home uninvited, I'll have an opportunity to fight back, with deadly force.

We walk to the café without incident. The sky is a wonderful light blue. And no clouds mar the vista. Richard and I find a table and I insist on having my back to the wall. I'm taking no chances although I can't imagine anyone coming in with a weapon and displaying it.

'Can anyone find me on the internet?' I ask.

'Only if you posted your details on social media,' says Richard.

'I haven't done that,' I say. I rarely log into my Facebook account and I have less than twenty friends, none of whom are avid recorders of activities.

After breakfast, I tell Richard I'm going for a walk. He says he's off to a rehearsal as there's a new show he's in. His audition for a character part the week before proved successful. I'm pleased for him. He deserves to be working in a play or some other live performance. It's what makes him tick.

On my walk to nowhere in particular, I come across men and women, all types, all different ages, walking their dogs or out by themselves. If I had a settled existence and a residence allowing dogs, I'd get one. But that's something to consider in the future. Currently, I'm too focused on survival and the successful launch of a drug which may have wide-ranging consequences on how humans evolve. Of course, it may prove impossible to achieve the dream I have imagined but at least I'm going to give it my best shot. Did Alexander Bell, Charles Babbage or Tim Berners-Lee, the inventors of the telephone, the computer or the world-wide-web give up when they struck speed bumps? I doubt it.

My phone vibrates. I pull it out of the pocket of my trench coat and look at the number. It's Liz. 'Hello,' I say, 'you're back?'

'I am. How are you?'

How much should I reveal? A lot has happened since I last spoke to her. 'Fine,' I finally say, not wanting to go into any details. 'Did you have a nice break?'

'Lovely. The wedding was fabulous. I wonder whether we could meet.'

'Sure. When did you have in mind?'

'Tonight,' she says. Her voice conveys a sense that the meeting is important.

'Okay. Name the time and place. I'm flexible.'

WHEN I WALK into the quiet, out-of-the-way restaurant in Kensington, I can't sight Liz anywhere. Not at the bar or at a table. I mention to the attendant at the entrance there's been a booking in Liz's name, and I'm taken to a table in the back corner. I wonder whether Liz requested the location. I also wonder why she didn't suggest meeting up at her place. However, I'm happy enough with the spot and survey the menu while I'm waiting.

Five minutes later, Liz strides in. She's looking radiant, hair done stylishly in a modern fashion, I guess, not knowing what's fashionable or not. When she gets to the table, she removes her overcoat and I see she's wearing clothes which I suspect are new. She sits down without giving me a kiss on the cheek or lips.

'New outfit?'

'Yes. You're observant,' she gushes, 'I bought a few things abroad.'

'The wedding was good then?'

'Super. You're looking good, too. Have you had a make-over?'

I can't resist laughing. 'No.'

'Still, I can't recall seeing you looking so young.'

A waiter interrupts. He asks what we'd like to drink. Liz orders a glass of white wine and I order a lager.

'I need to tell you now, Ethan. I've met a man,' Liz says, beaming.

'Good,' I say, not knowing what else to say. 'At the wedding?' I take this news calmly but wonder why she would ditch me, if that's what's coming. I know I have an exaggerated sense of my worth and find it hard that others don't see it.

'No. In Majorca. He's nice and he's got a great job and he's single and he likes what I like and he's also keen to have children.'

'Did you marry him?' I ask, tongue-in-cheek. How am I supposed to react? She'll find he's not so terrific after a short time together.

She blushes. 'No, but he's perfect for me. I don't think you and I have a future. I'm sorry. You're a great bloke but our relationship wasn't going anywhere, was it?'

'You mean marriage?' Liz is right, we were having fun, but I had no thoughts of a future with her.

'Well…yes, if I'm honest.'

'And you need to be honest. No point in pretending. I wish you all the best, Liz,' I say, not revealing I've met Kirstie and that I'm happy with her.

'Thanks. You're taking it very well.'

'Why not. We've made no commitment to each other. I'm pleased for you. Now, let's order. I'm famished.'

There's no pressure during the rest of the meal. No expectations. During our conversation, I ask whether she's told anyone about my change of address, which I informed her about in an email.

'No, I don't think so. Let me think. I may have mentioned it to Anne in passing. Why?'

'Just wondered. I had an unexpected visit recently, that's all.'

'Oh. A surprise?'

'You could say that.'

We part on good terms as we walk to the underground where we head to different platforms to take different trains.

ANNE AGREES TO meet me at the same West End pub in which Liz and I joined Warren and Anne for drinks on the Saturday night I became so intoxicated that I spoke about my anti-ageing work. Tonight, a worried looking Anne is wearing black leggings, a dark green jumper, and an overcoat.

'Hi,' I say when she finds me. 'It's not that cold anymore, is it?'

'I feel the cold. In fact, I try to get away for a couple of weeks to Spain when the winter is at its worst.' She takes her overcoat off and places it on a stool facing me.

'Not this year?' I ask.

'What do you want?' Anne asks, her expression blank other than lips tight.

'I just need to ask you ask you a question. Nothing to worry about,' I say. 'Are you not going abroad then?'

'No. Can't really afford it. Can I get you a drink?'

'You sit down, and I'll get you a wine. You like a glass of red, if I recall.'

'Thanks, Ethan. You have a good memory.'

I make my way through to the bar, zigzagging to avoid patrons standing, chatting and drinking. The bartender is serving someone but nods in my direction when he sees me. Perhaps he remembers me from my previous visit. I don't remember him.

Because of the increasing numbers, with more people coming in, the noise is worsening, and I expect that I will find it difficult to have the conversation I want to have with Anne. I'll suggest another venue once we've had this drink. The bartender is standing in front of me.

'What will it be, Ethan?'

He knows my name. How? I must have made an impression the night I was here. 'A glass of Pinot Noir and a half-pint of lager. You remember me?'

'Yeah, mate. You're that Aussie. Warren comes here all the time. He told me about you.' The tall olive-skinned bartender is pouring wine into a glass.

'What did he say?' I ask, intrigued. Does everybody know my business, I wonder?

'This and that. That'll be …thanks, that'll cover it,' he says, talking my ten quid.

I wander back to my table and I'm surprised to see Anne talking with the woman in black. I rack my brain and recall her name: Gina York. She is dressed in black again. Top to bottom. I wonder whether she washes her clothes or simply only owns black clothes. 'Hello Ms Snitch,' I say. 'What are you doing here?'

Anne intervenes, 'That's not nice, Ethan.'

'She called the police when I visited her,' I say, placing the glass of red wine in front of Anne. I decide not to ask Gina whether she wants a drink.

'You were a wanted man,' Gina says, 'I didn't know whether you were dangerous.'

I don't believe a word of it, but I don't respond with hostility as it will only lead to an unpleasant argument. 'Yes, I was wanted to help with enquiries. But the cops don't think I'm a suspect anymore, even if they thought so originally.'

Anne looks at me with startled eyes. 'A suspect for what?'

'Mass murder,' I say, annoyed. She wants to know everything, it seems, so I told her something to be shocked about.

'My God.' Anne drinks half her glass of wine in one gulp then shakes her head. 'Liz didn't say anything about that. She normally confides in me.'

I now understand what's happened. Liz talks to Anne and Anne passes on information to Warren. Where does Gina fit in? I turn to Gina. 'Where's your friend?' In the dim light, her dark clothes almost make her invisible.

'He's not well. Any news on progress of your anti-ageing invention?'

'No.' I recall the decrepit guy she introduced me to and I'm dying to understand the relationship Gina has with him. I can't get my head around the fact that they may be lovers. 'Is this your regular haunt?'

'On weekends. Anne mentioned she might pop in and I thought I'd catch up,' Gina says, looking at Anne who finishes her wine.

'So, you two know each other?'

'Is that a crime?' Gina protests.

'No. Anne never told me, that's all.'

'Ethan, you and I only met a few weeks back. You were out of it, totally spaced out.'

'I see. Then you became friends?' I don't recall Gina at the pub that night, only Matt and his girlfriend. But I was extremely drunk. Who knows what else I'll discover about that fateful night?

Somebody bumps into Gina and she's pushed against me. Her breasts, which I now realise are huge, cushion the blow.

'Sorry,' she says.

'Not your fault,' I say, holding her so that we don't fall into other people. 'Can I get you a drink?'

'Thanks, but maybe another time. I have to get back to my friend,' Gina says and stalks off.

I drink my lager and Anne sips her wine as we remain silent. It seems Anne hasn't digested the news that I was wanted by the police. She doesn't make eye contact, simply looks around at the people coming and going. The place is now heaving and noisier than ever. It is so crowded now that I can smell the body odour wafting off some of the patrons. 'Anne, can we get out of here?'

'Why?' she almost shouts.

'Can't talk here,' I shout back.

Reluctantly she dons her overcoat and we walk outside.

'Where to?' she asks.

We stroll along the streets until we find a quieter place, a more intimate wine bar. I order the drinks and sit beside Anne who has kept her coat on despite the central heating. I remove my trench coat and place it beside me. 'I'm no killer,' I say.

'But the police had reason to suspect you, right?'

'It was a mistake and it's been cleared up,' I say looking directly at her.

Anne pushes hair from her forehead. 'Who was murdered?'

'My flatmates.'

'Oh. Sorry to hear that.'

'And had I been home, I may have been shot as well,' I say, not wishing to go into more detail.

Anne touches my hand. 'Sorry for over-reacting at the pub. I've never met anyone suspected of any crime before.'

'That's okay. I understand,' I say soothingly. 'I guess you told Warren that I'd moved to a new flat?' I suspect this is the case, but I want to confirm the information, nevertheless.

'Yes. Was that wrong of me?'

'No, no, not at all. I had a surprise visitor the other day and I wondered who might have said anything about my new place.'

'Oh. Who was it?'

'Just some friends of a friend,' I say, not wishing to tell her about other grisly matters. She'd probably freak out if I told her the truth.

'And were they friends of Warren?'

'I didn't ask. Anyway, let's enjoy this place. It's much cosier than that other bar. Have you been here before?'

'No. I might get back to that other pub after this drink. I may have mentioned the change of address to Gina, too. Can't remember.'

This news shocks me. Now I wonder who else knows. Warren and Gina may have talked to others. Why would they though? What's the fascination with knowing I've moved residence? 'Okay. Have you met Gina's boyfriend?'

'No. Why?'

'Nothing. She has an interesting taste in men, is all.'

'I have no idea. Gina moves in circles different to Warren and me.'

'Goths?'

'I guess. She's a nice person, even though she dresses in black and has black fingernails and wears black lipstick.'

'I noticed. I don't trust her.'

'Because of her appearance?'

'Perhaps I'm being judgemental. How's Warren?' I ask, wanting to change the topic.

'He's fine. He's actually flying off again tonight. Brussels. Business.'

We chat for another ten minutes and finish our drinks. Then we make our way to separate destinations. On the tube, I reflect on the evening and realise that Anne is not somebody to confide in. She's leakier than a damaged water pipe. She's likely to tell anyone she meets about business which isn't any of her concern.

EIGHTEEN:
Tuesday

I AM BACK AT home. My door has been replaced and I intend to ask the landlord for a reduction in the rent due to the unsafe neighbourhood. Which is not true. He won't buy this story, but I need to convince him the damage wasn't my doing, or from people I know. He'll claim the cost of the new door on insurance after giving me a warning, I feel sure.

I've had a snack of smoked salmon on a fresh bread roll I bought on the way home. I note the time. It's a little after eight o'clock and I'm tired. I've had a busy day at work on a variety of experiments. I have music playing in the background while I'm looking at my notes on anti-ageing. My formula is still in a safety deposit box, but I've been recording daily observations about my condition on my laptop. So far, with the second pill, there have been no notable changes either externally or internally. My blood pressure is a little higher than I'd like but not elevated enough to be of concern.

A knock on the door interrupts my thoughts. At least this time, nobody's smashing the new door in. I peep through the spyhole. It's the Goth. The woman who is forever dressed in black. Gina. I open the door and wait for her to speak. She says, 'May I come in for a moment.'

'Okay,' I say and let her pass before me. We walk to the living room and I point her in the direction of an armchair. 'Would you like a drink?'

'Thanks. Wine, if that's okay.'

I go to the kitchen, wondering what the hell she is doing here. Perhaps she arranged for the previous gang to attack me. I don't really think she did, but one can never know what desperate people will do.

Carrying a glass of white wine and a bottle of Peroni back into the living room, I say, 'Hope this is okay.'

She accepts the wine. 'Look, let me apologise for calling the police the other day. I was concerned about the safety of my friend.'

I sit down. 'Okay,' I say, 'apology accepted. You say he's your friend. Previously you said he was your boyfriend. Which is it?'

'Actually neither. He's my son. He has progeria, the disease which causes accelerated ageing.'

'I see. Why does he live in an apartment above yours then?'

'My ex-husband lived there. He arranged for carers to be there while I got to live downstairs. At least I'm able to visit each day but it's so depressing to see what's happened to him.'

'I'm sorry to hear that. How old is he?'

'Eleven.'

I sip my beer. I can understand her anguish. Any chance of saving the boy would be welcome. But I have no way of judging how my pill would affect the boy.

Gina crosses one leg over the other. She's wearing tight black jeans and I note that she has long legs. She says, 'That's why when I overheard your discussion at the pub...you know...about working on an anti-ageing drug...'

'Yeah, I see. What I have is in the early stage of development. It may not be safe. In fact, it could kill your son.'

'Maybe. But we have no other options. We've seen doctors and specialists, spent most of the money we had. It even broke up the marriage. I'll try anything.'

I have a dilemma. If I provide the pill to Gina and it kills the boy, I could be liable for murder or manslaughter or reckless disregard for human life. If the authorities accept that I was doing a favour for medical reasons, Gina may then turn on me and sue me. I close my eyes, trying to find a way out.

'You're concerned that you'll get into trouble if it fails, aren't you?'

Gina has read my mind. 'It's risky,' I say, 'I'll have to be present if I provide the drug.'

'Why? Don't you trust me?'

'Well, that's another question but I need to be there should the boy start to convulse or act poorly. I'll need to bring other medication if that happens. Do you understand?'

'But you're not a doctor, are you?'

I peer at Gina. 'I know about medications, it's my job. Want to go ahead?'

'Yes. When can you come?'

'Tomorrow night. I'll get all the necessary items ready and I'll drop by after work. About seven o'clock. Is that okay?'

Gina nods. She stands, pecks me on the cheek and leaves the flat.

NINETEEN:
Wednesday

~

THE DAY HAS turned grey and misty. I walk into the office with a carton of coffee. Cappuccino with one sugar. I'm thinking about last night and Gina's sudden visit. Was she being truthful? She played the part well, but she might be a consummate liar. How can I find out, I wonder? I pass a colleague who smiles at me and I nod hello.

At my desk, I place my coffee carton on the right-hand side of my desktop computer. I log in and check out my emails. I see there's nothing earth shattering, so I decide to deal with those of some substance later. I research the disease Progeria using Google and I read what is available on the topic. The disease is extremely rare with one person in four to eight million contracting it. People with this disease rarely live beyond thirteen years of age.

As I finish my coffee, I digest this information. How likely is Gina's story? Also, I cannot believe that the so-called boy wouldn't be in hospital. Her story is too far-fetched to be taken seriously. So, is Derek simply old? Is he her father or grandfather?

The rest of the day goes smoothly as I dismiss the idea of providing my pill to Gina and her friend, Derek. But I will keep my appointment. When I leave the building at six o'clock, it is dark, and rain has settled in. The rain is light, like a mizzle, so it doesn't bother me as I pull up my jacket lapel.

I reach Gina's basement flat just before seven, having stopped off to buy a sandwich. I knock on the glass section of her door and wait. I'm about to turn away when the door creaks open. Gina is dressed in black tonight. No surprise there. She smiles, then invites me in, walking ahead and turning towards me in her living room.

'You're wet. Didn't you take an umbrella to work?'

'No,' I say. 'I should have but I decided to risk it. Bringing a briefcase was enough for me.'

'You've brought the stuff?'

'I have.'

'Good, let's go upstairs.' We leave her flat after she grabs a small umbrella. She guides me up to Derek's flat and enters using her key.

Tonight, the flat is dark, with only sparse light emanating from the end of the hall. I walk along behind Gina and wonder if there are any unexpected parties awaiting me. But there are no police or thugs who accost me. I'm asked to take a seat and Gina walks up the interior stairs, presumably to fetch Derek. As she'll take a moment or two to accompany him to get down, I go to a cabinet to the right side of the sofa and I open the top drawers, not expecting to find anything of interest. One drawer contains papers, receipts and bills. The other drawer seems to have a folder atop more bits and pieces: papers, pens and pencils, USBs and a batch of business cards. I'm about to shut the drawer when my hand comes across a leather folder. I take it out and open it. There's a passport inside.

I look around to see whether Gina and Derek have started to come down the steps. Then I hear footsteps. I pocket the passport and replace the leather pouch in the drawer. I wander around, trying to appear curious about the storage rack which houses music CDs.

'What do you like?' Gina asks.

'I like modern music as well as Beethoven and stuff from the eighties.'

'You won't find any of that there. Derek loves music from the sixties,' Gina says. This strikes me as odd, I think, for a kid of eleven.

Derek has finally managed to descend from the top of the stairs to the bottom. Gina helps him into an armchair. 'Hello,' he says.

'Hello, Derek,' I say. 'How are you feeling?'

'Wretched,' he says.

I'm more than a little suspicious now. What kid would say that? But I sit down and await Gina's plan.

Gina asks whether I'd like a drink, but I decline. Then she asks about the drug. I hand it to her, and she gets a glass of water and hands the glass and pill to Derek. He takes the glass in a hand which shakes slightly, puts the pill into his mouth and swallows it. Gina and I both watch him.

Nothing happens.

After five minutes, I get up. 'Looks like there's no adverse reaction,' I say. 'Just keep an eye on him. It may take overnight for something to occur.'

'Sure,' says Gina as she walks me to the door. 'Thanks for your understanding.'

Stepping outside, I turn and say, 'Remember, it's only a trial. Nobody else has tried it. I was hoping to develop it further after having white mice test it.'

'Of course,' she says.

'Any questions?'

Gina shakes her head and closes the door.

As I move down the steps I see, from the corner of my eye, a curtain draw back from the window in Gina's flat. Somebody is there. This explains why it took so long for her to answer. But why would the person be hiding?

Without further thought I catch public transport home. There I remove my jacket and remember the passport. I open it. It tells me it belongs to Derek Morrison. The date of birth is eighty-eight years ago. I smile. Just as well I gave him a placebo rather than the anti-ageing pill. I can't believe how devious Gina was. She's clearly desperate. The big question is - why.

Tonight, I lock the front door using the full panel of locks, the first time I've done this. I now realise how important the very idea of an anti-ageing drug is. If it were well known that this drug is available, there's no thinking what people might do to get hold of it. It means I need to rethink my strategy of making it public, should it get to that stage.

I fall asleep wondering what my next step should be.

At 3:10 a.m. I wake. I toss and turn for a few minutes before I decide I can't get back to sleep. I get dressed in warm clothes and boots. A walk will do me good. I slip my iPhone into my overcoat pocket, undo the three locks, and wander out into the corridor. I have one neighbour opposite me and presume he or she is fast asleep. I've not met my neighbour yet, so I have no idea whether one or more people live there. I make a mental note to introduce myself this coming weekend.

Outside I pop a beanie on my head. It's not that I'm feeling the cold, merely to ensure my anonymity and normality. I wander along the street, not sure where I'm headed. But the cool air clears my mind from thoughts of doom and gloom. Although it is dark, a few street-lights atop lampposts stand at reasonable intervals to guide me in my journey. I only come across one other person. The young man is rugged up, suggesting that the cold is biting. It seems my pill is still working to help me ward off the extremes of temperature. I need to record how long this will last.

Feeling more settled, I turn back. This time of night is so peaceful. Void, almost, of other bodies and vehicles, it's a perfect time to reflect. I take in my surroundings for the first time. Houses, closed shops, schools and parks. Rejuvenated, I take the stairs to my flat. I feel energised and wonder whether I should begin running at this time of day.

Then, reaching the door to my floor, I stop suddenly. Three men in balaclavas are exiting my place and are about to get into the elevator. I press my back against the door. Are these the same men who kidnapped me before or a new group? And who organised them? Only Gina knows my address and wants the drug. She must have observed that Derek hadn't changed and ordered a hit. Or am I jumping to conclusions?

Perspiration is running down my back and my heart is thumping. These men are armed. I can see a pistol tucked at the back of one man's trousers. I daren't move. I wait an eternity as the elevator finally opens and they enter. I wait a moment then proceed to my front door which has been closed. I use my key to enter and can only surmise that they picked the lock rather than smashing the door as before.

Inside, I wander through each area to see whether they've searched everything. It appears they were only interested in finding pills. As a precaution, I had mixed them into a bottle of other medication. Some drawers had been examined but I suspect they came to interrogate me. Or kill me.

I lock the front door again. Will they come back tomorrow night or during the day? I need to find a new place. But I've just signed the lease for this flat. What a nightmare.

TWENTY:
Thursday

~

T MY DESK at ten o'clock on Thursday morning, I sit back, lace my fingers behind my head and consider my plight. I should call the police but what can I say? Report a break-in in which nothing was taken? Report sighting masked men coming out of my flat? They will argue nobody was hurt so what is the crime? They'll need me to describe the men in detail, but I can't do that.

I call Kirstie and ask her how she is. Although she is still a cop with only one day to go before the resignation kicks in, I am not going to impose on her, to ask to have police officers come over for a visit. Instead, I ask her whether a big leaving function in her honour is scheduled for Friday night.

'I don't know, to be honest. There'll be a speech from my boss and booze and cakes in the afternoon but after that, I have no idea. Come over tonight. I'm not working late.'

'Sure. Why not,' I say.

I leave work at five, earlier than I usually depart. At home, I change into casual attire. Then I remember the guns I confiscated. I'd hidden them in three separate spots so, I check the freezer first. Shit, the gun, a Sig Sauer 380 Auto, is gone. The thugs must have removed it. Next, I check under a pillow in the bed but, The Sig Sauer 9Mn is also gone. I curse out loud. I try to think where I've placed the third one but, I cannot recall. Then, after a moment, as I wander about, I remember. I open a small Samsonite smart carry-on bag which I've left on top of a tall clothes wardrobe. I breathe a sigh of relief. This one, a silver piece, had not been discovered as nobody thought to open the bag. I leave the Glock 19 9 mm semi-automatic pistol inside for the time being. At least I have one weapon if needed. Perhaps tonight I will place the pistol under my pillow in case of intruders.

Having resolved what items had been stolen, I get ready for the evening. I take a tube to Camden.

When Kirstie opens the door, I hand her a bottle of champagne and a bunch of red roses. She smiles, gives me a kiss, and takes the flowers off me, but leaves me to bring in the bottle of champagne.

I place the bottle of Moet on the kitchen table that is cluttered with newspapers, a laptop, a leather satchel and an empty cup. Kirstie comes over to me after placing the bunch of roses in a vase. She embraces me, and we kiss passionately, her tongue searching for mine. In my arms, she feels so sensual, so soft.

'What's this for?' she asks once we pull apart.

'A celebration,' I say, 'prior to the official one tomorrow.'

She takes my hand and guides me into the bedroom. A queen-sized bed is centred amid a stylish bedroom. We explore each other's bodies as though we'd never seen them before. Our love making is urgent, like two teenagers enjoying forbidden fruit. Done, we lie side by side, looking at the ceiling. We do not speak for some minutes, to allow the physical experience to sink in. Her fragrance is intoxicating, and I turn towards her.

'Still happy about leaving the police?'

'Oh yes. I'll be free tomorrow night.' Kirstie moves across to me and puts her head on my shoulder.

I stroke her hair. 'I'm pleased you're happy about it. As long as you have no regrets.'

'Let's get something to eat,' she says, 'I'll order pizza.'

We dress. Kirstie asks what I want and places an order. She fills two glasses with champagne, then says, 'Any more dramas with hoodlums?' She says this jokingly as though she cannot imagine such a thing could happen again.

'Well, actually…'

'Really?'

I tell her the story of my early morning visitors.

'I'll have somebody call around. You may need protection.'

'I doubt your colleagues would take me seriously.'

Kirstie sits back and thinks. 'You may be right. You'll stay with me for a while though. I don't want anything to happen to you.'

'That's sweet. But I don't want to put you out.'

'Don't be silly. You're staying.'

'Okay,' I say, 'I like it when you're firm. Discipline is what I need.'

Before she can respond there's a knock on the door. The pizza man is here. As I reach for my wallet, Kirstie stops me. I wait while Kirstie takes care of the order. We share the large pizza while Kirstie awaits my decision.

I decide to stay the night which puts a smile on Kirstie's face. Tonight, I will focus on the here and now. And I will work out what I need from my apartment tomorrow. The prospect of being with Kirstie for even a short time excites me.

The night passes uneventfully but blissfully. My anxieties have disappeared. In the morning I explain to Kirstie that I will return after grabbing clothes and necessities from my flat.

During the day, I work on my current assignment with which I am totally focussed. The concerns with my new drug have gone. I've recorded data relating to my experiment on a USB which I'll transfer to my laptop when I get home. At six I leave the office. I haven't heard from Kirstie and hope she is enjoying her final hours at the station.

The weather has turned nasty again. Chilly winds blow. People are in a hurry to get inside. The tube is packed with commuters in heavy overcoats and pushy individuals. It's bad but I visualise the Tokyo underground which is no doubt considerably worse. Except that Japanese people are patient and more gracious. British people prefer to whinge about their lot. A cultural thing, I guess. A man bumps into me as the train halts suddenly.

'Damn driver,' he mutters. But he doesn't apologise for ramming into me.

I straighten up again, holding onto the overhead bar. It won't be long now. The next station is mine. I'm thinking about the evening ahead and hope Kirstie isn't held up too long.

I whistle to myself as I insert a new key into the front door which have had the locks changed. I push the door in, look around and wander in. But when I get to the end of the hall, a short dozen steps, I peer cautiously into the darkened living room because something doesn't feel right. I switch the lights on.

A gun is pointed at me.

'Sit down,' says a voice from a masked face.

I do as I'm told, choosing my favourite armchair. I see two other men with balaclavas standing at the back of the living room. They now move behind their leader. All are dressed in black outfits accompanied by heavy black boots. Footwear dirt has stained my lovely beige carpet. I'd make a comment but, in the circumstances, I'll hold back. 'What the fuck do you want?' I ask, speaking more confidently than I feel.

'I think you know,' says the leader, a tall man with a small head.

'How could I know? Are you the guys who bustled me into a van some weeks back?' I ask, wanting to know if they know about my enhanced strength.

'What are you talking about?' asks the leader. 'Don't play games. Where is that formula?'

'Of course, this is what this is all about. Why am I not surprised?' I need to keep them talking so that I can get them to lower their guard. The gun is the issue. Without that, I would take them on. 'I don't have it here. Is that why you raided my place yesterday?'

'I'll ask the questions, understood?' says Small head.

I nod. He puts his gun on the coffee table in front of the armchair he's sitting on. He feels confident I won't be a threat.

'Where is it?'

Without warning, thunder booms across the heavens. Then rain pelts down, streaming its force against my window. The storm rages and for a moment, nobody speaks. Nature wants to make a point. Unfortunately for me, this group also want to take charge.

'Are you keen on using it yourself?' I ask, conscious that I need to get Small head talking and distracted.

'What did I say about asking questions?' says Small head, irritation evident in his tone. 'Tell me what I want to know, or we'll beat it out of you.'

I observe how the two men behind him are positioned. The big beefy one has his arms crossed over his chest. The other man, smaller but fit-looking, has his arms by his sides. No weapons are visible although I suspect they also carry guns. 'Well…,' I say, suddenly getting out of my chair and, taking a short step forward, I overturn the coffee table with my left hand. The gun slides off the table but before the armchair man can gather it, I jump at him and strike his head with the side of my right foot, as though his head is a soccer ball. I had not tried this kick on a person before although I have performed a similar action in the gym on a basketball, after which I rolled onto a rubber mat.

Two men grab my arms, but I use my strength to push them back. Three of us are on the floor, all trying to gain an advantage. After some wrestling we manage to get back onto our feet. I punch the smaller man in the jaw, and he falls back down. The larger man gets me from behind in a bear-hug, but I stand erect and snap his embrace by smashing his face with the back of my skull. He lets go. I scramble aside to size up the positions of the two men I have knocked back, ready to kick and hit with my closed fist.

'Stay where you are,' says Small head, the leader who seems to have recovered.

When I turn, he has his pistol trained on me. I'm done. I may have enhanced strength but I'm no match for a bullet, as I've already experienced. The ease with which I've dealt with the two hooded men confirms the endurance of my greater strength but that's too bad. I won't have the opportunity to record this information, I'm certain. These men, if they don't kill me immediately, will no doubt cause me considerable harm through torture. And this is one experience I haven't had the misfortune to undergo. And I'm not keen to find out.

I stare at Small head while his two bruised colleagues get back on their feet.

'What shall we do with him?' asks the small fit guy, his voice slightly high-pitched. I'd recognise the whiny voice again if I ever had the opportunity to meet him in some future encounter.

'We are…'

Suddenly my front door crashes in and all of us are on alert, the leader forced to look back. The noise of an armed group shouting for all hands to be raised drowns out the sound of the unrelenting storm. I'm confused. I raise my hands as does Small head.

A SWAT team, numbering six men, submachine guns in full view surround us. The leader's gun, still in the air, is removed by one of the men. The masked men are paraded off, handcuffs applied in a brutal manner. I'm left alone.

The SWAT team leader says to me, 'You can thank Kirstie. We'll be in touch to talk with you about this incident.' Without another word, he follows his team out through the broken door. My landlord won't be happy.

I have a beer and sit down to calm my nerves. Afterwards I gather my suitcase and items for my stay with Kirstie.

Kirstie and I are sitting in her living room. She has a cup of tea in front of her on the coffee table. She appears relaxed. I am slouched next to her, holding a bottle of Becks beer. I take a drink and then place it on the coffee table.

'What a day,' she says.

'Absolutely. Thank you again. What made you arrange the rescue team?'

'After your story about the break-in, I didn't feel comfortable that you'd be safe when you returned to get your stuff. I had one of my colleagues watch the place. He reported an irregularity when he saw three men entering the tower and looking about. He raised the alarm. So, they were on their way before you even entered the building.'

'Wow. How did you manage to convince them to raid my place with a SWAT team?'

'My father. He called in a favour. He used to be a big cheese in the Met.'

I pulled her towards me, put my arm around her shoulders and kissed her. 'You are wonderful.'

'Don't get soppy.'

'Will I be told who they are and the person orchestrating the attack?'

'You'll be interviewed and informed at the same time. You'll have to come clean though.'

I sit up straight, retrieved my beer, and swallowed another mouthful. 'Of course.'

TWENTY-ONE:
Friday

T HE INTERVIEW ROOM at the Belsize Park police station is nothing fancy, I see, when I'm invited in by a uniformed officer. Then another police officer, a powerfully built plain-clothes man, pops in before I sit down and asks me to accompany him.

'Sorry, sir,' he says, as we walk along the corridor, 'That's for suspects mainly. We have an office where we can have a private talk. I'm DI Jim Callaghan, by the way.'

'I'm Ethan…'

'I know,' says Jim.

I follow the officer, a fair-haired man, to an office and he points to a vacant seat. A woman comes in and sits down near me. Jim takes the seat opposite us. The office has a large desk with a desktop computer and papers strewn about. Filing cabinets sit to my left. The room is painted a light grey.

Once we're set, DI Jim Callaghan says, 'My colleague here is DS Jean Drysdale. We can talk in this office without video recording. I will set up my phone for audio recording to obtain your story, if that's all right?'

I nod. 'Sure,' I add.

Drysdale, a woman in her thirties, nods to me. 'Hello. Did you find us okay?'

'Yes. I'm new to the area but I'm discovering more about my surroundings every day.'

Callaghan, a fit man in his forties, coughs to get our attention. 'Would you take us through the events of last night?'

I tell them my story. I can see that DI Callaghan has a strange expression on his face. He doubts my version, I believe.

'You challenged three big men, one of whom had a gun sitting on a coffee table?'

Without explaining my pharmaceutical background, my current experiment and the drug which gives me added strength and confidence, I can appreciate how the story seems far-fetched. I doubt I'd believe it if I were listening to somebody spin this tale. But I don't propose to tell the cops about this. They would probably think I'm delusional or on drugs, so I'd better come up with a more convincing story. 'It wasn't quite like that. As I said, the gun was on the table and I felt my only chance to prevent a beating or even death was to try to grab it. The rest of the events happened in a kind of blur and I would have died without the police intervention.'

'Okay. That makes more sense. Why were these men after you?'

'That's a good question. I don't really know. Did you happen to find out what the thugs said they were doing invading my place?'

DS Drysdale turns to me and says, 'We shouldn't be talking to you about our investigation, however, sir, if I may…'

'Go ahead Jean,' says Callaghan.

'The spokesman said they were given a contract to terrorise you so that you would reveal a secret. Do you understand what he meant?'

'Can't say I do,' I say. 'Did they say who put them up to this?'

'No. Thought you might be able to help us,' says Callaghan. "Do you have enemies? Anything that can help us?'

'I wish I knew,' I say. 'Have you arrested the men?'

'You bet. We're going to throw the book at them.'

'Great,' I say, thinking I would like to be the one doing the throwing. But I would throw something other than a book.

THE PARTY IS in full swing. Kirstie and I arrive at nine o'clock, later than the scheduled time of eight. We had enjoyed a curry at a restaurant near the house to which we'd been invited. The party venue is a large house in Golders Green. Told the place was in St Andrew's Road, we walked along the path. Tennis courts abounded in a street of fine houses, cars lining both sides of the narrow road. We finally reached the right address, a double storey white house with a well-kept garden visible from the street.

When we had entered, I noted the circular staircase to the right, winding up to the next level. Our coats were taken, and we were led into the main party room, a room designed to entertain. We'd brought two bottles of wine, but it was clear this wasn't necessary. There was so much booze on offer, our contribution would be lost amongst the vast array stored in the bathtub. But Anne had smiled and said it was appreciated.

'Warren's busy but he'll say hello soon,' says Anne, dressed in a sleek outfit accentuating her slim figure.

'Thanks for the invitation,' I say, 'Anne, this is Kirstie.'

The two women smile at each other and acknowledge the introduction. Anne invites us to mingle. Before we can say anything, she excuses herself to answer the door which has just chimed again.

'Will we run into your ex-girlfriend?' Kirstie asks.

'Probably,' I say, 'I hope you're going to behave.'

'Of course, darling, but I won't promise to be good to you when we get back home.' Kirstie grins.

'Understood,' I say, playing along. I like Kirstie's sense of humour.

Home is at Kirstie's flat. I am staying with Kirstie at present because my landlord has told me I'm no longer wanted as a tenant. He said during my last discussion he cannot keep fixing my busted front door. Although I could challenge him legally, I'd agreed to move my stuff out during the following week.

Kirstie and I accept a glass of champagne offered by a man in a waiter's outfit. As he continues on his way, the waiter maintains his dour expression. I'm wondering what kind of party this is and why I've been invited. The place is heaving. I guess there must be a hundred or more people wandering about, chatting, drinking or simply standing around and watching the activities. And, to my delight, the function is catered as I see a woman with a tray of finger food coming up to us. Kirstie takes a wrap of some kind off the tray. I select a stick of carrot. After my meal at the Indian restaurant, I can't bring myself to eat anything substantial. I don't know how Kirstie does it but she's a big girl and can probably manage to eat more, and more often than I can.

I lose Kirstie as we wander through the throngs of people, some dressed in costumes designed, I suspect, to present a fun appearance. Kirstie and I have come in smart casual clothes and I make a mental note to stay no longer than an hour. I'm still puzzled by the purpose of this function and, particularly, by the reason I'm here. I'm not a friend of Warren and Anne's.

'Hi,' says a familiar voice.

I turn around to see Liz who is dressed in a flowing, floor-length, polka dot dress. Her shoulders are bare, a couple of straps holding up the elegant gown. The heating in this house makes it possible for such outfits to be worn without worrying about the February cold. 'How are you?' I say.

'I'm fine. Glad you could make it. Great party, isn't it?'

'Yes. What's the occasion?'

'Warren is celebrating a couple of things, combining a recent business win together with his fortieth birthday.' Liz pulls out a small mirror from her purse and checks her lipstick.

'I see. He must be rolling in it.'

'Yes, he's well off. As an options broker, he makes a fantastic salary and his bonuses are monstrous.' Liz sips her drink, a Campari, I guess, judging from its red appearance.

'Did you get Anne to invite me?'

'No. She decided all by herself. As you can see, there are lots of people. Maybe she invited everyone she thought Warren knew. His work colleagues are here as well as school buddies and well, us.'

'And we're the important ones,' I say, tongue-in-cheek. Liz is a close friend of Anne's but now that I'm no longer with Liz, I find my invitation to be odd, mysterious even.

'Ah, I see someone I've been meaning to catch up with. I'll catch you later, okay?'

"Sure,' I say watching Liz wiggle through the crowd.

I walk out onto the balcony which has heaters keeping the cold from outside at bay. Lights shine across the back garden. Well-tended lawn and gardens of plants and flowers are visible. Beyond the immediate lawn are tennis courts. Two courts. I wonder how often Warren plays the game. He does not appear to be a sporting type, but I could be wrong. With his thick physique and prominent midsection, I would imagine him to be more comfortable in pubs and at fancy restaurants.

I look around and the balcony is less cramped than inside. I can't see Kirstie and hope she's having a good time. As I contemplate my next move, I sense somebody sneaking up on me. I've discarded my empty champagne flute and my hands are free. I'm leaning forward, elbows on the balcony railing. I ponder how many people can stand here, having heard of balcony collapses before. But this structure seems sturdy and I turn to face Gina, the woman in black. Even in this party setting, her severe black outfit accompanied by black lipstick and black nails is disconcerting. I wonder as I gaze at this picture of horror whether she's into black men too.

'Well, hello, Ethan, fancy seeing you here,' she says.

'Fancy,' I say now turning fully to see that she's dressed in a tight black dress, black stockings and black boots. Her hair is raven black, and I wonder whether she has it coloured like that or whether the colour is natural. I imagine she has tattoos under her clothing, all in black. Yet she possesses the most extreme white skin, an Irish white, I presume, that I've ever witnessed on a person. What a contrast any black tatts with her natural colouring would be. This is not a topic I will raise however, as she may assume, I would want to sleep with her. This is a fantasy even I cannot entertain. Yet, as I examine her closely, I see a beauty I've not noticed previously. The flawless skin and smirk make her a curious study.

'Where's Derek?' I ask, knowing that this might be a sensitive issue.

'He's at home. Dying.'

'Have you called an ambulance?'

'You're not a nice person, are you? Not sympathetic to other people's misery.'

'Sorry. But you lied to me about Derek and his age. Do you remember?' Gina is holding a can of beer which she crushes. She drops it on the tiled floor. 'What makes you say that?'

'I found his passport which I will return,' I say.

She seems stunned, her delayed response telling. 'You stole his passport?'

'Sorry. I was confused by your stories,' I say.

'You could've helped. I didn't know how else to prise a sample of the anti-ageing formula out of you. You have no compassion.'

I'm tired of this topic. It's always the same with her. She still hasn't told me what her real relationship to Derek is. I fail to accept that he's the boyfriend. 'How do you know Warren?' I ask, simply to change the subject.

'He's a friend.'

It occurs to me that it was Warren rushing off down the road when I'd visited her recently, when she took a long time to answer the knock on her door. 'A good friend?'

'Why do you want to know?'

A waiter with drinks arrives. Gina takes a can of beer off the tray while I grab a bottle of Heineken. I'll have this drink then I might take Kirstie home, I figure. I'm not someone who likes to make small talk so mingling with strangers is not really my cup of tea. 'How old is Derek?' I ask. I know this question is both impolite and annoying, but I want Gina to go away.

To my surprise she answers, 'Eighty-eight. Not that it's any of your business.'

This is true, according to the passport I nabbed. 'How does a young woman like you maintain a relationship with a man so old?'

Her expression is such that I think she's going to slap me. My impertinence probably deserves this punishment, but I don't care. As I wait for the reaction, Warren appears.

'Glad you could make it,' he says. He's dressed in a black satin shirt and white trousers. With his hair swept back, he reminds me of a playboy, keen to impress on people that he is rich and available. I wonder what Anne thinks of his slick appearance. Although with his fat gut, I can't imagine him having much success with the ladies.

'Happy birthday,' I say. I note that Gina is smiling at him. Did she know him prior to the Saturday night Warren, Anne, Liz and I were at that West End pub at which I disclosed my secret. What a night that was, one which subsequently has brought so much trouble.

'Thanks, buddy. Hitting this age, I realise I'm getting on. Wouldn't mind if somebody did discover a way to make me look and feel younger.'

'Of course. We'd all like that.'

'Getting anywhere with your attempts?' he asks, taking a party pie from the tray a floating waitress has presented.

She offers the goodies to me and Gina. I decline any food. Gina takes a fried chicken wing from the selection of fast foods.

I wonder why Warren has taken an interest in my invention. Previously, he'd made out the notion of anti-ageing was fanciful. 'Still trying. These things take time,' I say.

'Good luck with that. What do you think Gina?' he says, turning to the woman in black.

Gina almost chokes on her mouthful of chicken and can't speak. She simply nods.

'If you get anywhere with it, let me know, okay?' says Warren who turns around and heads off back into the house.

Gina finishes her snack and I'm pleased she hasn't thrown up. She says, 'How much would you charge if you get it right?'

'I haven't thought that far ahead and …,' I say. My phone cuts me short. I answer. It's Kirstie.

'Where are you?'

'Meet you at the door,' I say, 'We probably should make tracks.'

When I meet Kirstie at the front, she smiles. 'We both had the same thought. I've had enough mingling with these ponces.'

When we get to Kirstie's place, we go straight to bed.

TWENTY-TWO:
Saturday

~

FTER A BREAKFAST of eggs on toast, Kirstie and I drive to my flat in a hired van. We gather my possessions and place them in the back. I don't have enough items to hire a truck. I've always rented furnished flats, so I didn't have to worry about bedroom and living room furniture and refrigerators.

'Is that all?' asks Kirstie.

'I'll do one last check,' I say, 'you stay here.'

I return to the flat and walk through each room. In the bathroom, I investigate the cabinet which held toiletries. Suddenly I recall that I'd removed everything, but I don't remember clearing out the few bottles of pills. I try to think but no memory of actually packing the pill bottles returns. Would the police have taken them? I doubt it. I imagine I must have piled them into a box. It's not worthwhile worrying about. I'll find them when I unpack. I go downstairs and get into the van beside Kirstie. She drives off.

'How do you feel about living with me?' Kirstie asks.

'We'll see how long we last,' I say. 'If I pay half the rent, you'll save some money.'

'Is that all you can think about?'

'Of course not,' I say, wondering whether she's taking my flippant comment to heart.

'I hope you don't focus on money,' Kirstie says, easing to a stop at a set of red lights, minutes after leaving my flat in Belsize Park in north London.

'Are we having our first fight?'

She laughs. 'It'll happen sometime. May as well get it out of the way.'

'Interesting perspective. But being a cop, you're used to confrontation.'

'You better watch it. I might clasp some handcuffs on you.'

'Didn't you have to give them up?'

'Yes. But I have some personal ones,' Kirstie says, firing a cheeky glance at me. She continues driving on the A2 through Bloomsbury, across the Thames and then south through Lambeth, Peckham and Brockley.

We laugh and chat about nonsensical things until we reach her place in Catford.

When I unpack, I cannot find the pills. The anti-ageing pills were hidden in one of the bottles. Surely nobody went in and took them. The door wasn't locked as it was damaged, but I can't imagine anyone going inside. The men who'd broken in had been arrested so it couldn't have been them. It is indeed puzzling. Then, as I wander back to the kitchen to inspect the contents of the fridge, a thought surfaces. Who would know about the raid? Obviously, the person who put the gang up to barging into my flat. That makes sense, but I can't figure out who the mastermind is.

At noon, we have a snack then Kirstie says she'll visit her sister's store. She's going to start her new job on Monday but thought it would be useful to pop out there beforehand to observe how the place is run.

'Great,' I say. I'll sort through my books and music and organise them. 'You enjoy the afternoon and I'll book a restaurant for tonight.'

I walk along the streets to familiarise myself with the area. Kirstie lives in Catford, south-east of the city of London. Walking through the centre of Catford, I'm reminded of an article I researched on the internet, earlier that day.

"As Catford resident columnist Lucy Mangan put it, this is *the only place in all of London and the south-east set to remain impervious to gentrification*. Catford has its flaws. But it also has beautiful, reasonably priced homes (for London), good playgrounds, parks and schools, and smashing examples of what used to be called "continental grocers", of which Turkish Food Express is one."

I window shop and stroll in a leisurely manner. It is not as cold as the last few weeks, with people wearing warm clothes but few overcoats are on show. I feel wonderfully comfortable with a T-shirt and light jacket. I find a café and walk inside. Just as I pull a chair aside, my phone buzzes.

I sit down and look at the screen. The number is withheld. I answer, suspecting, it's an insurance salesman or a charity requesting a donation. But it's a voice I recognise, albeit in a hysterical state. I can't make out what is being said, so I say, 'Calm down. Who is this?'

'It's me, Gina.'

'What's wrong?'

'It's Derek, he's in hospital. He's in a serious condition,' Gina whines.

'He's old. Why are you calling me?'

'It's your pills. He took two. Do you have something to help him survive?'

I'm totally blown away as I pull the menu towards me. 'How did you get my pills?'

'I can't talk about that now. I need to save Derek's life.'

'I haven't produced an antidote, if that's what you're after,' I say, trying to imagine what I'd have to engineer to create an effective reversal.

Gina sobs. She's unable to take this in. She probably feels responsible for the man's demise.

'Where are you? I'll come over,' I say realising I have to witness this. I need to see the effect of a person taking two of the anti-ageing pills. It may sound morbid, but I'm a scientist, after all.

I hate hospitals yet here I am again. I ask for Derek and I'm told only family are permitted as he's just been released from intensive care. I can't pretend I'm family, so I walk away from reception. I text Gina who explains where she is. I ride up the elevator and when I get off on the right level, the one Gina said she's at, I find her waiting when the doors slide open. Dressed in her usual black garb, I have the unpleasant thought that soon she may be at a funeral and then she would finally be dressed appropriately. She doesn't look happy but, nevertheless, she takes me to the general area in which Derek's bed is located. A nurse queries us but Gina tells her that she is family and that I'm her husband. What a seasoned liar she is, I realise.

We walk into Derek's ward. He has all sorts of things attached to him. I dare not ask what they are nor am I interested. I recognise a drip for fluid intake, the ventilator to assist breathing and an arterial line for blood pressure monitoring but I don't focus on all the things sticking into him. I look at the man. He looks dreadful. His whole body seems shrunken. I look at Gina who appears quite distressed. 'This is your fault,' she says.

'What happened?'

She wipes a tear from her cheek. 'I gave him a couple of pills from one of your bottles.'

'You're at fault, you idiot. Since when are you qualified to administer medicine of which you know nothing?'

She tears up but I cannot feel sorry for her. She's stupid and dangerous.

'How did you know which bottle?' I ask.

'You only had three bottles in the cabinet, and I could tell which ones were genuine and which ones had nothing to do with the label.'

'So, you stole the bottle of experimental pills. Why?'

'Because I needed them.'

Furious but maintaining a calm exterior, I say, 'Tell me what happened. In detail.'

'I thought you may have kept some of your pills at home and the medicine cabinet seemed like a logical place to search. I asked some guys, mates of a friend of mine, to take everything you had in there which looked like pills. They also found guns at your place. So, if you call the cops, I'll tell them about you hiding weapons.'

'I see,' I say, happy to have resolved one mystery, 'then what happened?'

'Well, I gave Derek two pills to speed up the anti-ageing process. Watching him, I saw that it took a little time to work but magically, he went from looking in his late eighties to looking just over fifty. It was a miracle.'

I wonder, peering at the shrivelled body, why the effect on Derek is so different from mine when I took only one pill. Am I going to end up like this? But I say, 'Go on.'

'Derek felt better. He even smiled. He ate heartily and I was pleased. He said he felt stronger as well and he demonstrated this by lifting something he couldn't dream of trying to lift previously – an armchair. In fact, he felt so good, he wanted to do it again. So, I gave him another pill.'

'You gave him a third pill?' I'm astounded by this development. Was she telling the truth? Of course, when I experimented, I didn't take more than one pill. Then to have taken two in quick succession explains the different outcome. At least now I know that's something to avoid. But to have overdosed by taking three pills is lunacy. I don't know how I can get this message across to Gina. Besides, it's now too late to fix the error.

'Yes. We waited for the magic to kick in but instead, after half an hour, he began to tremble. Then he collapsed and I called emergency services.'

'You've experimented with something which you shouldn't have. You're not a scientist and you've done something so irresponsible, I can't believe…'

'I didn't know,' she blubbers.

A doctor comes in. 'Would you please go outside,' he says as he looks at the readings on the monitoring equipment.

We walk downstairs without another word. We find a café and I order a cappuccino for me and a tea for Gina.

'Can't you do something?'

I simply stare at her. I shake my head but refuse to console this cretin.

'You invented it. You must know how to fix the effects.'

'You don't seem to understand,' I say, 'it needs to be thoroughly tested and you've taken it without permission and administered an experimental drug without regard for safety.' I know I'm being harsh, but I had warned her before.

'I'm sorry. Will he die?'

'Probably but I'm no better able to guess the outcome than you are.'

Gina, in her severe black appearance in contrast to the white walls of the cafe, sips her tea. Today she is dressed in black jeans, a black top, a black overcoat and a black scarf, covering her head. Black strands of hair escape parts of the scarf. I wonder whether she'd like to have dark black skin like some Africans as well. 'It's in the hands of the Gods then,' she says.

'I guess,' I say, not interested in finding out what weird beliefs she may hold. I'm reminded of a Woody Allen joke I read where a couple were in conflict. One was an atheist and the other an agnostic and they didn't want to conceive a baby because they couldn't agree how the child should be brought up. But something was still bugging me. 'Had you arranged break-ins to my flat?'

'Of course not.'

'I don't believe you.'

'Derek may have hired people,' she says, looking innocent.

'You're lying. You said before you had enlisted some men, friends of a friend,' I say, wondering whether she ever told the truth.

'Alright. I did. Satisfied?'

'So how did they find my place?'

'Through Warren. I visited him to see if he knew where you lived. Anne had told him,' she says.

I drink some coffee. A couple near us are quietly consuming a meal. They seem sad and I wonder what their story is. A child or a parent dying of something, I imagine? 'Tell me the truth. Who is Derek?'

Gina looks at me. She seems torn. 'It's complicated. He's my grandfather.'

'What's complicated about that?'

'I promised to look after him. He's the only person who cared for me. He raised me and I owe him my life. My mother bore me when she was nineteen. She didn't know who the father was. She was addicted to drugs and died when she was thirty. But she never looked after me. My grandfather persuaded her not to have an abortion and he and my grandmother took me in. Nan died when I was thirteen. So, Derek looked after me and he did everything to make me feel wanted. We have a close bond.'

'I see,' I say. Now the whole business makes more sense. 'Don't you have a boyfriend?'

'No. I have nobody. Derek kept me sane.'

'What about other …'

'Goths?'

'Yes.'

We finish our hot beverages and I leave after telling Gina that I'm sorry this had happened because of my drug. I give Gina a gentle touch on her arm. 'You'd better get back,' I say. 'Another thing. Return the rest of the pills. They're dangerous.'

'I will. Thanks for coming.'

She looks pitiful as I walk towards the exit. I almost feel sorry for her.

TWENTY-THREE:
Saturday

~

Pavle Stanoski is playing tennis in Sydney. He strikes the ball fiercely, imagining hitting the head of somebody he hates. He hates a lot of people. That is his nature. The smash flies past his opponent for a winner. He raises his fists. The score is 6-2, 6-3 in his favour. He runs to the net and shakes the hand of Brian Milton.

'Well played,' says Milton.

'Thanks for the game,' says Stanoski.

The two men walk into the club house. 'A beer?' asks Milton.

'Wonderful,' says Stanoski, 'In this heat a cold beer will be perfect.'

Stanoski sits in a chair and awaits his beer. He nods hello to a couple of members who are waiting to play. Milton sits next to him.

'How long are you here?' asks Milton, handing his guest a bottle of Coopers.

'Just a few days. Here on business. Arrived two days ago. Thanks for letting me play. Needed some activity.'

'No problem,' says Milton. 'Hope you do the same for me when I'm in Germany.'

'Of course,' says Stanoski, 'Lena will be happy. Hasn't seen Judy for a year.'

'Judy talks to Lena once a month. So, you have just had another child, I hear. Congratulations.'

'Danke Schoen Brian. A little girl, Emma.'

Both men sip their beers from the bottle and look about. Some players are coming back from a court and today's court captain organises another doubles match, leaving the members sitting inside the clubhouse chatting, with others moving from their chairs out onto a vacant court.

'How's business?' asks Milton.

Stanoski grins, 'Okay.' He doesn't mention the unrealised loss he's sustained in options. His broker, an Englishman, has led him on, getting him to dedicate more funds into commodity trades. So far, the cost to him has been over two million US dollars. This has strained his cash flow that he needs to run his business in Germany. But Stanoski doesn't want to think about it nor talk about it. 'Thanks for the game and drink, Brian. Need to clean up before meeting a potential buyer tonight.'

Stanoski stands, shakes Milton's hand, and walks down the path to his hire car, a Ford. Although Stanoski is European and can't imagine living elsewhere, he enjoys Australia where the weather is usually sunny, even in winter. Once his business is humming, he'll book a holiday in Queensland, he says to himself. His wife and young ones will enjoy the break.

KIRSTIE IS SNUGGLED up against me, in bed. We've got the television on, but we are only watching the crazy talent quest intermittently. I've told her about Derek and his condition.

'Wow,' she says, 'it's dangerous stuff. Why did you ever think of using it yourself?'

'Foolish, I know, but I didn't have the lab to myself. I couldn't use the work facilities to conduct experiments in a measured way. It was a gamble.' I brush my lips against her cheek. 'Nice to know you care.'

'But it seems other people want the pill. How many times have you been assaulted now?'

I lean back, trying to recall the details. 'There's the original assault when my flatmates were murdered. Then I was kidnapped a few days later. Broke free with my enhanced strength. A week ago, men broke in, smashing my door down. They drove me towards my work, but I managed to get away after using one of their guns. Then two days ago, men were waiting for me. That's the occasion you got your colleagues to rescue me. So, four times. On top of that, there was the burglary which accounted for pills being stolen. God, when I look at the incidents in that light, I have to admit I'm lucky to be alive.'

'You're taking this in your stride. Are you sure you're not blocking the memories out? You need to see a psychologist, I think.'

Kirstie is right. I need help. These attacks have made sleeping difficult. Images of men in balaclavas have assailed me at night but I've tried to keep it under control. 'I'm not sure anything will help except catching the culprit who's been setting up these attacks.'

'I can use some of my police contacts to help you out,' Kirstie says.

'The police have already been pursuing the murders and the mastermind for the last attack. Nothing's come of it so far,' I say as I slip further under the covers. I bury my face between her breasts.'

'You're incorrigible,' she says.

TWENTY-FOUR:
Sunday

~

WHEN STANOSKI STEPS outside the North Sydney Harbourview hotel in Blue Street, he experiences the intense heat of an Australian morning. Such a contrast from the cold in Europe. He stands for a moment to look about. The time according to his iPhone is ten minutes after nine o'clock. Although the breakfast of bacon and eggs with black coffee was enough to satisfy him, he wants a stronger coffee. The hotel coffee was too bland for his taste.

He walks along Walker Street into the centre of North Sydney and he's amazed how dead the place is. In Germany, everything is open on Sundays. Apart from the coffee, he wants to buy some shorts. His jeans are far too hot in this climate. Still, a walk will do him good, he figures, if he does not melt first.

As he heads back to the hotel forty minutes later, he can't help thinking of the foolish decision he made, trusting Warren Buckley. The value of his account today, when he checked on the client platform, is now less than one hundred thousand US dollars. And to think his account was once almost five million dollars. Yet Warren kept saying he had another trade which would take him close to ten million dollars.

Stanoski rides the elevator up to his floor, unhappy. He is furious with Warren but also angry at himself. How could he have been so gullible? And here in Sydney the buyer had backed out, unable to commit to a delivery of women's fashion. He packs his bags when he is inside the hotel room. No need to linger. He may as well return to Munich and to his wife, Lena, their son, and their baby daughter. He looks at her photo which he keeps in his wallet. She is beautiful. Tall, slim, blonde with a lovely warm smile and radiant skin. She would have come with him if their new-born weren't so young.

He arrives at the airport two and a half hours before his flight. He returns the hire vehicle to Avis Rent a Car and walks languidly across to the departure area. He considers his options, then comes up with a plan. He will visit Warren in London. The surprise might give the man a heart attack.

~⁊

Tuesday

The cold is still biting. I'm wearing a trench coat and I feel the cold a little more than I'm used to. It occurs to me that something is wearing off. The pill may only be effective for a short period of time. When I return home, I'll check the detailed features of the formula and the current level of my strength and make a note in my special diary. If I can help it, I'm not going to risk taking another pill, given what happened to Derek.

Standing in front of Gina's door, I consider whether what I'm about to do is wise. She did say I could collect the remainder of the pills tonight. I check the time. 8:10 p.m. To hell with it, I can't worry about what she might say.

I knock on the door. Gina opens after a few moments. She's been crying, her eyes red. The rest of her is black, a different outfit from my last encounter with her but the same colour.

'Sorry,' I say, 'is this a bad time?'

'No, no. I've just called the hospital. Derek is not getting better. He's unconscious. Come in.' To my astonishment, she hugs me.

'Oh,' I say, the physical contact unsettling me. I follow her through to her living room. When she held me, I could feel how soft and womanly she was. Maybe I had misjudged her. The emotional outpouring of grief for an old man was nothing short of inspiring.

She goes into the bathroom while I stand, feeling numb. I'm partially responsible for the man's demise and I feel guilty. What have I done? Admittedly the pills were stolen and administered by somebody who knew little about what could happen, but it does not make me feel any better. Even if I stick a warning sign on the bottles of anti-ageing medication, I doubt thieves would heed the message.

Gina comes back and hands me the bottle. 'I have to visit him at the hospital although he won't be able to talk to me.'

'I wish there was something I could do for you,' I say.

'At least Warren doesn't need to worry,' she says.

'Why should he worry?'

'It doesn't matter anymore. I can tell you now. Warren arranged for you to be kidnapped to reveal where the formula was.'

I'm stunned. So, Warren, the man who dismissed the notion of an anti-ageing solution for humans as fanciful was behind the attack on me when I was staying at Richard's. 'Did he organise other break-ins too?'

'No, just the one.'

'Why? What good does it do him?'

'You'll have to ask him. Something to do with the effect of the price on pharmaceutical stocks, the way he tells it.'

Without another word, I leave her. Can I trust Gina, a woman who lives a dark life, in black clothing? I've never seen her in anything else. Even tonight she wore black leggings, a black top and a black cardigan. I'm surprised she hasn't painted her walls black. But surely Gina is not lying about Warren.

On my way to the tube railway station, I too am in a dark mood.

What should I do? Call the police? I only have Gina's word that Warren had me assaulted which wouldn't be good enough to have him arrested. There's no evidence, particularly as the gang who carried out the deed have fled. But the gang she referred to may not be the gang who murdered my flatmates. I am still puzzled by that attack.

I need to confront Warren to confirm what Gina had said. He may have suggested finding out if my invention were real or imagined, but would he commission a criminal act? For now, I need to remain calm and plan my next steps.

When I return to Kirstie's, I find she is sitting by the fire, playing a game on her phone. I decide not to tell her about Gina's revelation as she may jump to conclusions and have her cop friends involved.

'New game?' I ask as I join her on the sofa.

We kiss briefly and she says, 'Yes. It's addictive. So how was the visit?'

'She was in tears, but she gave me the pills. Her grandfather is in a coma.'

TWENTY-FIVE:
Wednesday

W ARREN IS SITTING on a hard chair in a basement. His hands and ankles are tied, and he has duct tape over his mouth. Pavle Stanoski views the scene from an adjoining room which has a two-way mirror. His people have finally succeeded in capturing somebody and keeping the person in place. Their attempts at capturing and hanging onto the scientist have proved futile.

Stanoski looks to the leader of the three-man team. 'Goran, I will go in and talk to him. Wait here until I give you a signal, thumbs down, then bring the tray. And wear the balaclava. Okay?'

'Sure,' says Goran, a muscular dark-haired English Serb.

Stanoski pulls a balaclava over his head and walks into the dank room Warren occupies. From the entrance, Stanoski peers at the English stockbroker before advancing to the foot of the chair. He sees fear in Warren's brown eyes. He notes that the Englishman's black hair is mingled with some grey strands.

The room is littered with cardboard boxes and old paint cans. It is dimly lit. Oil streaks are visible in one of the corners. The basement has a wall running down the middle dividing the large underground space into two rooms. It reminds Stanoski of an interrogation area used by spies. But he has no idea what this abandoned house had been used for previously. It may have been a bakery or a small manufacturing centre. Goran's team, familiar with London, had found it on the outskirts of the city.

It's cold. There is no central heating in the place and Stanoski sees that Warren is shivering but he doesn't know whether the man is freezing, dressed only in a white business shirt and trousers, or whether he's shaking from fear.

Stanoski pokes Warren in the stomach. It is soft and flabby, probably from too many business lunches. Stanoski rips the duct tape from the man's face. Warren cries out in pain.

'Good morning, Warren.'

"Who are you? What do you want?'

Stanoski slaps Warren's round, white face with his gloved hand. 'Shut the fuck up. I'll ask the questions,' he says, waiting for his captive to quieten from his pathetic cry. The man doesn't know real pain, the sort of pain he'd once administered to cowering Bosnians.

Warren stares ahead, pretending not to engage with Stanoski whose covered face is above him.

Stanoski does not mind this tame gesture. He'd experienced tough men trying to hold out on him and they'd caved eventually so this office guy wouldn't even be a challenge. In Serbia, before he married a German woman and settled in Munich, he ran a gun running enterprise. This earned him the funds he used to become a legitimate businessman in Germany. He smiles. He's going to have some fun. 'I want some answers and I want you to answer honestly. Understood?'

Warren doesn't respond. He stares ahead as though this is a nightmare he'll awake from soon.

Stanoski takes a knuckle duster out of his trouser pocket, slips it onto his right hand then pulls his arm back. He waits a moment to assess what registers on his victim's face. He allows time to pass to give Warren the notion that he is bluffing. Just when Stanoski believes

'Hi Ethan, it's Gina, sorry to trouble you but have you heard from Warren?'

'Not in the last few days,' I say, detecting mild hysteria in Gina's voice.

'My God. He was supposed to meet me last night, but he never showed.'

'Have you tried Anne?'

'Of course, that was the first person I called.'

I don't want to pry but I thought Anne was Warren's fiancée, the one person he would tell of his whereabouts. Was he being unfaithful? Or was Gina simply an acquaintance who would like to be more? What business was it of mine? 'Well, I can't help,' I say, 'No doubt he'll show up. He may have gone out with some mates and stayed at one of their places.'

'Maybe. Thanks.'

'Before you go, Gina, how's Derek?'

'Near death. He's not getting any better and the doctors can't seem to work out what's wrong. They have done all sorts of tests and nothing…,' Gina says, starting to sob.

'Sorry to hear that.'

'Sure.' Gina hangs up.

When I return to my computer, it occurs to me that perhaps only one component in my formula needs adjustment. If two pills are so strong as to cause a shut-down of the internal functions, and if one pill begins to wear out after a while, then the ingredient responsible for duration shouldn't be hard to trace. I make a mental note to check this after work today.

~

'Have you had a good night?' Stanoski asks when he's sitting in front of Warren.

'Absolutely dreadful. I'm starving, you bastard. Give me something to eat.'

Stanoski smiles at Warren. He takes the baton out of his briefcase and smacks Warren left leg with it. 'Don't whine.'

Warren closes his eyes as though he thinks he's in a nightmare and any minute he'll wake up. When he re-opens his eyes, Stanoski is amused by his startled expression. The gravity of the situation is sinking in. 'How can I help you?' asks Warren, defeat written all over his features. His shirt is torn. The rug has been removed. He's shivering from the cold and the fear.

'That's better,' says Stanoski. 'This is not random. You're going to account for your actions.'

'What actions?'

'Tell me why you used the funds of investors for your own purposes. I have it on good authority that you shorted the GlaxoSmithKline equities trade.' Stanoski watches Warren carefully. If he lies, he will smash his knees with the baton.

'It's complicated.'

'Well, uncomplicate the explanation,' says Stanoski. He whacks Warren's ribs with the baton and waits for the man to regain his breath.

Warren looks ill, his pallor almost grey. After a pause, he says, 'A man, a competitor, let's say, is working to introduce a product which will reduce the need for many pharmaceutical products, and this will hurt the share price of all major stocks in that category.'

'You know this how?'

'I know the man whose invention it is.' Warren sniffles.

'But the price hasn't gone down,' Stanoski says, infuriated with the man's incompetence. He takes his iPad out of his briefcase and finds the stock price chart for GlaxoSmithKline for the past three months. He turns it to Warren. 'The price is going up, you idiot. See.'

'The timing is the important thing. We can't predict that,' says Warren, looking weary. 'I need something to eat.'

Stanoski takes a Mars Bar out of his briefcase, unwraps it and forces the bar into Warren's mouth. 'Eat.' He leaves the man to his calories as he wanders back to the observation room.

'Joseph, make sure he doesn't choke. Pour some water down his throat once he's finished the Mars Bar. I'll be back soon.'

Stanoski drives to a café close by. He enjoys a black coffee and sorts out how to proceed with the next stage of his plan. A tall red-head, dressed in a long skirt, smiles at him as she passes and sits at a table further towards the back of the establishment, joining another woman. The café is busy, many people coming in to escape the cold.

Stanoski pulls out his phone and calls his wife. He enquires how her day is going and reassures her that his business will be over in a few days. He misses the family and wants to settle what he came to London for as soon as feasible, but he won't rush it. Lena is a strong, independent woman and will be able to cope without him for however long it takes.

As a respected businessman in Germany, Stanoski has no issues with authorities there. His exporting business, mainly in women's fashion and, to a lesser extent, in travel accessories, is a far cry from dealing in the gun running business in Southern Europe and the Middle East. That business was fraught with conflict and danger, but he had been masterful in selecting a group of tough men who dealt with opposition and the many enemies the business threw up. That's where he learned how to extract information and, when necessary, eliminate threats.

Back at the basement, Stanoski asks Joseph how Warren has dealt with the silence.

'He scream. Then he stay quiet.'

'Where's Luka?'

'He come in afternoon.'

Stanoski pulls his mask on, places his miniature voice-changer ball into his mouth, then walks back into the section Warren occupies. He sits in the chair in front of Warren. 'How is it? Comfortable?'

Warren glares at him. 'Absolutely not. I've told you what you asked. Now, let me go. I'm freezing and I'm so hungry I could eat cardboard.'

'Okay, Mr Buckley, let's get down to business. I want my money back. On top of that I want an extra ten percent for the fucking inconvenience and missed opportunities.'

'How do you think I can do that? I can't control the market,' Warren wails.

'As you've said to me on occasion - do what you can to get the money. It's a great opportunity.'

Warren shifts uncomfortably although he cannot move much against the restraints. 'There were opportunities. It's not my fault the market went the wrong way.'

Stanoski turns slightly and nods. He waits a moment then Joseph, fully masked, rolls in a tray with sharp implements. Knives, scalpels and needles. He leaves the tray a metre from Warren's chair with the items visible.

'Think how you can come up with US$ 2.2 million,' says Stanoski, standing. 'You have two hours. I'll be back.' Stanoski walks off. In the next section, where Joseph has a heater next to his seat, Stanoski says, 'Keep an eye on him. He'll be bleating and begging but ignore him. Also, no toilet breaks. Let him sit in his own excrement.'

As Stanoski goes for a drive, he smiles to himself. The bastard deserves what is coming to him. Often the prospect of torture and injury are worse than the actual execution of pain. Thoughts play on one's mind and images conjured up are generally much more sinister than actual physical force. For untrained captives, psychological pressure works incredibly well.

What Stanoski doesn't know is what Warren had done with the name of the contact Goran had given to him. Warren had asked for assistance from Stanoski, six or eight weeks back, in a casual conversation, if he recalled right. Wanted to know of people who might scare someone into revealing secrets. Stanoski had asked Goran to talk to him, by phone. He wondered whether this was when Warren had changed direction in his trading recommendations. Stanoski's account, after a brief downturn due to silver, had been brought back to its original value with a slight profit using oil commodity options. Then after the switch in shorted stocks in pharmaceuticals the account balance had gone pear shaped, straight down like a rock over a cliff.

Warren is going to be sorry he didn't allow Stanoski access to his account balance for over a month. It was something he couldn't comprehend at the time, but trusted that Warren's firm knew what they were doing.

TWENTY-SEVEN:
Thursday

~

HEIDI IS FUN to be with when we discuss chemistry and other science related topics. She may not be as socially adept as other women at the company, but she holds her own when work matters are discussed. She is bright and I find her vibrant and much more alive now. I'd given her details of my anti-ageing formula in a small spiral notebook which, being on paper, as far as I'm concerned is safe, so the information is not available electronically. We talked on the walk here about the pros and cons of making subtle changes and I could see how another mind worked through the problems and helped in the process of the creation of an anti-ageing solution.

We are sitting in a corner of a café, coffee cups in front of us, chatting about how the pill could be altered to make it less powerful but more enduring. She is smiling and I can see from the light in her blue eyes that she is taken with this work. Today she is also dressed differently, I feel. Less business- like, more feminine. Did she hope to lure me into bed? Am I more attractive now? She may be turned on by brains. Most women in my experience are attracted by wealth or power or, in Kirstie's case, by physical strength.

'Let's make the two key changes but not the third,' I say, wanting to be inclusive. The end successful product might well be the one in which we have collaborated. I don't know whether it will work, but I'm prepared to try.

'Fantastic,' she says. 'I'll stay on this evening.'

'Great.'

'I'd be happy to test it on myself,' she says.

'Really? You're only thirty-five.'

'Yes. But we're trying to reduce the reversal to only a quarter of the actual age, rather than a third when you trialled it.'

'True,' I say. 'Anyway, let's discuss that later. And I want you to sleep on it, okay. It's a big step and there may be other side-effects.'

'I know,' she says, 'but I'm excited.'

~

It is 2:30 when Stanoski confronts Warren Buckley again.

'Well,' says Stanoski, 'any thoughts?' He sees that, despite the cold, Warren is perspiring heavily. The man looks like he's aged overnight. He has wet himself, although it appears he's been able to control his bowel movements.

'What can I do? I can't simply send money to an account from the business. The firm is highly regulated and audited. I'll be dismissed and prosecuted if I transfer money without evidence.'

'Really. Is that all you can think of? Your life is worth nothing, but your employment status and reputation is? How pathetic you are.'

Tears flow from Warren's eyes. He can't brush them away, so they stream down his cheeks and onto his torn shirt. 'I don't know what I can do.'

'Doesn't the company have a slush account?' Stanoski is enjoying seeing the man in pain. As far as he's concerned, Warren is a liar and a conman. And if there's one thing that gets up Stanoski's nose, it is a business cheat and liar. Stanoski has killed men before for stealing from him, and for conning him. Warren is no different from a common thief.

'We have a small one, but I can't access it without authorisation from a higher level.'

'Well, that's too bad for you.'

Warren begins to sob, more tears streaming down.

Stanoski takes his baton and smashes it into the side of his midsection. 'Stop it. Act like a man.'

Warren yelps in pain and sits upright. Then he whines, 'Give me a chance. I'll do what I can.'

Stanoski waits until Warren has settled. 'All my team are here now. We're going to clean you up then my next-in-command will get you to access your bank accounts and investments. Understood?'

'You can't do that. I'm not at fault.'

Stanoski gets up and walks slowly to the tray of sharp instruments. He lingers, selects a bolt cutter, and returns. Joseph, who is powerfully-built comes out, sensing what his boss wants. He grabs Warren's hand and spreads the fingers. Stanoski places the cutter over the base of the middle finger, left hand. He nods to Joseph who takes over and presses down on the finger with force.

The basement echoes with Warren's hysterical scream. The cut finger is tossed aside, and Joseph blunts the blood flow with a rag he's brought with him.

Goran and Luka join Joseph and tend to the prisoner. Stanoski nods to Goran. 'You know what to do.' Stanoski departs as though he's late for a bus.

Will Warren have the funds Stanoski wonders as he walks to his vehicle. If there is a shortfall, he will have Warren subjected to the knives, cutting him but keeping him alive. He has had plenty of experience with this technique.

TWENTY-EIGHT:
Friday

~

Kirstie shakes me awake.

'What? What time is it?'

'It's six-forty. You look odd. Do you feel alright?'

I push a hand through my hair and open my eyes fully. 'What do you mean? I feel fine.'

'You're looking a lot older than yesterday.'

I pull Kirstie, wearing a short, white dressing gown, towards me and hug her. 'Good morning,' I whisper into her ear. I slip out of bed and walk into the bathroom, naked, not bothering to cover up. The central heating is great. Something I may not get used to, being Australian, having lived the bulk of my life there, where small heaters don't do the same job. I examine myself in the mirror and see what Kirstie has seen. A man more than forty years old. A worn face, wrinkles evident at the edge of the mouth and eyes. My hair sports grey strands.

I peer at myself. If I am not mistaken, I look older than I did prior to the experiment. So, the first pill reverses age but when it's undone, it turns back with a vengeance. I look forty-five, I reckon. I'm thoroughly disappointed. My thirty-nine-year-old body has taken some punishment, it seems. I sit on the toilet seat and bury my head in my hands. What have I done? I need to call Heidi before it's too late. She may be foolish enough to try the new version of the pill. And it may have even worse side effects.

Before going back to the bedroom, I brush my teeth then shower as though my new, old body needs to be cleansed. I stand under the hot shower wanting it to dissolve my body. If only I didn't experiment with chemicals, and to think I thought it was a good idea. And then I had been mad to use myself as the guinea pig. How stupid am I? I had no way of knowing what might happen, did I? I'm worse than a gambler who stakes his house on a game of cards. A theory, that's all I had. Why? Angela is long gone. If I did this crazy experiment to reduce her age and bring her closer to my own age, it was daft. She has moved on, totally. She has a new man, a new family, a new life. I sense another presence. Kirstie has joined me. She puts her arms around me.

'What's wrong?' she asks.

'The effects of my wonderful pill have expired,' I say with heavy sarcasm. 'Can't you tell?'

'You look fabulous to me. A gentleman with a lived-in face. But a lovely one. I feel like we truly belong together now.'

Her statement takes me by surprise. She wants me to look my actual age or even older. It makes her feel comfortable. Maybe I should let it go. Stay with who I am. Don't chase the impossible dream or the big bucks. I'll need to think this through, though. It's hard to simply abandon the experiment. And should I be deterred by one set-back, or even by what somebody else wants?

I embrace Kirstie and we play in the shower.

~

AT TEN O'CLOCK, Stanoski strides into the room where Warren is held captive. Stanoski sits on a chair in front of him and sips coffee from his take-away carton. Then he smiles. Warren is looking pale, his eyes half-closed and his body sagging from the weight of sitting for so long.

'My men have searched your bank accounts and details of your investment assets. Thank you for providing the information.'

'You bast…,' says Warren.

'Bring some water,' shouts Stanoski.

Goran brings a bottle of water and administers it to Warren, who drinks greedily.

'Good. Now we can converse properly. What were you saying?' Stanoski drinks the rest of his coffee and tosses the carton aside.

'You bastard. When can I have something to eat?'

'Right, I understand. Have you figured out who I am?'

'You must be one of four people but I'm not exactly sure who yet.'

'Okay. Best to keep guessing. You see, if you do know or find out then we'll have to get rid of you. At least if I'm one of four possibilities, you can keep guessing forever.'

'You're going to kill me, aren't you?'

Stanoski doesn't want to show his hand at this time because he hasn't worked out what's to his best advantage. 'Who knows? Back to business. We need you to transfer your funds across to an account number I can give you. You'll also need to dispose of your shares and your fixed interest account.'

'You won't get away with this.'

'We'll see. After all, investing with you means I'm a risk taker. So, I'll organise some food and we'll allow you access to a laptop.'

'It'll take three days until settlement for the sale of shares takes place.'

'Alright, so you'll be our guest for a little longer. Lucky for you the debt will be paid without having to sell your house.'

'I won't do it. You can't make me.'

Stanoski stands. He goes to the instrument tray and toys with a knife. 'You're right, but I can manage to extend your life so that you will suffer and die slowly and painfully.' He advances to Warren, removes his left shoe, then pulls off the sock.

'Wait, wait,' wails Warren. "Alright, I'll do as you ask.'

Stanoski walks into the observation room and instructs Goran to feed Warren, shower him and bring him to the computer. Meanwhile, he will calculate the shortfall. All up, Warren has around US$1.5 million. Stanoski opens an Excel spreadsheet. He needs to factor in the cost of this operation, including payments for his men, other expenses and what he believes Warren should pay to compensate him for financial opportunities foregone.

AT 7:25 A.M., Kirstie blows me a kiss as she leaves for work while I'm still watching the morning news with a bowl of muesli and banana in front of me. A call interrupts my concentration. I take my phone off the coffee table in front of me and answer without looking at the display, my eyes focused on the volcano in Hawaii.

'Hello,' I say.

'Hi, Ethan, how have you been?'

'Ah, Liz. I've been okay. And you?'

'This is not a social call. Anne is frantic. Warren is missing. Nobody knows where he is. You haven't heard from him, have you?'

'No. Gina asked me the same question. Do you think Warren and I are buddies?'

'No, but we have run out of friends and relatives to call. I guess we're covering everyone he knows.'

I switch off the television. 'That's too bad,' I say. 'Might be a job for the police.'

'Yes. Sorry to disturb you.'

'No worries. I wish you luck and If he contacts me, I'll let him know he's missed,' I say, tongue in cheek. I doubt Warren would call unless he wants something from me.

An hour later I walk into the office, looking for Heidi. On the way through the open plan room, a couple of people have done a double-take, wondering whether it's me or an older brother. I guess it's hard to explain. All I can say is I've had a few hard nights.

After dumping my belongings, a leather bag and an overcoat, on top of the desk in my cubicle, I visit the kitchen. Heidi is filling up a cup with coffee. Her back is to me and I note she's wearing a red skirt, rather than her usual trousers, and a matching red and yellow top. Blazing colours for the usually dull Heidi, and this is a workplace, not a disco. Perhaps she is going out tonight, it being a Friday, and she's already dressed for partying. She turns around.

The shock on my face must have transmitted instantly as she smiles, obviously pleased with my reaction. She is a decade younger looking. She looks fabulous as she has helped it along with make-up and clothes.

'What do you think?' she asks.

'You look beautiful,' I say.

'You've never said this to me before, have you?'

'I've not thought about it. You look so much younger. You took a pill despite my warning, didn't you?' I avert my gaze as I realise, I may be giving off the wrong signal. She is younger-looking and more beautiful, but she may be in for pain and disappointment. I take my mug from the overhead cabinet and pour percolated coffee into it.

'Sorry. I was so excited, I simply had to try it. Be positive. Nothing happened to you except the first pill simply wore off. This one, as you know, was modified and made less … well, for a better word, extreme.'

'You mean less powerful or potent.' I turn to her. I move closer and I study her face. 'I can't get over it. Have any of the others commented?'

'The lads have stared at me and the women have frowned, as though I was from outer space.'

I laugh. 'It's done now, I guess. Can I take a photo of you with my phone? I want to record changes to your appearance over the next few months. And you need to tell me how you feel. Is that okay?'

'Sure. I know I'm your guinea pig. Tonight, I'm going to have fun. Go out to a night club or something. Want to join me?'

'Let me think about it,' I say, tempted but knowing I need to talk to Kirstie first. After all, Heidi needs to be watched for a period before I can accept the idea that she is completely safe.

TWENTY-NINE:
Friday

~

THE WEATHER OUTSIDE is bitter, the temperature having plummeted during the day. The basement is cold but is protected from the extreme wind which makes the exterior to the property many degrees colder. Warren is shaking with cold, despite having been given a light jumper to pull over his torn business shirt.

'How are we doing?' asks Stanoski, sitting down and observing his adversary's discomfort.

'I'm fucking freezing.'

'I see. For being co-operative, I've asked my men to buy a heater and put it in here for you.'

'How much longer are you going to keep me tied up?'

Stanoski waits a moment. 'I have some good news and some bad news. What would you like to hear first?'

'Stop playing games. I want to go home. I need medical attention for my finger.'

'You'll live. Well, the good news is that we may be able to release you in a few days and we won't need to take your girlfriend prisoner.'

'What? What's she got to do with this?'

'Nothing. We've looked at your home computer and found that you have a woman you communicate with regularly, called Anne, and another, called Gina, with whom you also trade emails. Do you go out with both? Lucky man.'

Warren splutters. 'You've broken into my house?'

'We needed to check some things. So, Anne and Gina are safe, for now. But one never knows when that could change.' Stanoski enjoys the feeling of having this hideous man squirm. He hates con artists with a passion and now this one is paying for his treachery.

'So, what's the bad news?'

'Oh yes. After disposing of assets and transferring cash holdings, you are still half a million US dollars short. So how do you suggest making up the shortfall?'

'What?' Warren yelps like a dog being kicked.

'Should I repeat it?'

'I don't have any more money.'

'Who's the other broker who called me? You know the one giving me the bad news. When you wanted to avoid telling me the bad news about my account yourself.'

'Pavle Stanoski. That's who you are, isn't it?'

'Correct.' Stanoski removes his mouthpiece so that Warren will recognise his voice. To date, there is no evidence that Warren can use should he go to the authorities. But Stanoski retains the mask. If Warren sees him, Stanoski believes he will need to be eliminated. 'So, the name.'

'Why?'

Stanoski stands and wallops Warren's right hand with the police baton. 'Next time, we will cut your hand off. Name?'

'Denny… Denny Tomas,' Warren whines, struggling to keep tears away.

'We'll give you a phone to talk to him. Naturally, if you try anything silly, you will suffer. Understand?'

Warren nods. 'What do you want me to say?'

'Get him to transfer my money, the half million dollars, into my account in Germany. You must have the details in the office as I've emailed them to you previously.'

'He doesn't have the authority. Your account shows about five thousand US dollars so that's all he can transfer.'

'Figure something out. I don't care what, but do it or we'll grab your girlfriends.'

Warren's head slumps. He closes his eyes. He looks like a thoroughly defeated man, a man who would do away with himself if he had the chance. Stanoski smiles.

THE NIGHT AIR forces me to pull up the collar of my trench coat and I'm grateful when we reach the nightclub Heidi has selected. It's called Nightclub Kolis and is on Archway Road, north of the Westend where I'd imagined Heidi might choose a place. We'd had a bite to eat earlier and I'd called Kirstie to tell her why I'm out with another woman. Kirstie laughed when she heard Heidi had taken the ant-aging pill. Told me she thought the woman was crazy.

'Noisy joint,' I say.

'There's a table,' says Heidi who leads me to a far corner where we squeeze into an alcove of sorts.

Settled, I offer to buy her a drink.

'Can I have a Baileys on ice?'

As I wander to the bar, through the crowds of men and women, standing, talking, moving around, I find myself fearing the worst. Heidi has not been her usual quiet self. I've never heard her talk so much and certainly, previously, nothing about her personal life. Over dinner, she told me she'd grown up in a boring middle-class home in Surrey. Her father is a lawyer and her mother a radiographer. As an only child, Heidi was protected from the outside world, attending a school for girls. She had no contact with boys until age eighteen. Yet tonight, she said she wanted to party.

I order drinks and head back to the table. But when I place the beer and Baileys on the table, Heidi is missing. I look around. The loud thump thump of the music makes it difficult to talk and that suits me. So, where is she? Perhaps she's gone to the bathroom. As I sit down, I see Heidi in the distance. She seems to be gyrating to the rhythm of the hip-hop or whatever it is that's playing.

After ten minutes, Heidi returns. 'Having fun?' I ask, intrigued by her change in behaviour. Is this a side-effect of the modified anti-ageing pill? I observe Heidi's face to see whether there are other mysterious indicators. She hasn't had any alcohol or drugs so the animation and general high can't be attributed to such substances.

'Absolutely. Want to dance?'

'In a moment. I need to ask you some questions first.' I'm sitting on the right of Heidi in the alcove, close so I don't need to shout to be heard.

'Fine. Shoot.'

'How do you feel?'

Heidi peers at me as though I'm talking to a disturbed child. 'Great. Why do you ask?'

'Are you normally like this when you go out?'

'I don't know what you mean. I'm feeling good. Better than usual. Why?'

I take her hand to see whether it's hotter than it should be. 'Could the pill be affecting your mood and general happiness?'

'Who knows? Let's dance.'

She pulls me up and we join the teeming couples already jumping or shaking about. We copy the others on the dance floor as Heidi slips through a small opening between two couples. I follow her, wondering what is happening to this blonde madwoman. It's so crowded that we can't help bumping into others. If only I were experiencing what Heidi is, I might be able to record the effects more accurately. When somebody stands on my foot accidentally, I realise that the slight pain I feel is what I would expect, rather than when I experienced enhanced strength from the first experimental anti-aging pill.

Waves of perfume and body odour assail my nostrils. I want to escape but Heidi is frenzied. I stay with her, fearing she might collapse. I can't ask her what she's experiencing now but perhaps I might get a better picture of her state tomorrow, or in a few days. I rock into another woman and apologise but there's no response. People are inebriated or stoned, I imagine, and totally unaware of what's happening.

With the dancing over for now as the band is taking a break, Heidi and I go back to our table, our drinks minding the space. Heidi seems suddenly exhausted. So, has the madness worn off, I wonder. I finish my beer, watching my partner closely. Heidi doesn't talk. Not that much can be heard above the other voices and music. When Heidi has finished her drink, I persuade her to leave. I hail a taxi, drop her off at her place which is not far from the nightclub, then I have the driver take me home.

I pay the taxi driver, then with my key, enter Kirstie's flat. I wander through to the bedroom. Kirstie is watching television. I embrace her, pleased to be with a sane and well-balanced person again.

THE NIGHT AIR clears Stanoski's troubled mind. He walks along the street, trying to think. What to do if this Tomas guy cannot manage to do what his colleague asks. Stanoski's already in deep with the kidnapping and assault of one man. Ordinarily, this wouldn't bother him. But he's trying to live a decent life after the activities he was part of back home in Serbia. He's married with two kids. He can't afford to have police pursue him. Now that Warren knows who has taken him captive, he will spill to the cops, who will try to track the German-Serb down. There is no way out now, except to kill him. And Denny Tomas might need to be taken care of as well.

This is a dilemma. He thinks back to an earlier time when it appeared things were working out. Then, a lack of communication from Warren made him furious. When it dawned on him that he might be the victim of a scam, his mood turned into a murderous rage.

Luckily, he had friends who found Warren Buckley via social media. But he had been extremely difficult to pin down. It seemed the address he gave as his business address did not exist. Also, the website which looked legitimate turned out to be a fake website. For these deceits alone, Stanoski felt the punishments Warren currently experienced was justified.

Stanoski checks his watch. Nearly five o'clock. He goes back to talk again with the English captive. Goran intercepts him at the door and asks him to pop into the observation room.

'Warren say Tomas will meet him at six o'clock in city,' says Goran.

'Did he give an address?'

'Yes.'

'Go get him. Take one man with you.'

'He say, he only meet with Warren.'

'Get his description. You can use Warren's phone to get a picture. The device should be amongst his stuff in the observation room.'

Goran walks to where Warren's belongings are stored while Stanoski seats himself in front of Warren. 'So, how can your colleague help us?'

'I don't know. But he won't talk to anyone except me.'

'Really.'

'You have to let me meet with him,' says Warren.

'Everything you've ever said was a lie. Why would I trust you?'

Goran comes in with Warren's phone. He shows a picture of a man to Warren. 'Who this?'

Warren who had previously told Stanoski's gang the password to his phone peers at it. 'A friend.'

Stanoski's patience has dissipated like water left in a bowl in the sun. 'Tell us which picture shows Denny Tomas. Otherwise we will cut you in the stomach, slowly and painfully.'

For a moment, Warren appears stoic. But when Goran moves the tray of sharp instruments closer, he nods.

Stanoski looks at Warren, seeing if there are tell-tale signs of deception. 'If I find you've lied, you will be in for some harsh treatment.'

Stanoski waits until Goran has swept through images on Warren's phone and found the right picture of Denny Thomas. Then Goran leaves the house and Stanoski gathers his wits. 'I have some questions for you which I'm curious about.' He waits. 'Right, now let's start with your business address. There is no such thing, no address for JBT International Services, is there?'

'An address is required to set up a business, but we can work from anywhere with a phone and a laptop. Doesn't mean we can't service our clients.'

'How did you come up with the name?'

'I'm cold. Can I have a rug?'

Stanoski sniffs. The air in the room is thick with the smell of oil, or urine. 'You will get one after you answer my questions.'

'You're treating me like a dog. A reward if I do what you want.'

'I would never treat a dog like this.' Stanoski doesn't add that a dog does nothing but be a friend. He doesn't lie and cheat.

'The name is made up of three of us partners. Jefferson, Buckley, and Thomas.'

'Are you all licenced brokers?'

'Well…not exactly,' says Warren grudgingly.

'So legal action against this fictitious entity would be difficult?'

'I don't know. Nobody's wanted to sue us. Not yet, at least.'

With mild disgust, Stanoski peers at the broker who now looks like a homeless man. He departs without another word.

THIRTY:
Saturday

~

IT IS JUST after midnight when Stanoski, after a meal and an hour's sleep, returns to the basement the gang had found for these interrogations. When he goes into the room occupied by Warren, he sees that another figure, bound and gagged, is present and sitting a few metres from Warren who is asleep. He assumes this is Denny Thomas, different in shape and size from Warren. Thomas is still suffering the effects of the chloroform administered on him.

Goran had gone back to the hotel to rest. He has left his two mates in attendance. They have put a couple of electric heaters in the basement which is now relatively warm. Stanoski had told his men that he doesn't want anyone to die, not just yet.

Stanoski looks at Thomas who is leaning forwards. He is slighter than Warren, grey-haired and probably ten years older. But he is no athlete. Soft from an easy life, he figures. Stanoski won't get anything from these men now. He'll try again later in the morning.

~

I WAKE TO find Kirstie's right arm slumped over me. I'm warm. I need to pee but I'm reluctant to move from the bed. I wait a moment then slowly manoeuvre out of Kirstie's embrace. I slip out of bed and walk naked into the bathroom. I decide, since I'm up, to brush my teeth and shower too. With hot water streaming down, I think about plans for today. I need to check how Heidi is doing and to record what happened last night.

When I get back to the bedroom, I see that Kirstie is awake and gazing at me.

'When did you sneak out of bed?'

'I had to go…you know.'

'You've been in there for a while.'

'Thought I'd start the day early, although I see its eight-thirty already.'

'Do you have somewhere to go?'

'No, but I need to check up on Heidi,' I say, keen to see Kirstie's reaction.

'Oh. Do you have a thing for her?'

'Of course not. But I feel responsible as she took an experimental pill.'

'Come back to bed then,' she says, pulling the bedcovers aside.

There's no rush to follow up with Heidi so I relent and join my friend. She's actually my girlfriend, I realise. Sleeping together, cohabitating. Yes, we're more than just friends.

After a breakfast of eggs, bacon, tomato, toast and coffee, I'm ready to embark on my adventure. I call Heidi and she answers after the third ring.

'Yes?'

'How do you feel?'

'Fine. I think I did some dumb things last night, though.'

'You remember?'

'I do. I'm still in bed and I'm ravenous.'

'Let me see you. I need to conduct a few tests.'

'Okay. Give me an hour.'

I load my backpack with a blood pressure monitor, a thermometer, an iPad and pain killers. Then, an hour later, I take a taxi to Heidi's flat in Camden.

'Come in,' she says, almost immediately after I knock on her second-floor door. She is dressed in slacks and a loose, white cotton top. The central heating is warm but not too hot.

I follow her through to a living room at the end of a hallway with doors closed on the rooms running on either side. The flat is tidy. Like Heidi who always presents as fresh and neat. I'm invited to sit, and she offers coffee. I place my backpack on the floor next to the coffee table.

'Let's get the tests done first,' I say.

'Sure,' she says. She leads me to a study which contains a desk, a bookcase crammed full of books and along one side is a narrow bed. I guess this room must double as a guest room. I put the backpack on the floor. On top of the desk is a laptop. She sits on a chair in front of her desk and I pull another chair close to her.

Blood pressure and temperature are taken, which I record on my iPad. I also take another photo of her, although I can't detect any change from the first time she appeared younger, after taking the experimental pill. That done I ask questions about any changes she's noted and how she feels.

'Today I feel like I always do, but I have to admit yesterday I was euphoric in the evening. My moods were swinging during the day and I guess it must have been the pill. I hadn't thought about it too much, until now.'

'What about strength. Are you stronger?'

Heidi gets up and walks over to the bed and lifts it from the long side. She turns to me. 'I'm a little stronger but not much. Probably only because I'm younger.'

'Good point,' I say. At least it's not the super strength I experienced.

'Anything else? Don't worry, Ethan, I'll let you know if there are signs which are adverse.'

'That's good but I need to record how you feel daily, together with changes in blood pressure, heart rate, temperature, weight, general feeling of well-being and so forth. I'd like you to inform me by personal, not work, email. Is that alright?'

'Of course. Now, let's have some coffee,' she says.

Just after ten o'clock, Stanoski has had breakfast near the hotel and is full of energy. The weather is milder than the previous day and Stanoski is seated in front of his new captive who is sat further towards the far wall in the basement. Stanoski has arranged for his men to place headphones over Warren's ears and to have his face covered with a sack so that he cannot see what's going on.

'What the hell? Where am I?' asks Thomas when he sees Stanoski.

Stanoski has the voice changing device in his mouth. 'You are a broker at JBT, aren't you?'

'Yes, so what?'

'Don't be so hostile,' Stanoski says, annoyed with the arrogance.

'Go fuck yourself.'

Stanoski stands and wallops Tomas's shins.

Thomas screams in pain.

Stanoski goes into the observation room and tells Goran to toss cold water onto Thomas. After a short walk outside, Stanoski returns. 'Have you settled down, you scum?' Stanoski's mood has changed for the worse.

Thomas nods. 'What do you want?'

'You were responsible for losing my money. I want it back.'

'That's not my fault. The market may have turned. Who are you, anyway?' Thomas looks bedraggled, his hair still wet, but he sounds more confident now.

'That doesn't matter. What I'd like to know is why, as a broker, you don't look after your clients.'

'I do.'

'Then explain how it is that you allow trades to diminish rather than selling them when in profit?'

'Until I know the case, I can't answer.'

Stanoski raises his right hand as a signal, then Goran and his two companions come into the room. Stanoski watches as the previous arrangement with his men is carried out. The men secure Thomas' hand so that it is tied flat on a side table. Then Goran's muscular off-sider smashes the hand repeatedly with a mallet until it is well and truly broken and limp.

Stanoski takes his police baton and strikes a wailing Thomas across the face, breaking the man's nose. 'Shut the fuck up.'

Stanoski leaves.

THIRTY-ONE:
Saturday

~

KIRSTIE AND I are watching a West End play. I'm leaning back, relaxed, not paying too much attention to the stage. Kirstie seems to be enjoying the show and that makes me happy. She's been incredibly supportive, and I couldn't ask for more, particularly due to the stress I've encountered of late.

Suddenly music breaks out and I'm startled back to what's happening on stage. The production is first class. But soon my mind goes back to earlier in the day. Heidi knows exactly what is required to discover whether the pill is a viable solution. If a lay person had taken the pill, the results would probably not be recorded accurately. And if an adverse situation presented itself, that person might panic. As a scientist, Heidi is definitely better qualified to detect subtle as well as significant changes.

The performance is over. Everybody applauds and I follow suit. I glance towards Kirstie who is smiling and clapping as though she thoroughly enjoyed the show. She turns to me and I smile to acknowledge that I, too, enjoyed the musical.

Outside, we walk together slowly, arm in arm, soaking up the atmosphere. The night is cool rather than cold and my trench coat is more than adequate to battle the elements. Bright lights abound. Tourists and locals cram the footpaths in these parts of the West End. I wonder what Heidi is doing when I see a woman who looks a little like her, eyes wide with excitement. Then I turn to Kirstie who seems content to be with me, as myself. I'm lucky, and I wonder whether pursuing my dream of looking younger will become a curse. Why can't I be satisfied to be myself, ageing naturally?

A man accidentally bumps me as I focus on a restaurant which appeals to Kirstie.

'Sorry,' I say.

'Watch your step,' he responds.

I dismiss the remark but now I realise it would be advantageous to have the extra strength I previously enjoyed. Just to reply with a witty remark and possibly invite a physical reaction. But I decide it's best to move along. I ask Kirstie about coffee and dessert. She nods approval and we enter the lit-up establishment she seemed interested in earlier.

THE DAY HAS been pleasant. Not too cold, a light drizzle but no substantial rain. Stanoski likes these conditions. Australia was too hot for his liking although he enjoyed the tennis. He walks through the park, alone with his thoughts. He's not concerned about anything or anyone, walking in the dark by himself. If a mugger did emerge, he'd either fight back or shoot him. He had always been a tough fighter, rarely bested in one-on-one skirmishes. If anything, he missed the rough and tumble of street fighting. He grew up in the wild streets of Serbia and feels quite capable of looking after himself.

Stanoski reaches the edge of the park and observes a homeless man almost hidden by the bushes. He ignores him and walks along the street, then he hails a taxi. On the way back to the abandoned house, Stanoski thinks about the arrogance of Thomas and why he appeared so certain he'd be released after some preliminary questioning. However, Stanoski has the time to change this man's attitude. Stanoski needs to hang around in London until Warren's investments have been converted into cash so there's plenty of time to plan what to do with Thomas.

When Stanoski asks about the day's progress, Goran informs him that Thomas doesn't have enough funds to pay the shortfall. He also tells him that both prisoners have been given food and drink and had bathroom breaks. Apparently, they tried to communicate with each other but, before much happened, gags were placed over their mouths.

Stanoski wanders into the basement with the small electric bar heater positioned between the two men. He notes that Warren has his eyes closed as he passes him. Stanoski watches him for a second and is satisfied the man is asleep. He continues on to where Thomas is tied and sits on the chair in front of him. A rat scurries off into a corner where a heap of rubbish is piled up.

'It's good to see you again,' says Stanoski. 'It's also good to see you can't talk. Now when I allow you to speak, I want you to answer my questions without any smart-arse answers. Is that understood?'

Thomas nods. His eyes reflect a hint of fear, Stanoski detects. Stanoski rips the gag off his captive and waits for the effect. But Thomas only emits a small cry.

'You don't have the resources to help pay my account. Tell me how you are going to deal with it,' Stanoski says, keeping his eyes fixed on Thomas' expression and body language.

'I don't know. I just don't have enough assets. You could bankrupt me, but what good is that?' Thomas has perspiration running down his face. He tries to wriggle his busted, swollen hand but the movement from it is almost indiscernible. And it's extremely painful.

'How are you going to resolve this? If you can't come up with a solution, we will need to crush your other hand and feet. You'll be able to function, just, but you will be considerably inconvenienced, and in a great deal of pain.' Stanoski sits back and places his hands behind his head.

Thomas's face turns red and he looks like he might suffer a heart attack. 'Please, please. I'll do anything but I can't pay the money.'

'Doesn't your firm have a slush fund?'

'It can't be touched. I'll be arrested.'

'You're more afraid of touching the firm's slush fund than what we're going to do to you?' Stanoski laughs. He can't believe what he's hearing. His phone buzzes. He looks at the ID. It's his wife. He stands and walks away from Thomas and into a corner but not the one into which the rat fled.

'Ja?'

His wife speaks in German. 'Rudolf called. He wants to know when you'll be back.'

'Tell him I'll get in touch soon, in a few days. How are you?'

'Good. I miss you.'

'I miss you, too. I'm in the middle of a meeting so I'll have to go. Goodnight.'

'Goodnight, darling.'

When Stanoski resumes his seat facing Thomas, he sees that the man is shivering, and he doesn't think it's from the cold. 'So, tell me what you people have been doing with the money your clients provide?'

'We arrange trades, mainly in commodity options and sometimes in CFDs or equities.'

'Easy. Liquidate some trades.'

'Our silent partner wouldn't allow this. We cannot execute the trades. We have to go through a process.'

'Who's the silent partner?'

'I don't know. Warren knows.'

Stanoski signals for Goran to come in. He says, 'Gag Thomas and hood him.'

Stanoski waits while his order is executed then walks over to Warren, rips off the gag and slaps him awake. 'Silent partner. Who is it?'

'What?'

'You heard. Answer or I'll cut off your balls.'

THIRTY-TWO:
Sunday

~

KIRSTIE WAKES ME from a dream which I cannot recall entirely except that, at the moment I wake, I am shaking Heidi. I open my eyes. 'What time is it?'

'Seven-forty. Take this call, there's a hysterical woman asking for you.'

I rub my eyes and reach for the phone which Kirstie hands me. 'Hello,' I say, wondering who the hell would be calling so early on a Sunday.

'Derek,' the woman says, her voice shrill. 'He's getting worse. You have to do something.'

I realise it's the crazy woman, Gina, the woman who always wears black. 'You have to let your grandfather go. He's old.' I don't know why she's so upset. People die. Old people particularly. In fact, I can't understand why lots of terribly ill old people aren't assisted to escape the tyranny of life on earth. I may be working on trying to reverse age, but I don't see benefits for the incredibly old.

'He's not my grandfather,' she blurts.

I'm thoroughly confused now. Am I dreaming? Perhaps I've woken from one dream only to enter into another. I sit up and look forward and see Kirstie dressing. 'Why did you lie to me?' I ask, now more awake than ever.

'It's a long story. I'm at the hospital. The doctors called to say Derek could expire in the next few hours. Please help.'

'I'd like to but I'm not a medico. I'm sorry.'

'You're a chemist so you must know how to reverse the effects of anti-ageing.'

'I wish I could but so far, I haven't come up with the solution,' I say exasperated.

Gina ends the call.

'What was that all about?' asks Kirstie, fully dressed now.

'Gina's friend Derek who took two of the anti-aging pills stolen by Gina's friends is about to die. There's something strange about the whole saga,' I say.

Kirstie comes over and sits on the bed beside me. She's wearing black leather trousers, a tan top and a beige cardigan. 'I need to go and help at the store today. A big sale is on. I should have told you earlier, but it skipped my mind. Will you be okay by yourself for the morning?'

'I'd be happy sleeping if someone hadn't woken me,' I say, smiling.

Kirstie pushes me flat on my back and kisses my forehead. 'You sod. See you later.'

STANOSKI STANDS OUTSIDE Derek's flat. He is accompanied by Goran, leaving the other two members of the gang at the house with the two captives. He knocks on the door. The street is deserted and the area smells of poverty. All the houses appear to be exactly the same and all lack any evidence of maintenance. Stanoski wonders whether Warren has lied to him. Pity him if he has. They wait then Stanoski knocks again, only harder.

Stanoski turns to Goran after another two minutes have passed. 'The man's either not in or not answering. Use the tools.'

Goran sets about opening the front door with special tools he's used to break into places. It takes all of a minute and the front door gives. The two men saunter in. Stanoski calls out, 'Derek, are you here? Mr Warren Buckley sent us. Derek, where are you?' They wait a moment but there is no response.

'Goran, you check the rooms on this level. I'll check the ones upstairs.'

After five minutes the two men meet near the spiral staircase. 'No one in,' says Goran.

'Fuck! I found papers telling me a Derek lives here but he must be out.'

'What now? Wait?'

'We've tried his number and he's not answering and he's not in. What sort of man is he?' Stanoski scratches his head, bewildered. 'Goran, you wait inside for a while. I'll return to the basement and ask Thomas who this Derek is. I'll call you, okay?'

'Okay.' Goran stretches and yawns.

As Stanoski exits the flat, a woman with extremely white skin dressed in a severe black outfit stares at him. 'What are you doing in that flat?'

'What business is it of yours?' Stanoski moves onto the pavement and is facing the woman. He's seen this sort of person before but is intrigued. What kind of demented personality has black painted nails, black lipstick and a tongue stud which he glimpsed when she spoke? And that in addition to all-over black clothing.

'He's my friend,' she says, a hostile tone in her voice.

'You live here?' Stanoski wonders whether this woman is going to cause trouble.

'I live in the basement flat, but Derek and I are close friends. So, I'd like to know what you're doing coming out of his place. And if you don't tell me I'll call the police.'

Stanoski cannot believe the gall of this woman. Rather than talk to her of his interest in Derek, he punches her in the face so hard she falls onto the ground, hitting her head hard. He then calls Goran. The men carry the unconscious woman upstairs and lay her on the sofa in the living room.

'Get a big container of water, Goran. We'll wake her.'

When Goran returns, Stanoski accepts the large pitcher of water and holds it. 'Try to wake her,' he says to Goran.

Goran shakes her but she remains still. He stands up again and looks at Stanoski. Stanoski pours the entire contents of the pitcher over her head, letting the liquid spill over the sofa and carpet. The woman opens her eyes.

'Good,' says Stanoski. 'You awake.'

'What…' says Gina. Shaking, she puts her arms around herself.

'Where is Derek?' Stanoski asks.

'I don't know,' she says.

'Do you want us to beat it out of you?' Stanoski is tired of these English.

'He's in hospital,' she blurts out. 'He's near death.'

'Convince me. You call hospital, on speaker.'

AN ARTICLE ON breast implants gone wrong disturbs me. Science may not be the answer to the medical issues that humans face, after all. I move on to another piece of investigative journalism.

Lying on the bed, Sunday newspapers spread about, I wonder how Heidi is faring. I'm a little concerned that my experimental pills haven't been tested appropriately. Admittedly I should have thought of this before but, after the initial test on myself, I felt I'd hit the jackpot and I was anxious to take the product to the next phase. But it seems it won't be ready for approval for some time and, in the process, I may be responsible for harming people. Sure, Derek is in hospital and may die and I wonder how much is due to his swallowing three pills, despite my warnings, and how much is due to old age. But one thing is clear: I cannot allow another person to test my work.

I call Heidi who answers on the second ring.

'Hello Ethan.'

'What's up? You sound a little stressed,' I say.

'Can you come over? Something's not right.'

'Be there soonest,' I say, ending the call and organising myself to get to Heidi's place.

When I arrive, Heidi is dressed in slacks and a loose blouse. She is barefoot and fidgety.

'What's wrong?'

'Can't you see? I'm even younger looking than yesterday.'

I follow her inside and feel the heating which has been turned up. 'Let's see,' I say, waiting for her to face me in the sunlight streaming in from the balcony. 'You do look a bit younger than last time I saw you. Is that so bad?'

'Maybe the pill is reversing continually. Maybe I'll look like a child soon.'

I don't know what to say. The situation is distressing. We tinkered with the formula, without really knowing the extent of the change. 'Any other physical changes?'

'No, but the way I look makes me feel scared.' Heidi comes to me and puts her arms around me while I wrap my arms around her.

This is unlike her. Usually Heidi, the cool detached scientist, is now an emotional wreck. And I can't tell her to stay calm and examine the ingredients in the formula. Her emotions would blind her to assessing it rationally. I hate myself for getting her involved. It's all my fault. Talking about it has cost lives. Having it stolen will most likely cost a life. And now my eager assistant has been adversely affected. 'Let's go out and get a coffee.' I need to explore this development rationally.

Heidi releases me and rubs a tear from her eyes. 'Alright. Best not to think about it. Let me get dressed in suitable gear.'

I watch her stroll to her bedroom. Then I wander to the window, peering out, before going outside onto the balcony. Sun is sneaking through the grey clouds. Heidi returns and stands beside me.

'What are you thinking?' she asks.

'Nothing, really,' I say, not telling her that I wish I'd never let her know about my work.

We go for a walk. Being out and about may take Heidi's mind off her situation. The overcast sky, its steel grey strengthening, matches my mood. Gloomy. We pass shops and crowds of people. Heidi is attracted to a women's fashion store. We stand at the window while Heidi inspects the offerings. I gaze at the women inside checking out the dresses, trousers and tops.

'Hello Heidi,' says a voice.

Heidi and I both turn towards the voice together. It belongs to a petite dark-haired woman of around thirty-five. 'Hi, Susan, long time no see,' says Heidi.

'Oh my God, you look so young. What's your secret?'

I watch Heidi to see how she responds.

Heidi blushes, 'It's not a special diet. Maybe walking. I don't know.'

'You must come around soon. We haven't seen you for ages. Bring your friend,' says Susan, eyeing me.

I smile.

Heidi says, 'I've been busy at work, so I haven't been socializing much.'

'Call when you're free and we'll set something up. I'm meeting up with Tim and the girls. See you. Nice to meet you…,' says Susan.

'Ethan, likewise,' I say.

Susan heads off and I invite Heidi in for a coffee at the next café we come across.

~

STANOSKI IS SITTING on a sofa in Gina's flat. Goran is floating about, looking at the sparse offerings of music and photos scattered around the living room. Gina is making tea.

Stanoski pulls at his nose, thinking about the next step. Gina's call to the hospital has proved her claim that Derek is in hospital and still in a coma. And after some probing questions, he's convinced she doesn't know who Derek's partner is, the man pulling the strings at Warren's firm.

Gina comes into the room with a tray holding three cups, a white sugar bowl and a carton of milk. She places the tray down for everyone to help themselves. Goran joins the pair, sitting on an armchair near Gina who has positioned herself opposite Stanoski.

'What now?' she asks.

'How well do you know Derek?'

Gina hesitates. Finally, she says, 'A long time.'

'And you have no idea who his friends are,' persists Stanoski.

'No,' says Gina, sipping tea.

Goran pours some milk into his tea and lifts the cup to his mouth. He tests it then returns the cup to the saucer on the coffee table. 'Why he sick?'

'He swallowed too many anti-ageing pills,' says Gina.

Stanoski stares at her in disbelief then says, 'You're joke. There's no such thing.'

'It's true. A chemist I know invented these pills and they work. I saw the result with my own eyes. But Derek took more than one pill and that's when it all went pear-shaped.'

'What is pear-shaped?' Goran asks.

Gina looks at the muscled man beside her. 'Things go bad, downhill, you know.'

'Is he the mystery partner?' Stanoski asks. He now recalls something that Warren said, about shorting some companies like GlaxoSmithKline. But he can't remember why. It had something to do with health benefits for the aged and the fact that many traditional medications would become redundant. But he did not understand what it meant, and he let Warren run with it.

'I don't know,' says Gina.

'Where can we find him?'

'He keeps moving so I don't know where he lives. But I could call him,' Gina suggests.

'Let me think.' Stanoski needs to plan before rushing into anything. Was this chemist an inventor or a business partner? He needs to find out first.

THIRTY-THREE:
Sunday

~

WHEN I ARRIVE back at Kirstie's, around six o'clock, she has changed into a dressing gown. She's spread out on the sofa, fiddling with her phone. The news is playing on the television but, on seeing me, Kirstie switches the TV off with the remote.

'Looking for an early night?' I ask.

'Just had a shower so I couldn't be bothered getting dressed. We're not going out, are we?' Kirstie shifts to let me sit beside her.

I snuggle up to her and plant my lips on hers. It ends up being a passionate kiss. Before long, my hands explore under the gown which leads to a quick session of love making on the sofa. We both shower together, each of us soaping the other. I hum a tune as I towel down. Kirstie takes longer to dry herself and I open the bathroom door to get my clothes which are in the wardrobe immediately to my right.

'I'll order pizza,' says Kirstie, as I leave the bathroom. 'Okay?'

'Sure,' I say.

'Tell me what you did today,' Kirstie says, when we are both in the living room.

'Will do as soon as I have a beer,' I say, heading for the kitchen. Whilst inspecting the contents of the refrigerator, I plan my evening. Seeing Heidi distressed and uncomfortable was disconcerting. She had also complained of being weaker than she recalled. This was particularly bad news. From having added strength to losing strength is a dramatic outcome. Obviously, when we tampered with the formula, we overcompensated with the use of certain ingredients.

I choose a bottle of Peroni, thinking how I can save Heidi from getting younger and weaker. Dressed in jeans and a black T-shirt, I join Kirstie in the dining room. We set out plates, appropriate cutlery and wine glasses for our pizza delivery. I drink half the bottle of beer and place it on the table.

'Okay, fill me in,' says Kirstie, as we sit on our chairs.

The doorbell rings before I can utter a word.

Settled with pizza and wine in place, I tell Kirstie about my meeting with Heidi and the stress she is undergoing. At the end of my story, there are two pieces of the family-sized pizza left in the box.

'Wow, that's terrible. What can you do?' Kirstie pours the remnants of the red wine into our glasses.

'I'm going to review the formula tonight on my laptop. I have to figure something out.'

'While you're doing that, I'm going to bed to watch a police drama.'

'Feeling you'd like to be back working as a cop?'

'No, no. Watching the show will do me fine.'

We clean up and I set up my laptop on the living room table while Kirstie leaves the room. I place both formulas side by side and examine them closely. There must be a solution, I figure. Trial and error is something which is part of many inventions. I have to remain patient.

After thirty minutes of examining a variety of options to the formula which featured in Heidi's pill, I am stumped. I stand up and swing my arms about. Next, I do some sit-ups. Finally, I walk to the drinks cabinet and pour two fingers of Johnny Walker Black Label scotch into a tumbler. I take this back to my desk. With the assistance of this magic fluid inside me, I rethink what I'm aiming to achieve.

~

DARKNESS HAS DESCENDED. Stanoski likes the dark. Some of his best work, before the fashion business, was in the dark. Leaving Goran with Gina, Stanoski gathers Luka and Joseph together. Talks to them about his plan. Then he asks how the prisoners had been doing during his absence.

'Thomas anxious. Fidgets a lot,' says Luka.

'And Buckley?' asks Stanoski.

'Asleep mostly,' says Joseph.

'Luka, you stay here. Joseph, you gag and apply earmuffs to Thomas while I talk to Buckley. I don't want him interfering. Okay?'

'Sure, boss.'

When Stanoski sits in front of Warren, he pokes him.

Warren opens his eyes. 'What now? When can I go?'

'Here, I have coffee for you. Joseph, untie his good hand.'

Warren takes the carton and begins to drink. He sighs after taking a few gulps. 'That was good,' he says.

'Tell me about the man who invented anti-ageing medication,' says Stanoski, turning to his assistant. 'Thank you, you can go.' He is careful not to say a name in front of the captives.

'Why?'

'You wanted to short GlaxoSmithKline shares, remember?'

'Yes. So?'

'Is this man Derek's partner?'

Warren laughs. 'No.'

'How do you know about him?'

Warren finishes the coffee. 'Through a friend. He has produced pills which work. Sooner or later he will market the product and then it will affect other drug companies. That's why I shorted the stock as I expect all major pharmaceutical stocks to fall.'

'Thank you.' Stanoski accepts the explanation for the time being.

'How long do I have to stay like this? I'm cramped and it's affecting my blood circulation and general health.'

Stanoski stands, secures Warren's free hand with cuffs, and says, 'Once the proceeds of your investments are transferred to my account then, and only then, will I let you go.'

THIRTY-FOUR:
Wednesday

~

OUTSIDE, THE BREEZE was making everyone freeze. I felt immune to it, walking along Threadneedle Street in the City of London, in a simple collared shirt and suit jacket. I'm on my way to a bank, the NatWest, to establish the possibility of obtaining a loan for a start-up business. I'm feeling terrific. I've worked extremely hard over the past two days and nights. I've figured out how to create an antidote to Heidi's situation and she is much happier. She is back to looking her real age and has expressed gratitude. She even wanted to have me make love to her, but I said I'm living with a woman to whom I'm going to remain faithful. Besides, fucking a work colleague brings with it all kinds of problems.

I like London's financial district. The buildings are ancient, unlike Australia's large cities, its architecture intriguing. Modern buildings are likely to be the same throughout the world, towers dominating. I walk casually as I'm early for my appointment. I told my boss I'd be in late. He didn't have any issues with it as I'm a trusted member of the team and often achieve results within specified deadlines. On top of that, I stay late on a regular basis.

But today is special. I've managed to manufacture two additional kinds of pills. I have samples at home in different bottles. There's the original in a bottle marked A. This was the first anti-ageing pill which enhanced strength, but it didn't sustain the ageing process. Then the one Heidi and I worked on is marked B. This one created ongoing ageing and made the person weaker. The next one is the antidote to B, and I marked that bottle as C. Then the latest one I produced is in a slimmer bottle, and marked D.

Currently, I'm trialling D. This pill has reduced my age, in terms of appearance by roughly eight years. So, I look around thirty instead of thirty-nine. This one also makes me feel great. Strong, positive, as though I could conquer anything. I haven't tested it to see whether I'm as strong as I was with the first pill, but I need to do so thoroughly. To date, I've found I can lift Kirstie with ease. I've updated my notes progressively. I worked until 3:20 a.m. and then woke at 7:30 a.m. I don't feel tired. Is this another property of the new invention? Still, there may be side effects which will surface over the next few days or weeks. I'll have to see.

Heidi is happy not testing any more pills. She's pleased to be alive and is curious to see the effects on me. My colleagues haven't seen the new me yet nor has Heidi. But Kirstie has and she's amused by the changes in the various appearances I present. She thinks I'm nuts. I can't argue with that. Now that I've come this far, I'm going to see it through. I know the end result might be death, but I don't care. Did inventors in the past pull out before finishing with their works? The Wright brothers created the first aircraft and tested it. Benjamin discovered electricity probably fiddling with things he shouldn't have. And Tim Berners Lee developed the internet amid scepticism.

I'm nearly at the bank. I need to rehearse my pitch. The wind is picking up and people are pulling their over-coats around themselves more tightly, pushing up collars to cover their necks. I feel the cool, but I'm definitely not cold.

STANOSKI SIPS HIS carton of coffee, feet up on the desk in the observation section of the abandoned house's basement. He peers out at Warren Buckley and Denny Thomas who both still seem drowsy. Both men had been drugged overnight to prevent needless complaints. Recently, both men have been given enough water and food to keep them as healthy as possible. Mattresses and bed coverings have also been installed in the room for better sleep.

Coffee finished, Stanoski asks Goran whether settlement of Buckley's investments has taken place. Joseph and Luka, who had the overnight watch, are back in their hotel rooms. Luka will visit Gina after a nap. Soon, phase one of this operation will be over.

'I will check, boss,' says Goran who opens a laptop.

Their ongoing issue will be Gina, that strange woman, always dressed in black. Stanoski wonders what kind of cult she's following but he's not going to ask. Presently, she's secured at her Camberwell residence and locked in one of the rooms upstairs. She hasn't been tortured. She's been looked after in relative luxury, although she would dispute this. She's been tied down flat, to have her lying in a bed, so much nicer than sitting on a hard chair for days. She's been provided decent drink and food, albeit McDonalds and other fast food. And she's been given regular bathroom breaks. She has a role to play and Stanoski needs to keep her reasonably happy and functional. He still hasn't decided what to do with Buckley and Thomas at the conclusion of their business. Although Buckley has seen his face, Stanoski can't see Warren tracking him down after Stanoski has left the country.

And finding the money will be impossible. Stanoski has channelled the funds into one account which automatically diverts those funds to multiple accounts. With the women's fashion business not operating as he expected, Stanoski wants to make money from some other enterprise. Which is what originally prompted him to deal with Buckley and company. The women's fashion business was his wife's idea and she was meant to be a large part of that business. Leaving it in the hands of a manager while his wife did baby things wasn't a good strategy. The business is barely keeping afloat.

Goran speaks but Stanoski doesn't hear. 'What did you say?' says Stanoski.

'Equity account shows all is in cash,' says Goran.

'Good. Now we need to transfer the money. We need to get the password from Warren, so that I can execute the transaction.'

'Did we not get password?'

'That was for his bank account. There'll be another for the share account,' says Stanoski. He looks up at Goran. 'Why don't you take the car and ensure all is well in Camberwell. I'll stay here with the men and when Warren is awake, I'll get the password.'

But suddenly Stanoski has a thought. 'No, Goran, I'd actually like to visit the woman to check on things. You stay here, okay?'

'Sure, boss,' says Goran who rubs his two-day growth.

~❀

AFTER STANOSKI HAS begun driving, he reflects on his team, Goran, Luka and Joseph. Goran is his long- time lieutenant who served with him in Serbia and has proved trustworthy and competent. The two men become friends in Serbia and kept in touch when Stanoski migrated to Germany and Goran settled in England. Luke is Goran's cousin and was born in Manchester. Joseph is a friend of Luka and has been a petty criminal. He is being paid by Stanoski and is happy with the work. Goran leads them well, Stanoski feels.

Stanoski now wants to think about his overall mission and he does not want to deal with the captives which is why he is keen for his team to carry out his routine requests. It occurs to him that the scientist might be onto something which could generate large profits. He watches the road and concentrates on the next step. He arrives outside Gina's flat and sits in the car. He closes his eyes to collect himself.

After a moment, Stanoski goes upstairs and visits the woman in black.

I'm sitting in an office with no windows. The manager I made the appointment with is due any minute, I'm told. I pull out some documents from my leather satchel and place the papers on the table in front of me. I leave the satchel on the floor beside my polished black shoes. Then I reread the application form I'd emailed to the bank.

A woman appears and asks whether I'd like a drink.

'A glass of water would be fine,' I say.

'Mr Robinson is on a call. He won't be much longer,' says the middle-aged woman. She is neither slim nor overweight, nor friendly or unpleasant.

A glass of water is placed before me and I continue waiting. I check my phone. It's ten past ten, ten minutes after the scheduled meeting time. I check the news app on my phone.

Finally, after another five minutes, a man enters the room. He is in his fifties, slick grey hair combed back, and he wears round spectacles.

'Sorry to keep you waiting, Mr Stone, I'm Darcy Robinson,' he says extending his hand.

I shake his hand and sit down again while he moves to the comfortable chair opposite me. I see he has a folder which he places on the table.

'You're here for a loan, is that correct?'

'Yes. A business loan.'

Robinson adjusts his glasses and peers at me as though I'm a goldfish in a tank. 'What sort of business, Mr Stone?'

I'm wondering whether he thinks I'm too young due to my now youthful appearance. 'Pharmaceutical products,' I say.

'I see,' says Robinson. 'Do you have a business plan?'

I pass across another document I've taken out of my satchel. Robinson scans it. 'Drugs to help people look younger. Are you serious? Have you got evidence of this tested and approved?'

'Tested, yes, but I'm in the process of having it approved. I'm here to see what your lending process is and to understand how much I could borrow.' I'm stretching the truth a little but I'm hoping that the bank will see an opportunity.

Robinson runs the palm of his hand over his head, ensuring, I guess, that his hair is smooth. 'I'll get you to complete some forms and you can return them when you have proof that the drug has been approved by MHRA.' He hands me a batch of forms which I slip into my satchel.

'You didn't tell me how much I can borrow,' I say.

'You show the amount you'd like to borrow, and it'll be reviewed at the appropriate time,' says Robinson pushing my Business Plan back to me.

'So, it's unlimited?' I ask, tongue-in-cheek. This man is a pen pusher and does not help at all. I hate bureaucrats.

Mr Robinson smiles. 'Of course not.' He stands and stretches his right hand. The meeting is over.

I shake his hand although I would rather tear it off.

I CHECK IN with Heidi when I get to the office. 'How are you feeling?'

'Great. That antidote did the job.' Heidi is looking at a screen with equations running down the page. 'How did you get on?' She turns to me, smiling.

'This will be a long process,' I say, 'but it's just as well to start early. I didn't expect it to be easy,' I say, sitting on a roller chair next to Heidi. I've told her about my plans and asked her to join me once we have funding for a new company. 'I'll also have to engage an accountant who may be better placed to arrange a loan and prepare a professional submission.'

'What about your friend, Warren whatsit?'

'No. That guy is a shark. I wouldn't trust him.'

Heidi grins and stares at me hard. 'I can see the change. You look younger. So, the new pill works.'

'Well, I …'

At that moment, my phone buzzes. I stand and walk out back to my cubicle. 'Yes?'

'Ethan, Gina, you remember?'

'Of course, Gina,' I say, wondering whether she's going to tell me that Derek has died and she's wanting me to feel guilty. What's strange is her question, as though my memory of her has disappeared. 'What's up?' I want to ask whether she's dressed in anything other than black, but I don't as her tone is serious.

'Would you be keen to discuss a business deal for your invention?'

I'm suspicious of this out-of-the-blue question. And I don't see the lady in black as being a businesswoman. But then I might be totally off the mark. 'I thought, given Derek's situation, you'd be wary of my pill.'

'Well, I was, but I've thought about it. One pill worked wonders. The second one and then the third one produced the bad results,' she says, 'What do you say?'

'I'm open to the idea. What do you have in mind?' Should Gina or whoever is asking be prepared to fund my work, I can't see that as being a problem.

'Maybe I can come over and we can talk about it,' she says.

'I'm happy to talk but not at my place. Why don't we meet at a quiet restaurant?'

There's silence for a moment then Gina suggests a place and time. I agree, but I realise I'll have to check the location on Google.

STANOSKI TAKES THE phone from Gina. 'You did good,' he says, putting her phone in his pocket. He didn't know if this Ethan Stone, the so-called anti-ageing chemist, had her number on his phone or not but he didn't want to take the risk of her alerting him that something was amiss.

'What now? Will you release me?'

'Soon. Don't whinge.'

'Why are you keeping me here? You've drugged me and I wake up in this room. And there's no explanation. You haven't raped me or killed me so there must be something else you want.'

'Do you know Warren Buckley?'

'Warren, oh yes. Do you know where he is?' Gina sounds genuinely excited.

'He's in a place which I know. He's safe. You're insurance.'

'What for?'

'Never mind. You do as you're told, and all will be good,' says Stanoski, standing. He rubs his tired eyes. 'I'll collect you at seven o'clock. I'll make the booking for eight, okay?'

'Alright. But I look a mess. I can't go out like this.'

At that moment, Goran walks in. He nods at Stanoski to suggest that he's done the job, and all is okay.

'Don't worry. Goran will collect new clothes and things you need from your flat downstairs. Give him the keys. Use the bathroom here so you can clean up.' Stanoski marches out, slamming the door as he exits.

THIRTY-FIVE:
Wednesday

~

KIRSTIE AND I ask the black cab driver to stop a block from the designated location. Kirstie and I had discussed the meeting and we both thought it's best to be cautious. Why would Gina be interested in a business proposition? First, she's never conducted herself as anyone vaguely aware of investment. Second, she's poor. She wouldn't be able to raise enough for a modest party, let alone the funds required for starting a business.

The area is not one either of us are familiar with. It's dark with few streetlights in a street which appears to be mainly residential. Then I see a street sign. Osborn Terrace. It's in Lewisham, I think. I didn't want to get out too close to the restaurant as I need to suss out the surroundings.

'It's cold, even with my overcoat on,' says Kirstie. 'Of course, you don't notice, do you?' Kirstie bumps me playfully.

I smile. 'Sorry, it must be off-putting.'

We walk along the street, observing the neighbourhood of terraces. Nobody is on the street. At the end of the road, we see activity. The restaurant sits on one corner, a convenience store on another and a couple of businesses on the other two corners, across the road. The Carola is on Lee Street and I press Kirstie's hand.

'You prepared for anything?' I ask.

'You bet. I have my private gun in my handbag, and you have your super strength.'

'What kind of pistol do you carry?'

Kirstie puts her mouth close to my ear. 'A SIG Sauer P238. Why do you ask? Since when have you taken an interest in firearms?'

'Just curious. Ever since I've been shot, I've taken to researching guns.'

We walk into the restaurant which is only a quarter-filled. I can understand selecting this venue as it appears quite private with many tables in a large area and few patrons. I check the time. 8:13 p.m. I didn't want us to arrive first. Looking around I see Gina in the back corner. A waiter strolls towards us, his smile suggesting he's happy to see more customers. I inform him that we are with a group and point to where they are. He allows us to pass.

Gina looks in her element in the darkened corner, dressed in her black clothes. One could imagine the corner table to be reserved for romantic couples but the man beside her doesn't seem remotely like a romantic companion. His expression is severe, much like Gina's overall appearance and he looks distinctly Eastern European. He stands and shakes my hand. He doesn't bother with Kirstie. We sit opposite them.

'How are you, Ethan?' Gina asks.

'Fine. This is Kirstie.'

'Nice to meet you, Kirstie,' says Gina.

Kirstie nods. I wait to see what the man says. He hasn't been intro duced and before I can say something, the waiter brings two extra menus.

'What's good here?' I ask to break the ice.

'I've only been here once. The lamb is nice,' says Gina.

'Let's order so we can talk business,' says the nameless man.

'Who are you, sir?' I ask, not impressed by his lack of manners.

'You can call me John,' he says, 'I'm a friend of Gina's.'

Orders placed, I fill Kirstie's glass with water before doing the same to my glass. I've ordered a glass of red wine which I'm looking forward to. 'Okay,' I say, 'I understand you're interested in investing in my invention.'

'No investing,' says the man called John, 'I am interested in buying some units of your product.'

'Oh,' I say, 'how many are you after?' I don't believe this man is genuine. He wants to find out how far along the process we are at.'

'Let's talk price first. Cost per hundred units?'

His abrupt style annoys me. 'I'll send you the price, by email, once I've factored in the costs to develop a batch. At the moment, I only have a small sample. I should tell you that what I'm really interested in is finding a business partner to help fund my operation.'

'We can't do a deal now. When will you have a commercial quantity?'

I scratch my head. I don't know when a large enough number of pills will be available. Besides, I need to think about safety. I can't simply sell the product unless the tests prove the pills to be reliable and completely absent of side effects. But what can I say to this moron who sees an opportunity to cash in? 'It's hard to say as I'm still developing the product. Which is why I need funding.'

The drinks arrive, preventing John from talking freely. When the waiter departs, I glance at Gina who seems unusually subdued. Almost as if she doesn't want to be here. I wonder how she got involved with this man, the unsmiling John, someone who isn't her type of friend. But maybe I'm being judgemental.

'How's Warren?' I ask to draw Gina out of her fugue.

Gina glances at John. 'Fine.'

We chat about nothing in particular and when the meals arrive, we eat in virtual silence. It's a laborious process and I question how Gina has managed to tell another person about the formula which has all but killed Derek. Since John can't get what he wants, he seems to have shut down. I glance at Kirstie who is making the most of her meal.

The waiter arrives after we have demolished our food and asks whether we'd like dessert or coffees. I take the initiative and say we'd like to pay. Nobody contradicts me. John agrees to pick up the bill, using a credit card. He's probably keen to get out of this very boring encounter.

John orders a cab. We say goodbye without any physical contact and stroll out the door. As we stand outside, the cool caressing my face, I feel invigorated. What a night. I still can't get over Gina's extended silence. John and Gina stand alongside us.

'Can we drop you off?' asks John.

'No, we're okay,' I say.

The cab comes to a smooth halt in front of us and I open the back door for Gina. She looks at me imploringly while John gets into the front seat.

We hail a cab of our own.

With Ethan Stone and Kirstie waiting for a taxi, Stanoski looks at Gina. 'You did good. Nobody had to get hurt.' He then pulls out his phone. 'Goran, follow them and keep me updated.'

After another moment, Stanoski tells the driver to stop. He and Gina walk back to the restaurant and take the rear entrance to fetch a piece of paper Stanoski had dropped. They find it under the table they'd sat at. After retrieving the page, from a small notepad he'd used, which must have slipped out of Stanoski's pocket when he withdrew his wallet, he checks that it's the one with important details of his UK contacts. He tells Gina he has another plan.

'Where are we going?' asks Gina.

'Back to the house, after I stop off somewhere first. If you behave, we'll let you go tomorrow. Okay?'

Gina doesn't say anything, simply walks towards the restaurant door at the front. Together they go outside, to see a cab with Kirstie peering out, turning a corner. They continue walking to where Stanoski had parked his vehicle.

'Why did we order a cab before when you've got your car? I'm confused. Did you forget?'

'I wanted to drop off Stone so I could check where he lived but not with my car,' says Stanoski.

When the pair reach Stanoski's car, he opens the back door and ushers Gina inside. Luka is there waiting. The second car, occupied by Goran, is gone, as Stanoski expected. He also has Joseph back at the abandoned house monitoring the two male captives. So far, everything is going to plan. Stanoski had no intention of paying for the pills. As Stone wouldn't disclose his location, this was his plan all along – to have him followed.

Stanoski likes to drive. He drives the vehicle making sure to abide by the road rules and speed limits. He can't afford to have traffic police stop him. Gina might suddenly become bold and do something stupid. Naturally, he would use the pistol inside his jacket to kill any cops, and the whole affair would then become messy and unpredictable.

As Stanoski gets close to their destination, he ponders the next steps. If he kills Gina, Buckley and Thomas, the result would be a determined effort by the police to track the killers. Also, Ethan Stone and his girlfriend are now witnesses to the restaurant meeting. Better to release these people and threaten them with retribution if they inform the authorities.

Stanoski parks the car and then instructs Luka to escort Gina back to her room. He goes for a walk and calls Joseph to ask about activities, if any, during his absence. He is told that Warren and Thomas were quiet, occasionally nodding off because of a sedative in the food they had for dinner.

Satisfied with progress, Stanoski returns to his car and drives back to his hotel. All the cash from Warren's bank account and Warren's investments converted to cash have now been transferred to Stanoski's special bank account in Germany. The only issue outstanding relates to the silent partner Thomas alluded to. Warren, when questioned with menaces, didn't know who that partner was, saying the man contacted him, by phone, from time to time. Apparently, this man had ordered the capture of Ethan Stone previously but without success.

Asked how the silent partner was originally involved, all that Warren could explain was that the firm he worked for had been founded by two men, one in London and one in New York. When Warren took over from Toby Gillian, the London partner who died in a car accident, Warren said he never met the New York man who went by the name of George.

Stanoski grabs a beer from the mini bar and sits on the bed, gazing at the flat screen television. He's not interested in watching British television but his thoughts flow to Stone and the anti-ageing pills. He must get his hands on a sample so he can take it back to Germany. There he'll have the concoction analysed and possibly reproduced. Yes, that would be satisfactory, and he might then make up the losses sustained by Warren. Then he realises that Thomas has contributed next to nothing and that this broker was instrumental in getting him into a commodity which sank like the Titanic.

Unable to sleep, rage still dominating his thoughts, Stanoski calls a number he sourced from the internet – Kitty Galore. Having informed the service of his preference, Stanoski takes a Scotch Whisky from the mini bar and drinks it straight. He settles back and waits.

Thirty minutes later, Stanoski hears his phone. It's the girl. He takes the elevator down to the lobby and sees that the service has provided the choice he made. She is Asian, petite with a lovely face. Completely different from his German wife who is tall, buxom and has the creamy complexion he first admired. Stanoski nods to the woman who is in her twenties, and takes her to his room, using his key to ascend the floors to level ten.

THIRTY-SIX:
Thursday

~

I ROLL OVER AND give Kirstie a playful nudge with a rampant uncontrollable extremity. She grunts but I know she's awake.

'What's got into you?' she asks, 'We did it twice last night.'

'I don't know. I just want you,' I say.

Kirstie turns towards me. 'You're just horny. I think it's the new pill. Dangerous.'

'What about me? I need to release this energy.'

'I'm tired. It's only six o'clock.'

'Seven minutes after six to be precise.'

We kiss and soon our bodies get carried away, passion winning through. I'm consumed by my desire and find I'm able to maintain my erection for longer than before, before taking the latest version of my anti-ageing pill. This feature is a welcome aspect of my latest pill. It would replace Viagra. Certainly, a marketing plus for males. What about females. If only Heidi would try this. I'd like to understand the effect. If it were to work so gloriously for females, as for males, this pill would cure all the world's ills. Making love because one wouldn't have time for fighting. I'm getting ahead of myself, I know, but in this euphoric state, I'm not thinking clearly.

Exhausted, we both lie back and study the ceiling, which could do with a coat of paint, I feel.

'Let's shower together and have breakfast,' Kirstie says, 'I have a full day coming up.'

In the shower, as I soap Kirstie's back, I ask, 'What did you think of that John character?'

'I wouldn't trust him as far as I could throw him. A sleaze. And I've come across many in my time as a copper.'

I soap her thick thighs and find concentrating on her words an effort. 'I agree. I can't see myself doing business with him.'

At breakfast, Kirstie asks, 'What's with that woman dressed in black? She seemed afraid.'

'Yes. Something was not quite right. I might call and see if she's okay.' I'd wondered, too, about Gina who, in my previous dealings with her, was usually chatty and not afraid to express her opinions. It was consoling to hear Kirstie's take on the matter.

I arrive in the office at 8:50 a.m., carrying a carton of flat white coffee, and place my satchel on the ground. I check my emails as Heidi comes into my cubicle and sits opposite me. Today, she is dressed in her usual dark trousers and white blouse. Flat shoes.

'How's the pill going? Any side effects?'

'Only positive ones so far,' I say explaining about my morning. 'It's a shame you're not comfortable trying this one.'

'Maybe I will,' she says. 'Let me think about it.'

'Okay. I've brought these pills with me, should you want one,' I say, pleased with Heidi's response. At the same time, I don't want to push it if she's reluctant. I've caused enough misery.

'When will you hear about your business loan?'

'I've completed the forms with the help of my accountant, and I'll post them today, but I know that these institutions take their time, so I wouldn't hold my breath.'

'I'm really keen to work with you. The work I'm doing for the company is routine and boring so anything to give me a purpose is welcome.' Heidi stands up and wanders off.

~

STANOSKI IS NOT in a good mood when room service knocks on the door. His night with Amy, the pleasant-looking, petite Asian woman did not go as planned. She was prepared to do a slow striptease and she was good at it. She had a trim figure and blemish- free skin. No tattoos or piercings. Stanoski hates women with voluntary disfigurement. He cannot understand the need for people to have their skin coloured with ink or pictures. So, the evening had started off well. Amy smiled during the show which she seemed to have performed before, a rehearsed routine, he suspected. But then, when he suggested she be tied up, she baulked at the notion, saying she did not like the idea. He didn't force her, and they had vanilla sex with him on top, thrusting his member vigorously into her. After he'd done with her, he told her to get out in a tone indicating he wasn't satisfied. She dressed hurriedly and fled as though the hotel was on fire.

The breakfast tray is wheeled in by an older man, someone Stanoski suspects is in his fifties, who deposits the cloth-covered table containing plates of food and coffee in the centre of the room. The silver-haired man lingers, waiting for a tip but Stanoski is not about to reward him for doing his job. The waiter departs without a word and closes the door behind him.

Stanoski tries to understand the purpose of the silent partner involved in the London-based brokerage firm. It appears that the captives are more frightened of him than they are of Stanoski's men. Who is he? Nobody seems to know. Perhaps he needs to be drawn out. Stanoski eats his Eggs Benedict while mulling over the pros and cons of releasing Buckley, Thomas and the woman in black clothing.

Stanoski wipes his mouth with a napkin then phones Goran. 'Did you find where Ethan Stone lives?'

'Yes, boss. It's a flat and Luka went into the block and discovered which floor Stone and the woman went to. Also found out there are two flats per floor.'

'Okay. Have Luka break in and find the pills. Knock first to see if the neighbour is at home,' says Stanoski, pouring more coffee into his cup. 'Also, let prisoners go. Tell them if they talk to police, they will be killed. Oh, and have Joseph follow Thomas.'

'Okay.'

Stanoski ends the call. None of his men have exposed their faces. He is the only one who has been seen. So, identification is confined to only himself, but he knows he'll change his appearance once he gets back to Munich. He feels comfortable he'll be abroad soon enough and doubts the brokers have the resources to track him.

~

AFTER AN UNEXCITING day at work, I arrive home to find Kirstie cooking and listening to the radio. She's singing along to a tune I don't recognise.

'You're in a cheerful mood,' I say, giving her a hug and kissing her cheek.

'Yes, we had a good day. Sold more items than usual. Clean up, dinner will be ready in ten minutes.'

I change into casual clothes in the bedroom as, I believe, we will probably spend the night at home. I have come to accept Kirstie's abode as home, at least for the foreseeable future. My desire to get a place of my own has evaporated since Kirstie wants me to share everything with her. I go into the bathroom and wash my face and hands. Looking into the mirror I see no change in my appearance. I still feel great so I can record other measurements after dinner. I've left my current pills at the office. Heidi indicated she'll think about trying one since I've noted no side effects thus far.

Stroking my face, I feel the stubble is rough. Should I shave for later in the evening? I open the bathroom cabinet and see that all three of the anti-ageing pill containers are missing. I check around. Other medications are in place, but the boxes marked A, B and C, are gone. And the pill box B, the one Heidi tried is extremely dangerous if not used for the right purpose.

I rush to the kitchen in long strides and ask Kirstie whether she's taken any of the missing bottles and wonder why I hadn't disposed of these dangerous pills. She denies even opening the cabinet tonight. I feel relieved. But then it occurs to me that someone's been here. I mention this to Kirstie. We both go to all parts of the flat to see if anything else has been taken or whether there is evidence of an intrusion.

'I think you're right,' says Kirstie. 'Someone has rummaged through my top drawer. I remember how my make-up was positioned this morning and it's different now. But nothing, other than your pills, seems to have been taken.'

I come into the bedroom. 'That's good. Looks like only the anti-aging bottles of pills have gone missing. Who would… hang on? Gina's mate John. Did he follow us or have us followed? That's the only explanation.'

'I agree. You'd make a good detective, Ethan. Want to change careers?'

'Not yet,' I say. 'Let's eat.' I'm too furious to speak. How dare they, whoever? My residence has been breached so many times in the last few months and I'm thoroughly sick of it. As much as I'd like to move again, at least to keep Kirstie safe, I'm reluctant to bow to the demands of criminals. There has to be another solution.

Over dinner, I raise the topic with Kirstie.

'I'll call one of my contacts in the police tonight,' she says. 'We'll start with Gina. You know where she lives, right?'

'Good idea,' I say.

THIRTY-SEVEN:
Tuesday (The Following Week)

I STARTLE AWAKE AT the sound of a bird. I cannot sleep anyway. I've been tossing and turning for ages, wondering when the nightmare is going to end. I have had visions of masked men breaking in. Of Derek dying. Of Kirstie being assaulted. And of Heidi getting younger by the day. At five o'clock in the morning, a time I would never think of waking up, I've had enough, and I slide out of bed, making sure not to disturb Kirstie. Getting up so early in the morning is something other people do, but today it's the right thing for me to embrace. I glance at Kirstie who seems at peace. I will resist the temptation to kiss her and leave her sleep.

Dressed in black jeans, a grey sweater and blue sneakers, I decide against breakfast. With an overcoat on my arm, I leave the flat. Outside I reconsider taking the overcoat as the cold is not penetrating. I return to the flat and dump the overcoat on the sofa. Then I realise I can't just walk out so, before departing, I leave a message for Kirstie, giving her the address in Camberwell I intend to visit. Using public transport, I make my way to Gina's flat. I'm not going to wait for the police to question her further. I need to ask her some things first.

Although the cold today is evident from people huddling together or wrapping themselves tightly, the breeze is lowering the temperature considerably, making many pedestrians disappear indoors. Standing outside Gina's front door, I look at my iPhone. The screen shows twenty minutes after six. No way would she have gone to work yet. I knock on the door. Once. Twice. Then I remember she might be upstairs where Derek lived. I walk up the stone steps and knock on the door loudly.

Gina, dressed in a black robe, opens the heavy door. 'What,' she stutters.

I barge in, brushing past her and walk down the hallway to her kitchen. I put the kettle on. 'Coffee good?' I ask.

'What the hell?' she splutters. 'You can't just push in here and take over.'

'Sit down,' I say. I finish making coffees for both of us. When I bring the cups out to the table, I see Gina watching me, arms across her chest. The dressing gown is slightly open, revealing a sliver of white thigh skin, so white that I cannot imagine snow being less white.

'What do you want?' Gina finally sits down.

Just as I'm about to pose my questions, a man walks out of the bedroom. He has a gun and it's pointed at me. 'Who the hell are you?' he commands.

In his dressing gown, he still looks intimidating. Tall, bulky and middle-aged, he stands two metres from me.

'Anton, please, no violence. This is Ethan Stone,' she says.

'The anti-ageing scientist?'

'Yes,' says Gina.

I hadn't spoken during this exchange and I wonder who this man is. Is this Gina's boyfriend or lover? And what about Derek? But I don't ask, given the pistol aimed at me. I realise I should have brought my own gun and then we'd be able to have a shootout like cowboys in the gunfight at the OK Corral. The shootout did occur in 1881 but this is not the Nineteenth century and not the American Wild West either.

'Those damn pills killed Derek,' says Anton. 'What do you say about that, Mr Stone?'

'Let me explain…' I begin.

'Don't bother. Gina told me,' says Anton, lowering the gun, no doubt feeling unthreatened.

'When did he die?' I ask, curious more than anything else.

Anton brushes his greying hair back. 'When was it, Gina?'

'When I was kept captive by that man, John,' she says. 'I have to make enquiries with the hospital to find out exactly.'

'Derek was my partner, you know,' says Anton.

'Not Gina's grandfather?'

Anton laughs, a deep disturbing sound. 'A good story.'

'Derek was the silent partner Warren and his partners worked with. But Anton was the man behind everything,' says Gina. 'Derek couldn't deal with the business once he got sick.'

'Don't say any more, Gina. He doesn't need to know,' Anton says. Then scratching his head, he seems to relent. 'Let me tell the story. Warren doesn't know that I used Derek to pass information on to him. I live in New York and originally Derek was my partner. When Warren became a partner, he was not told my name. For security reasons, he received messages from me by phone or email or through Derek.'

'I see. It's all so complicated,' I say, not fully understanding why the broking business needed to have such secrecy.

'Now, where are these pills of yours? I assume they work if taken as directed,' says Anton.

'This is why I came. To find John. My place was broken into and the pills stolen,' I say. I'm not about to reveal which pills are safe, trusting label D pills are okay, and which category of pills are unsafe. I also don't know how the antidote pills affect people if they haven't taken label B pills, the ones which made Heidi sick.

'How do we find this John?' Anton asks. He sits down in an armchair, facing us.

I drink some coffee. It's been a rough morning. I look at Gina.

'I don't know where he is. He blindfolded me when I was first kidnapped by his gang and also later when I was driven back.' Gina looks to Anton.

'No problem,' says Anton. 'I have connections with some French colleagues. They will find him.'

I wonder whether these French guys are the men who killed my flatmates. Now I realise that Warren was the guy who informed Gina of my invention. Gina would have passed the information on to Derek and hence Anton. A weird web of people, all out to gain by deceit and manipulation. And who is John? Was he wronged or was he told of my work?

A banging on the door interrupts my thoughts.

'Who the hell...?' says Anton, clearly annoyed.

'Police, open up,' says a voice.

Now I'm pleased I left a message with Kirstie. I watch while Gina answers the door and, a moment later, I see two police officers follow her into the living room where Anton and I sit. Anton places the gun into the right-hand-side pocket of his dressing gown.

'What's this all about?' asks Anton, not bothering to stand.

'Sir, I'm DC Bower and this is DC Kartik, we'd like to talk with this lady, in private,' says the tall thick-set man. His Indian partner simply observes the exchange.

'I'll take these gentlemen upstairs, to the study,' says Gina.

Gina and the two policemen take the stairs to the next level where they'll be assured of privacy. I look at Anton to see if he's going to raise the gun again. He doesn't.

'Any idea why the cops are here?' Anton asks. He shifts in his seat.

'None,' I lie. It appears I won't get to talk to Gina further, but it does not matter as she has no idea of John's whereabouts. However, the visit has revealed that Anton is involved with Warren. I stand. 'I have to go,' I say, not keen to be in the same room with this guy.

'Hey, I haven't finished with you,' says Anton in an authoritative voice.

I remain standing. 'What are you going to do? Shoot me? I'm sure the cops upstairs will hear the shot.' I don't know why I'm acting courageous. I don't feel it, that's for sure. Again, if I can reach Anton should he try to take the gun out of his pocket, I'll easily overpower him. I'm simply aware that Anton may not want to shoot up Gina's flat, given the potential problem it would cause.

'I'd like some of those pills. I'll even pay you. I'm very rich. Warren and his team have produced some great results,' he says with a smirk on his face, the smirk of an extremely confident person.

'This John fellow stole them. That's why I'm here. To see whether Gina knows where he might be.' I stare at the man, wondering whether he's buying my story.

'Well, let's see what's she has to say,' Anton says.

I sit down again, opposite Anton, and cross my legs. It appears he's being rational. He seems to be a businessman through and through. I doubt I'd be able to trust him by having him invest in my project. He's the sort of guy, summing him up after only twenty minutes, to want to take control. He'd screw everyone else in the process. But I can see why he would want to look younger. His wrinkled face needs help. 'Alright, I'll wait another ten minutes,' I say, not knowing what to talk to him about. I survey the room to see if changes have occurred since my last visit. None have.

'Let me see your photo ID,' says Anton, after he's had enough of me ignoring him.

'Why?'

'I want to see for myself how old you say you are,' says Anton.

'Okay,' I say. I take my wallet out of my jacket pocket and hand him my driver's licence. This has my photo and date of birth.

He looks me up and down. 'Whatever you've done works. You don't look thirty-nine. Jesus, I need this. Can you produce more pills?' He hands back my licence.

'I know nothing about you. You don't even sound British,' I say.

'I'm American. I live in New York, as I've already said. I met Derek three decades ago at a conference. Want to see some identification?'

Before I can respond, Gina returns with the policemen and sees them out to the door.

'Thank you for your help,' says DC Bower.

Gina walks back down the hallway and stops on the side of our seats so she can see both of us. 'Thank God, that's over,' she says.

'What did they want?' asks Anton.

'Asked about the abduction, but I didn't give them anything.'

'Why not?' I ask.

'Because I'd like to live. When John had his hooded mates drive me back here, blind-folded and handcuffed, I was told it would be very unwise to discuss what happened to me with the police. John said he had the means to hurt my friends and kill me.'

'Good,' says Anton. 'I'll have my associates deal with it.' He levels his stare back at me. 'Now, how can I get some of the anti-ageing pills?'

~

STANOSKI WAKES FEELING energised. He stretches his arms and then stretches his legs underneath the covers. He feels great. Looking at his phone, he sees the time is already 8:30 a.m. That was the best night's sleep he's had in such a long time, he thinks, remembering he'd taken one of the pills from Stone's cabinet. He pulls the blanket aside and rolls out of bed and stands, allowing the unfamiliar feeling to run through him. Was this the effect of the anti-aging pill? He goes into the bathroom and checks his features in the mirror which stands above the basin.

Stanoski cannot believe it. What a miracle. He looks more than ten years younger. Perhaps nearer twenty years off his forty-eight years. He feels like jumping up and down, but he contains his enthusiasm. He calls his men in, keen to see their transformation. Only Goran declined to take one of the pills. Stanoski had taken a pill from bottle A, while Luka chose bottle B and Joseph used a pill from bottle C.

When his three comrades visit his room five minutes later, Stanoski is shocked. They size each other up – they all look different and not all in a positive way. Stanoski tells them they need to see this Ethan Stone. On the trip to Stone's girlfriend's place, Stanoski recalls the trouble he underwent to find the anti-ageing pharmacist.

Warren had revealed where Stone worked but didn't know his current address. Gina confirmed that Stone worked at GlaxoSmithKline but didn't know where he currently lived either. However, Warren had mentioned Stone had brought a woman along to a party. A policewoman. From there Stanoski found her address through a contact he had in the police. Then it shouldn't have been hard to find her apartment, but she had moved. But Goran had found the address when he followed them in the taxi.

'We know where Stone and the policewoman live. So, let's plan what we need to do,' says Stanoski, angry that he has to deal with another problem.

THIRTY-EIGHT:
Friday

~

WORK KEPT ME from thinking about what had transpired earlier in the day. But now, leaning back and enjoying a coffee break, I wonder how I should handle Anton's request. I'd left him in the morning at Gina's flat, saying I would arrange a couple of pills for him, from my office. Of course, that did not sit well with him and I needed all my negotiating skills to get him to see that I couldn't just produce as many as I wanted as though I was some baker, producing loaves of bread. He persisted, asking whether I kept a bottle of pills at home. Although I denied having a batch at Kirstie's, I don't think he believed me.

But my mistake was telling Anton to meet me that evening with money to pay for the sample I was going to give him. We planned to do the trade at ten o'clock at a pub in the West End. I had no qualms selling him pills as I knew he was wealthy. What I didn't understand was what his involvement was with Gina. Did Warren introduce him to Gina by phone? Why was he fascinated by this woman in black? Did her dark garb turn him on? And did she sport black tattoos on her extreme white body? This I didn't need to know.

Heidi comes into my cubicle and sits on my visitor's chair. She smiles. 'So far, so good,' she says.

'What are you talking about?' I ask, snapped out of my dark thoughts about the risk of meeting with Anton. Heidi looks very appealing in her light-blue outfit. It lights up her eyes and suits her colouring overall.

'The pill. It works fine and there have been no side-effects. Can't you tell that I'm looking so young?'

'Of course. I was immersed in something else but yes, you do look so much younger,' I say, speaking with exaggerated enthusiasm. 'Want a coffee downstairs?'

She agrees and we walk downstairs and to the café situated on the ground floor of the building. 'I promised to sell a couple of the pills to someone. What do you think I should charge?' I ask.

'Why? I thought you wanted to thoroughly test it by waiting a sensible period of time.' Heidi brushes hair off her face.

'I know. But I have a very persistent client who knows about Derek's death and he could cause trouble if I decline.' I sip my coffee. I check my iPhone for the time. It is nearly twelve-thirty. 'Are you hungry?' I ask.

'Not yet. I don't have any clue what it might be worth on the open market. Bear in mind it's not currently able to be mass produced; it has cost a lot of development time, so I'd say it would have to be expensive for a buyer.'

'I agree. And this man can afford to pay. I'll text him, putting the price at such a level that he might decide it is too high.'

I decide to leave Heidi to go back to work while I take a walk outside. I wander down the road and feel the sun. It's a nice change from the past few weeks. When I turn back, I observe the huge glass structure of the company's building with the 'gsk' sign alongside the full name emblazoned across the top of the building. It occurs to me that GlaxoSmithKline might be interested in my invention. I hadn't considered the company previously as they might wonder if I'm using their time to enhance a personal product. Should they express interest, it will save having to find backers or borrow funds from a bank and take the risk of starting a business. The company would also have the benefit of a huge marketing arm. I will need to prove that I developed this formula in Australia.

I will sound out some key players at the company. They may think I'm crazy. They may buy the formula from me and shelve it because it might reduce the need for other drugs, many of which are needed on an ongoing basis. I won't know until I talk to executives. But who can I trust?

Stanoski knocks on the door. No response. He nods to Goran to do his stuff with his tools while his other team members, Luka and Joseph, keep a lookout both sides of the corridor.

After barely a minute Goran has managed to open the front door. Stanoski and his men step inside, guns drawn. Stanoski signals for them to search the premises. He goes into the kitchen and checks out the refrigerator. He takes out a beer and positions himself in the study. He tells his men to do the same. The study only contains two chairs, so Goran takes two more from the living room. They wait.

At 6:20 p.m., Stanoski hears a key in the door. He signals for all to be quiet and alert. With the study off to the side of the living room, and with all lights off, nobody who enters can see the intruders. They wait. Footsteps move gently, the sound almost inaudible. Then a light is switched on.

Stanoski signals for his men to follow as he walks out into the light, gun drawn.

'Whoa…,' says the woman.

'I'd advise you to be quiet,' Stanoski says as his men also emerge from the study. 'Goran, tie her up.'

'What is this?'

'What's your name?'

'Kirstie. What do you want? You can have my purse. There's no other money here.'

'Just sit in that chair,' Stanoski says pointing to a kitchen chair. He nods for Goran to do his bidding.

Kirstie complies, watching with interest.

'You're a cop, huh?'

'Ex-cop,' says Kirstie.

Goran binds her hands and feet with duct tape, after removing her high heels. Stanoski, and his men lower their pistols. Each finds a seat in the living room. Stanoski chooses an armchair facing Kirstie. He looks at the solidly built woman and is grateful he came with men and weapons. She would probably be difficult to subdue otherwise. 'When does your partner arrive?'

'I don't have a partner,' says Kirstie.

'Don't bullshit me. Ethan Stone lives here, doesn't he?'

'Yes, but only temporarily. I never know what time he comes home from work,' says Kirstie.

'You're lying, but it doesn't matter. We'll wait. All night if we have to. Luka, go make coffee. Or would you like tea?'

'My hands are bound so how I am going to drink it?'

'We'll help, don't worry. Joseph, go to the door and signal when someone comes.'

'Yes boss,' says Joseph.

Finished for the day, I look forward to events planned for tonight and the weekend. Kirstie and I have arranged to meet up with some of her friends at a local restaurant. I call her to check whether we should meet at the restaurant. It's already 7:15 p.m. and our booking is for eight o'clock at Il Sugo, Camden Town. But she doesn't respond. I leave a message and catch transport to her place. She's no doubt occupied getting ready although, working at the fashion store, she's always well-presented and sometimes downright glamorous.

On the tube, I text Anton Jefferson telling him the pill is not ready but that I will postpone our meeting until tomorrow, same time, same place. I also say the cost of one pill is ten thousand pounds.

I reach the apartment just before eight o'clock. Kirstie will have to call Bob and Samantha Davis to say we'll be a tad late, I would imagine, and I hope Kirstie will be cool with that. I put the key into the lock and click it open, surprised to see the place is in darkness. I worry that something may have happened to Kirstie. It is unlike her to not answer her phone. She's generally so reliable. If anyone's tardy, it's me.

I fumble for the light switch, and after a few seconds, connect with the button and press it. Then I observe a scene from my worst nightmare. Kirstie bound and gagged. Men with guns pointed at me. I close my eyes. Surely this can't be happening. Am I waking from a deep sleep? But I'd just caught a crowded tube, I remember, and that ride was real enough.

I open my eyes again and nothing has changed.

'Come join us, Mr Stone,' says a dark-haired man sitting in an armchair.

I drop my leather briefcase on the carpet and wander into the living room. 'What is this?' I ask but suspect it has something to do with my invention, the anti-ageing pills which have created all my recent problems. I should have left it alone; this dream I had. But it's too late now and I have to deal with the consequences.

The man who spoke looks familiar. I try to recall from where I've come across him, but the memory eludes me at the moment. Then it dawns on me. 'John…is it?'

'I have used that name, sure, but my real name is Pavle,' says Stanoski. He waves his gun and points me to the sofa. I sit down.

'We tried your pills,' he begins, peering directly into my eyes. 'As you can see, I am well and healthy. The pill worked for me and I look younger. Goran here did not want to try the stuff and he's as he's always been – right looking for his age, forty-two. Then there's Luka who looks like a teenager. He tried the pills and he's ageing backwards in decades and feels sick. Finally, there's Joseph over there who has aged up and looks like he's eighty. What have you done with these pills? Why all the differences?'

I gaze at these men and I'm stunned, realising I had no concept of the power of the chemistry I had toyed with. None of these pills should have been used. They are unsafe and should have been tested properly. 'I'll explain, but only if you release Kirstie.'

'This is my show,' says the leader.

'No, it's not,' I insist, 'If you want these men to survive, you'll let me handle it.'

The leader, Pavle or John or whatever his real name is, stares at me, shifting in his seat. I can tell he's not used to being told what to do. But I need to be firm now, otherwise these gangsters will walk all over us. 'Goran,' says the leader, 'untie the woman.'

I wait until Kirstie is free and standing. She rubs her wrists and asks if she can go into the kitchen. Pavle nods. 'Luka, go with her.' Then he looks at me. 'Can you fix…put things right?'

'First, I should point out that you stole my pills, some of which are dangerous, and you guys have taken them without proper advice. They were experiments. And…'

'I don't want a lecture,' says Pavle.

'Give me the bottles,' I say.

'We didn't bring them,' says Pavle, looking less comfortable now that he's not totally in charge.

Of course, they didn't bring them along. Somehow, they think I can wave a magic wand and make everything better. I don't know whether my theory would work but I expect the antidote could help the guy looking like a teenager the same way it helped Heidi. And the old-looking guy who took the antidote pill might be helped if he took the pill the youthful-looking guy took. 'Okay,' I say, 'I need…'

The sound of my door thundering loose stops everyone in their tracks. I turn to see three more men approach. They wear black outfits with balaclavas and guns drawn. When they reach me, the man in front says, 'What's with all these people, Stone?'

The lights suddenly go off. I fall to the floor and hear shots fired. I roll to the side of the living room, knowing that none of the first group are in this vicinity. I'm guessing Kirstie pulled the plug to 'off' on the control box for electricity. I feel my way into the bedroom. Then staying crouched, I get to where I hid my pistol and wait. The gunshots continue but there are fewer shots. I presume some men have been hit, reducing the number of guns in play.

Suddenly, everything goes quiet and I await an explosion or some return to the noisy chaos. Have they run out of bullets? Or are they taking a break? I wait a moment, then see light. I creep to the edge of the darkened bedroom and peer outside. I see a couple of bodies lie on the ground. Then a shot is fired. The lights go off again. Kirstie is playing a dangerous game, but it allows the survivors to reset their plans.

With my back against a wall, I feel scared. This is madness. I only hope the noise has made a neighbour or somebody who's heard the commotion call the police. My phone is in the satchel I dropped when I walked down the hallway, so I cannot make the call.

The occasional shot rings out but for the next two minutes there's not much activity outside. I presume Kirstie is safe, and hope her police training has been useful.

My throat is dry. I've been running on adrenaline, I realise. At some point I have to be pro-active. Hiding in the bedroom won't resolve anything. I wait a while longer, hoping the intruders have died or run out of ammunition.

I'm about to chance fate by yelling to Kirstie to power the lights again when I see a beam of light penetrate the room. Then a voice, identifying itself as being police, tells everybody to raise hands their and stay still.

The lights return and I hear footsteps made by solid boots crowd the already crowded flat.

I move outside after placing my gun on top of a bookshelf. My hands are raised. I see a dozen cops looking at the damage. Two men are hand cuffed and four bodies lie on the floor. Someone is missing but I don't have time to dwell on it as I, too, am pulled aside to be cuffed. Kirstie joins the group and tells the cop that I live here.

Looking about I see Kirstie's furniture has been ripped to shreds. Bullet holes have also smashed the flat screen television and penetrated most of the prints hanging on the walls. One cop who knows Kirstie asks her to explain what has transpired. She confirms I'm with her and that the others forced their way in. She tells her part of the story and I add parts as well. I don't mention the anti-ageing pills, simply say the intruders wanted to hurt Kirstie. I'm told we'll have to come to the station to have a formal statement prepared.

THIRTY-NINE:
Saturday

~

AFTER SOME HOURS at the police station, Kirstie and I are released. As it is nearly two in the morning and, rather than go back to Kirstie's flat, I suggest we spend the rest of the night in a hotel. After all, we were driven to the police station and we now have no personal transport.

When I wake, I see it's seven o'clock. Kirstie is sleeping. I've not slept well despite an overwhelming tiredness which still plagues me. The man who eluded the police is on my mind. We mentioned this to the interviewing officer at the station and included the fact in our statement, but we couldn't provide a description which matched with anything they had on their data bases.

I recall the night before and our decision not to return home. The hotel we're in is comfortable but, as I look around, I realise the hotel is not a five-star job. I get out of bed.

Looking in the bathroom mirror, I note no changes to the day before. Will this version of the pill stick? The other versions seemed to alter at various points in the cycle. As I stretch, I'm aware of footsteps. It's Kirstie.

'Up already?' she asks.

'Couldn't sleep. I've been thinking of your apartment. Sorry, if it weren't for me, you wouldn't have your home smashed up.'

Kirstie comes to me and gives me a hug, from behind. 'Don't be silly. I love you. We'll sort this out together. Besides, I have insurance.'

'They may not cover the damage as it was caused by crooks and law enforcement,' I say, taking her arms and wrapping them around me more tightly.

'Don't worry. We'll have an assessor estimate the cost to make it new and what we can claim. I also need to read the policy,' she says.

'I'll pay for any excess or whatever does not get covered by insurance,' I say to let her know I will support her.

'Don't worry about the money. I love you a lot, you know.'

Cheered by this comment, I say, 'I love you, too. Why don't we start looking for some real estate together?'

'Let's have breakfast first,' she says, a smirk on her face.

Instead of ordering room service, we wander outside and breathe fresh air. There's a breeze but otherwise it looks like a fine day with only a few clouds marring the perfect blue sky. We find a café a few doors up and find a table near the front, allowing us to view the passing foot traffic. We order egg dishes and coffee before Kirstie looks at me.

'Do you know who the missing man is?'

'No idea. But I'd recognise him again. Once we find a place, we'll have to keep the location secret until this man is captured. The good news, I guess, is that the other intruders have been killed or arrested.'

'Well, that's comforting,' says Kirstie as coffees are delivered.

I sit back and laugh. 'Did you see what happened to two of the first group of gangsters? One noticeably young and weak and another old and weak. Serves them right for stealing.'

Kirstie sips her coffee. 'That's what I like about you. So compassionate.'

'Just remember, these men wanted to hold you hostage and possibly do you harm. I can't forgive that.'

Kirstie places her hand over mine just as our food arrives.

~⸱

STANOSKI ALLOWS THE hot water to run over him. This is bliss. He realises he's lucky to be alive. How he escaped being hit by bullets or captured by the cops is still a mystery. He tries to think back. Yes, he hit the ground quickly and got off some shots. His military training came in useful. Then when the fuse was deactivated and darkness hit, he slid across the floor and, in the general commotion when the police invaded, he somehow managed to evade everyone.

He steps out of the shower and towels himself with one of the exceptionally large, white hotel Sheridan sheets. He enjoys the sensation. Soon he'll have to plan his travel back to Germany. Did anyone manage to identify him? Probably Ethan Stone could offer a description. This means, it's not likely he can leave by air. Better to don a disguise and use the Eurostar to Paris, then take a hire car to Munich. Hiring a car in London will be too dangerous, he imagines. Ferry crossings could be monitored by the police, too. Yes, he will need to be careful, despite calculating the risk of each escape route. Interpol might be contacted too, but once he changes his facial appearance, he should be safe.

But first he has some business to take care of. At least he looks younger and, it appears, that he's stronger, perhaps a side effect of the pill. So, the burglary hasn't all been in vain. And he knows who tipped off the second gang. His team is gone, captured, or killed, and he can't do anything about that, but it's not important. Now, he'll have to rely on his own ingenuity.

Stanoski puts the gun in his jacket pocket. It's not cold today but he's going to wear his thick jacket anyway. This has more pockets and his belongings – keys, wallet, phone and pistol – are not obvious.

He reaches his destination an hour later. He'd been careful, keeping a lookout for the cops and also checking for anyone following him. At the end of the street, he looks around. Not many people about. Only an old lady wandering to the shops and a black kid skating down the road. Walking along, three blocks of apartments away from Gina's basement flat, he's surprised to see a man emerging from upstairs. A tall, suited man with grey hair.

Before the grey-headed man is aware of Stanoski's presence, Stanoski reaches him. 'Inside,' says Stanoski, pointing the gun at the man's head.

Startled, the man protests but Stanoski shoves the barrel into his midsection. 'Hey, I've got money,' says the middle-aged man.

'Shut up and go inside' says Stanoski.

The man uses a key and enters the flat. Gina rushes up the hall, and says, 'Have you forgotten something?' Then she sees Stanoski and retreats with the two men following her.

'Sit down, over there,' Stanoski commands.

Gina and the man do as they're told. Gina looks at her friend, but he stares straight ahead.

Stanoski threads a silencer onto his pistol. He sees that the man seems unintimidated and wonders whether this is Warren's silent partner, the man he was so afraid of. Does he know his henchmen have been killed or arrested? 'Who are you?' Stanoski asks.

'Who the hell are you, barging in here like this?' asks the old man.

'I've got the gun, shithead, so I'll ask the questions,' says Stanoski. 'How is Warren Buckley linked to you?'

'I don't know what you mean,' says the old man, brushing his hair back.

Stanoski waits. He knows the man is lying. Yet time is running out and he doesn't have the luxury of using the same facility, the abandoned house, to question this man. Having held the other captives in the house's basement to interrogate them had been ideal. Looking at the grey-haired man sitting beside Gina, the treacherous woman in black, Stanoski realises he needs to act decisively.

'Love, can you get us a cup of tea,' says the old man.

Gina stands and begins to move. 'Okay, Anton.'

'Hey,' says Stanoski, 'who told you, you could get up. Now, sit down.'

Gina moves back and slumps into her armchair. 'Thought you might like some tea,' she says.

'If I do, I'll let you know,' says Stanoski. He waves the gun about, the silencer secured. He's inclined to shoot the man in the knee to make Anton realise he's dealing with a serious man.

'I could certainly do with a drink. My throat is dry,' says Anton.

'Okay,' says Stanoski, 'you can have a drink but then I expect answers and no bullshit. Otherwise I will use this.'

Gina gets up and heads for the small kitchen, visible to the two men. Silence permeates the room while Gina gets three cups of tea onto a tray. She offers a cup to Stanoski first. He takes the saucer and deposits it on a table beside him, whilst still standing. Stanoski then sits down and places his gun on the table.

Gina then moves to her friend, offering him a cup from the tray. Anton reaches for a cup, but it slips and crashes to the floor, spilling the contents. He bends to pick up the dropped cup.

Stanoski sees Anton pull a gun from his trouser pocket, so he grabs his pistol off the table.

A shot fires and Stanoski sees the flash as the bullet grazes his shoulder. At the same moment, Stanoski depresses the trigger of his weapon, the bullet striking Anton in the neck. Blood gushes out. Gina screams and runs away, dropping the tray and the third cup of tea, shattering the porcelain. Stanoski fires at Gina and she falls to the ground.

FORTY:
Sunday

~

HAVING FINISHED OUR room service breakfast, I tell Kirstie we should go to an internet café to search for property. She tells me of a café nearby and agrees it's a good idea. But first she needs to shower. As she closes the bathroom door, my phone buzzes.

We'd been back to Kirstie's during the day yesterday to assess the damage. The extent of damage and breakages were so extensive that Kirstie advised she would deal with the situation on Monday when she'll have insurance assessors to visit. Having spent the rest of Saturday enjoying ourselves, we agreed to book into a local hotel for the night.

'Ethan, it's Liz, Gina got shot yesterday. I also understand there was a gunfight at your place. Are these incidents connected?'

I walk to the window and look outside. Birds fly past. 'How should I know? What happened to Gina?'

Liz proceeds to explain that Gina suffered a gunshot wound to her back and is currently in hospital. I get details and decide to visit. Gina may be able to tell me if the person who shot her is Pavle, also known as John, the man who is missing, the one who escaped from my place.

When Kirstie comes out of the bathroom, dressed and ready to go, I inform her I have to see Gina.

'Really, why?'

'She's in hospital. Why don't you go to the internet café and scout out some properties to rent or buy?'

'We're not going to buy straight away. Better to rent, then take time to search for places, don't you think?'

'Absolutely. But you could get some idea of prices in the areas which are suitable,' I say, keen to leave.

'So, what's wrong with Gina?'

'She was shot.'

'My God. Is it life-threatening?'

'No. Anyway, I better run. See You.'

When I arrive at Gina's bedside, telling staff I'm her brother, I sit beside her. Today she is not dressed in black. Her eyes are partially closed, and I can imagine she is in pain, not from the wound due to painkillers she would have had administered, but from having to wear a gown which is not black. The white dressing gown is lying on the chair near her bed. I sit in an unoccupied chair.

She opens her eyes fully. 'What are you doing here?'

'Come to see how you are,' I say.

'Sure,' she says, sarcasm heavy in her tone.

'Really, I'm sorry you were shot. You look okay though.'

'I was hit in the shoulder. It was operated on and I'll be right in a few months.'

'Did you see who did it?'

Gina looks at me strangely. 'Why. You're not with the police, are you?'

'Of course not. It may be connected to a break-in at my place,' I say, leaning forward. Now I can see the heavily bandaged shoulder on the opposite side of the bed I'm sat at.

Gina hesitates then describes the man and tells me he looked like

248

the man she knew as John, but she wasn't sure because her memory went blank. I determine he's the same man who escaped from Kirstie's flat. But she doesn't know where he's living. Warren told her his name was Stanoski, a Serbian national, living currently in Germany. Apparently, he's a disgruntled client, according to Warren. She tells me of the torture Warren and his business partner suffered.

John, who's actually Pavle is taking his disenchantment to another level. 'Have you told the police?'

'Not yet. They'll be interviewing me this afternoon, I was told.'

'Did Warren inform the police about this man?'

'No. He was threatened with death and Warren wants to forget about it.'

I find it hard to believe but, considering that Stanoski has associates in London, maybe Warren is being smart.

I get up. 'Hope you get better soon,' I say, smiling. I leave just as a nurse appears.

THE BEAUTY OF having contacts is immeasurable, Stanoski realises. He may have lost some men in the gun fight at Ethan Stone's place, but he had more resources available in England. Over decades of doing business, supplying weapons and drugs to many parts of Europe, he'd built up an extensive network. To escape the law, he'd arranged for a sea crossing to France at night via the English Channel.

Stanoski sits in the cabin, sipping whisky, while the vessel negotiates the waves. He reviews his English experience. He'd achieved some business success during his visit but he doesn't feel satisfied. Retrieving a substantial portion of the money he invested is useful, but he still smarts at being duped.

He takes a decent slug of whisky from the bottle. Was the woman in black, Gina something-or-other, the person who betrayed him? At least he shot her. Or was it Warren who betrayed him? He should have ended Warren and his business partner's lives. Being soft has backfired. He's learned his lesson. Never again.

The alcohol combined with the rocking boat lulls him to sleep.

He's shaken awake by the captain. 'Almost there,' he says.

Stanoski tries to focus. His head feels like it's been beaten with a hard object, like a baseball bat. He nods. 'Good. I'm keen to find a hotel. Later I will get transport home.'

The captain leaves Stanoski alone.

FORTY-ONE:
Thursday (April)

~

THE SUN IS shining and I'm in a good mood. Today is the first day of the first test between England and Australia at Lord's, the home of cricket. I'm in the queue at St John's Wood waiting for the gates to open. Kirstie is at work, but I'm accompanied by Heidi. She and I have both resigned from GlaxoSmithKline and have started our own company. The last pill that I've tested has shown no negative side effects and Heidi is considering taking it. But she's not sure she wants to look younger.

She has no image issues at present, she says, and will await further refinements on the invention. She had taken a pill some months ago, but the effects wore off when she had a minor car accident.

'How much longer?' Heidi poses the question whilst we queue in St John's Wood for the Lord's Test Match

'Be patient,' I say. 'You can't go to a cricket match if you're not patient.'

'I can leave early, can't I?'

'Naturally,' I say. 'You have watched cricket before, haven't you?' Although I'm pleased to be here, particularly as tickets were so hard to come by, I want the experience for my business partner to be uplifting. We will be having champagne when the match begins and an assortment of cheeses on fresh bread during the first session. I skipped breakfast except for coffee but Heidi mentioned she had fresh fruit on muesli at her regular time of 7:30 a.m.

'I've seen snippets on television, but I've never been to a live match and I wonder if I'll get bored.'

'How could you? I'll be with you,' I say, smiling. She knows how arrogant I can be. Having succeeded in developing a variety of pills, I've been able to get my former employer to invest in the production for mass distribution. They indicated that further testing will be carried out on animals and if successful, my start-up company will be taken over by them for a handsome sum. They were talking hundreds of millions of pounds as they see incredible medical potential. With this good news in the air, we're both taking a day off from work.

Heidi and I, dressed in smart casual clothes, finally get into the cricket ground and we find our seats. The next few hours pass without incident. We watch as Australia start batting. We hear champagne corks pop. At 11:05 a.m. we do the same and fill the two plastic glasses we'd brought. I see members in their colourful jackets strut about. The stands fill up to capacity, the game being sold out.

After the first session there is a mass exodus to the restaurants and bars dotted about the ground. Heidi and I find a place to sit and we have wine with a sandwich. Heidi, dressed in light blue jeans and a pink jumper, laughs at one of my jokes.

'Hello,' says a stranger who peers down at Heidi, 'Thought I'd heard that laugh before. How are you?'

'Oh, hi Josh, I'm fine,' says Heidi, 'this is Ethan.'

I shake Josh's hand. 'Hello,' I say as I note the tall thin man has ginger hair and I wonder whether he was teased at school.

'When did you get into cricket?' Josh asks.

'Just here with Ethan who's the cricket nut,' says Heidi, 'is Kathryn with you?'

'Yeah. She'd love to see you,' says Josh.

Heidi turns to me.

'Go,' I say, 'I'll be fine.'

Heidi follows Josh, leaving me to finish my white wine. With ten minutes until the second session begins, I walk around to stretch my legs and also to watch the people who have graced the occasion with their variety of fashion. I'm intrigued to see more women at the ground than I'd previously witnessed. But perhaps it's because I'm at an English ground and women take more of an interest in the game than women in Australia do.

Watching a leggy blonde who strides into the Lord's cricket museum, I don't see Warren immediately. Once the tall blonde woman disappears inside, I see him. He is chatting to Gina who, unsurprisingly, is dressed in black. What should I do? Say hello or ignore them?

Before I can decide, Gina sees me and frowns. She says something to Warren and then both come over to where I'm standing, avoiding the other patrons wandering around.

'I didn't know you liked cricket,' says Warren, 'but you're an Aussie so that shouldn't surprise me.'

I smile at the pair. Warren is dressed in smart casual gear - white cotton pants, a white collared shirt, a navy chino blazer and blue boat shoes – contrasting with Gina's more severe black look. I also wonder whether Warren has ditched Anne and is now Gina's lover, his bulky frame more suited to the not-so-slight Gina. 'England have a job ahead of them,' I say, 'the Aussies seem to be digging in.'

'Too early to tell,' says Warren.

'How are your experiments coming along?' asks Gina.

'I see you've recovered from the gunshot,' I say, avoiding the question. I have no intention of discussing my invention in a crowded venue.

Sun glints off Gina's dark sunglasses. 'My shoulder is still not fully functional but I'm okay generally. Do you know if they caught the shooter?'

'No idea,' I say, suddenly brought back to memories of the past.

Warren looks around then says, 'The shooter was Pavle Stanoski, a genuinely bad piece of work. He wanted your pills badly.'

'I know. He stole some bottles with mixed results. His men suffered set-backs before being killed.' I gaze into Warren eyes, assessing whether he brought the men to my door.

'Have you enhanced the formula? You look good, young and strong, or is that from the gym?'

Warren wants to know how close I am to marketing the product. The knowledge will help his business if he has inside information. But I'm not going to give him anything. 'I work out. The pills were only temporarily useful. Anyway, I need to find my friend. Enjoy the cricket.' I wander off.

~

Pavle Stanoski holds his daughter, Emma, up and smiles at her. But then he needs to put her down, his arms aching with the effort.

'Careful,' says Lena, rushing to grab the baby, 'you'll drop her.'

Stanoski lets his wife take the baby. He is really pissed off. He noticed a change come over him a few weeks ago. He was getting weaker and his appearance was changing, his features looking older. What had he done, to take that pill which he knew little about? All his men, except for his trusted lieutenant Goran, suffered ill effects from swallowing one of Stone's damn pills. 'Sorry honey, I don't know what's happening to me.' He hasn't told his wife about the anti-aging pills so she cannot suspect any medication to be the cause of his recent ailments.

'You need to see a doctor, Pavle, like I told you days ago. Something is very wrong with you,' says Lena, smelling the baby's bottom, and wrinkling her nose as though the smell is unpleasant takes Emma to the child's bedroom.

Stanoski sits on the sofa and rubs his face. Friends have also commented that he's not looking well. Only one has said he looks years older than his late forties. This made him self-conscious, a feeling he'd rarely experienced. Growing up, he had always been confident. He had been someone who took charge, become the leader, and acted when threatened. And he'd prevailed in most situations. Only his father made him feel inferior. But his father was a brute who used his fists to dominate his family and others.

Staring at the print of a famous painting by Salvador Dali – the Persistence of Memory completed in 1931 – Stanoski is inspired. He needs to resolve the problem of his accelerated ageing. He calls a man who owes him a big favour.

'Gunther, how are you?'

'Up and down, you know how it is.'

'Of course. I need you to help me with a problem,' says Stanoski.

'Tell me,' says Gunther, sounding pleased to be tempted away from his mundane factory job.

FORTY-TWO:
Saturday (Two Months Later)

GUNTHER RINGS THE bell and waits, Stanoski observes. Stanoski, realising it is only eight o'clock on a weekend, trusts that the options broker is not sleeping in. Hidden by shrubbery in the large garden, Stanoski watches to see who will open the door. He doesn't want Warren to see him yet. Stanoski had called the house minutes earlier to ensure Warren was home. Now he feels justified in his thorough gathering of information when he had his captives held at the abandoned house.

The day is cool and overcast, warranting the wearing of a jacket, particularly for him in his current state. Typical London weather, he thinks. Soon it will probably drizzle. He sees the front door of the large house open a fraction. Of course, in Golders Green, residents would be security conscious and careful not to open the door fully. Stanoski watches as Warren speaks and Gunther suddenly takes a pistol out of his jacket and points the gun at Warren who steps back. Stanoski joins the two men.

'Hello, Warren,' Stanoski says, 'it's been a while.'

Warren looks horrified, his facial expression a testament to undisguised fear. 'What do you want? I gave you all I could and now my mortgage is at the maximum the bank would permit.'

'Go inside. Is anybody else here?'

'Only Gina,' Warren says.

'Call her,' Stanoski commands.

Warren calls as the three men walk along the corridor to the living room.

'What…?' Gina stops short when she sees the gun and Stanoski.

They proceed into a large living room and Stanoski points to where he wants them to sit. Stanoski takes a comfortable armchair and sits opposite the pair who are on a three-seater sofa. Gunther, arms folded across his barrel chest, stands beside Stanoski's armchair. He hands the pistol, a Colt Commander, to his boss.

Stanoski places the gun on a side table, a polished mahogany piece, which he imagines has real value. 'Tell me, Warren, why am I looking so poorly?'

'I don't know,' says Warren.

Stanoski nods and Gunther approaches Warren and slaps him across the face. Stanoski informed Gunther earlier not to punch until he gave the order. He knew a punch from Gunther could kill a man or severely hurt him.

'John,' screams Gina, 'what are you doing? What have either of us done to you?'

'Keep quiet, woman, unless you want similar treatment.'

Gina opens her mouth but then shuts it again.

'It's your friend, the anti-ageing chemist,' Stanoski continues. 'I want information. Lie again, Warren, and I'll have my man break your arm.' Stanoski waves away a flying insect from his face.

'What have I got to do with that?' Warren whines.

'The pills,' Gina says.

'Correct, lady in black. What is your name again?'

'Gina.'

'I need to talk to the chemist, Stone, is it not?'

'Yes,' says Warren, 'but I don't know where he lives. He keeps changing address.'

'Where does he work?'

Warren stares at the man. 'I can tell you that but it's a huge place with complex security.'

'I won't be going inside, you dumbass.' Stanoski runs his hand through his hair. 'Just give me the fucking name and address of the place.' Stanoski suddenly places a hand on his chest, his breathing laboured. He is not feeling well, and his temper is barely kept in check.

Warren provides the information. 'But he may not be there on Saturday.'

'Maybe, maybe not. But I'll take that chance. If all else fails, Gunther may come across somebody who knows him,' Stanoski says.

Warren and Gina remain quiet. Gina straightens her black skirt.

Stanoski waits until his breathing is nearly normal then talks again. 'Gunther, you take Gina with you to identify the man if he's there this morning. Cuff her and get her to point the man out. I need him alive so he can be of use to me. I will stay with Warren as we need to talk. Understood?'

'Yawohl,' says Gunther, 'Come, woman.' He nods to Gina.

Gunther and Gina leave the house.

Stanoski had briefed Gunther earlier about what he needed, and his friend had always been reliable. Gunther will get the job done. He is calm and efficient and will take no nonsense from the woman, Stanoski knows.

Stanoski glares at Warren. 'Have you been working on how to get the money you still owe me?'

'Yes, I've been trying but the market is tough currently,' says Warren slumped in the sofa.

'It wasn't tough to con me. Surely you can do it to other clients to make up the half million US dollars you owe me,' says Stanoski who feels he might throw up. He is grateful for the gun. He doesn't think he has the strength to subdue anyone physically at the moment. He needs the chemist's medication to carry on.

'What can I do today?' Warren protests.

'You have a phone. That's all you needed, as I recall. So, get working. Grab your device and sit down again. I'm not in a mood to be fucked about.'

Warren stands and retrieves his phone from the kitchen island a few feet away. Stanoski watches him closely. Warren moves back to the sofa cautiously and sits down again, then begins to press buttons.

'What are you doing?' Stanoski asks.

'Finding names of clients,' Warren says.

'No funny business or I won't hesitate to shoot,' Stanoski says.

THE NEW APARTMENT we've moved into has been freshly painted and carpeted. It is a large two- bedroom place in St John's Wood. Waking, I stretch my legs and find nobody beside me. I slide out of fresh sheets and see Kirstie, semi-naked, looking inside the walk-in wardrobe. I glide behind her, put one arm across her back and the other under her knees. I lift and carry her back to bed.

'What are you doing?' she asks.

'You disappeared without a morning kiss,' I say.

'Feeling strong, are we?'

Without further comment I toss her on top of the bed then move beside her, showering her with kisses. We make hurried love then shower together.

Dressed, we wander casually to the tube station. The skies are steel grey but don't threaten rain. On the tube, which is not as packed as on weekdays, I allow myself to feel joy. Kirstie sits beside me, and we hold hands. I haven't felt this way since I'd been with Angela in Sydney in the now distant past. I can still see her auburn hair shimmering in the sunlight as we strolled through the Royal Botanic Gardens in Sydney.

And as we gazed across the harbour, I thought, as we held hands, that this was a love which wouldn't evaporate. But I was wrong.

Now, sitting next to Kirstie, anticipating a day filled with activity and closeness, I wonder whether this relationship will finish abruptly, as it had with Angela. But that is no way to contemplate the future which holds so much promise. The irony, when I think about it, is that, as I'm looking younger, to others it would seem I'm dating an older woman. How will Kirstie deal with this, going forward?

But enough introspection. We're going out for brunch then a movie.

~

STANOSKI REALISES THAT he doesn't need to point the gun at Warren; the man is too frightened. Their discussion about clearing the balance owed by Warren hadn't gone well. Warren had not been able to convince enough clients to invest enough money and he'd tried most of his regular clients. Warren found that he was still USD390,000 short.

'What about Thomas?' asks Stanoski.

'I can't call his clients because I don't have their numbers.'

'Then get him to come over,' Stanoski says, his bitterness evident. But he does not feel well. He is wondering whether he's going to vomit, so unsettled is his stomach.

Warren is standing but hesitates. Then Stanoski raises the gun.

'Alright. Calm down,' says Warren, 'I'll call him.' Warren tries his colleague, hoping he's not on the phone. He calls and eventually Thomas answers. Warren chats with Thomas about a variety of topics then asks him to visit. But it seems Thomas is reluctant, saying he has chores to do. But after a while, Warren persuades his colleague to change plans. When Warren is off the phone, he sighs then announces, 'He'll be over in a couple of hours. He's grocery shopping.'

But before two hours pass, Gunther arrives with Gina and another woman.

'Who is this?' Stanoski exclaims.

Gunther gets the women to sit next to Warren on the sofa which is getting crowded. Gunther turns to Stanoski and talks in German. He explains that he and Gina waited in the car which had a view of the entrance to GlaxoSmithKline and when it was obvious few people were at the company, he decided to ask a woman who had emerged whether Ethan Stone was inside. When she told him to 'nick off', he produced his ankle gun and forced her into the vehicle. He then had Gina drive with the captive in the passenger seat. Gunther stayed in the back to ensure the women behaved themselves.

Stanoski looks perplexed. But he doesn't want to show that he's worried. He asks Gunther to sit and keep an eye on the captives while he goes outside to think. With his gun in his jacket pocket, he watches the street. It is quiet. Cars are parked on the street but, presently, it is devoid of human traffic. The situation is beginning to get out of hand. He returns to the house and sees that the three captives are sitting calmly. Stanoski has a drink of water directly from a container in the fridge and is beginning to feel a little better. He can't afford to be ill now. Too much is at stake. He needs to get to the scientist. He also wants Thomas to help with the shortfall by calling his clients. These two crooked brokers should be able to con enough people to get the money. He wonders why nobody has had them sued for fraud. Obviously, his solution is more extreme, but it is the only one he's comfortable with. He could undertake legal proceedings, but he doesn't trust the process.

Back outside, feeling fidgety, Stanoski takes a cigarette from his Benson and Hedges packet. As he breathes in the smoke, an idea comes to him. He finishes the cigarette, a fairly rare occurrence now, and returns inside. He then talks to Gunther in German about the plan. Gunther nods and searches the house for appropriate material.

When the doorbell chimes, Stanoski goes to open it. He waits a moment, draws his pistol, and stands aside. Thomas calls out, 'Warren, I'm here.'

'Step inside,' Stanoski instructs as he comes into view, gun prominent.

"Wha…,' mutters Thomas.

'In. I haven't got all day,' says Stanoski.

Thomas walks in and Stanoski pushes him to go down to where the captives, now tied and gagged, are sitting. Gunther looks on, bemused.

'What's going on?' Thomas asks.

'Take him to another room,' says Stanoski. 'Tie him up while I watch this lot.'

FORTY-THREE:
Saturday (April)

As Kirstie and I walk out of the cinema, drizzle greets us. The weather has turned. But the rain is so slight that it almost feels refreshing. I look at Kirstie who doesn't react. No doubt she is so used to it; it must be like water off a swan's back.

'Did you enjoy it?'

'Well, let's say…'

My phone vibrates. Kirstie waits while I take the device out of my jacket and switch it on from silent. 'It's somebody from work,' I say.

'Take it,' says Kirstie.

'Hello, Ethan Stone,' I say.

'Ethan, hi, it's Sarah Brown from accounts. Sorry to bother you on the weekend but I need your help.'

'Okay, what's going on,' I say. I'm puzzled as I cannot conceive of Accounts wanting something, particularly on the weekend. If it were a problem relating to chemistry, I could understand. But I won't express surprise until I've heard Sarah out. As I recall, she is a middle-aged woman with fair hair, a few wrinkles and sporting a kind face.

'Listen up, Mr Stone,' says another voice. 'I want you to come to

Warren Buckley's house. Bring with you something to help reverse the effects of your bloody pill.'

'Who is this?'

'Never mind. I have four hostages and they will be harmed if you call the police or disobey my instruction.'

Suddenly, it dawns on me that this is the man who escaped when two sets of gangs confronted each other at my place. Pavle, as I recall. It seems that my invention is more a curse than a benefit. 'I don't think I can help,' I say. The last thing I want is to get involved with this criminal.

'Don't lie to me. You have a variety of pills. I know that from experience with my men.'

'I don't have them on me and I'm out now and I'm not back for hours.'

'I don't care about where you are. Just bring them here. I will kill one hostage every two hours.' The phone went dead.

'What was that all about?' asks Kirstie.

I tell her and explain what I've been told to do.

'I don't believe it. What are you going to do?'

'I don't think I have a choice,' I say.

'He could be bluffing,' Kirstie says.

'He's gone to extraordinary lengths and, from the sound of it, he's desperate. He would have taken one of the original pills, an unsafe one.' I take Kirstie's hand and look her in the eyes. 'I've got to do this, you understand?'

Kirstie nods and gives me a hug. 'Just be careful.'

STANOSKI COMES INTO a study and sees that Gunther has secured Denny Thomas to an office chair. His hands have been pinned back and tied. Legs are tied to the base of two of the chair's steel spokes supporting wheels. Stanoski nods and lets Gunther return to the living room to guard the other captives – Warren, Gina and Sarah.

'Now, Mr Thomas, have you managed to obtain cash to reimburse my shortfall?' Stanoski stands in front of the thin broker.

Thomas looks up timidly. 'I've tried but so far I haven't been able to get anywhere.'

Stanoski wants to slap him but he starts to feel ill again. He realises if he strikes the man and it's a weakened hit, Thomas may feel emboldened and continue to hold out. He knows from his previous sessions with Thomas that the man lives by himself, having been divorced from his second wife, and that he has few assets which could be converted to cash. He doesn't even own the flat he's in. 'I see. That's bad luck. I'm going to arrange for you to call your clients form a speakerphone. If you don't succeed in raising the cash I'm after, I'll hurt you. Understood?'

Thomas nods.

'And I won't kill you. I'll cut you up so that you'll feel real pain. So, don't think you'll get out of this with a quick death.' Stanoski goes outside and returns with four sharp kitchen knives of different sizes. He sets Thomas up for the job by taking his mobile phone and having Thomas tell him who his clients are.

FORTY-FOUR:
Saturday (April)

I ARRIVE AT WARREN'S Golders Green house at two o'clock in the afternoon. I look up at the sky and see it has grown darker, not the comfortable, dull colour it was in the morning. Before ringing the bell, I gather my thoughts. I didn't bring a gun as I expect to be searched. I wonder how many men are inside, guarding the hostages. Finally, after realising I'm here to save people, I press the bell.

A moment later the door opens, and I'm confronted by a large man with yellow-blond hair. He has muscles like a superhero. He reminds me of the actor playing Thor, Chris Hemsworth with blonde hair. He also has a pistol pointed at me. 'Kommen,' he says.

My elementary knowledge of German tells me he wants me to step inside, as in 'Come'. I comply. He presses me against the wall and searches me. He shoves me forward, along the hallway. When I enter Warren's large living room, I see Warren, Gina and the woman who called me: Sarah.

'Sit,' says the rude German.

I sit opposite the group on the sofa. I wait. I expect to be tied up, too. Then, emerging from another room, comes the man I suspected is behind this- John or Pavle. He doesn't look well and now I understand his desperation. He must have taken the pill I first trialled which worked well until it wore off. He looks older than his actual years and he must be getting weak. I recognise him as the leader of the gang who invaded Kirstie's apartment. He's the man who got away.

'Gunther, have you searched him?'

'Yeah. Clean,' says Gunther, who has placed the pistol in the back of his waistband.

Pavle, the leader, confronts me, looking down, as though he believes I'll be intimidated by him in this position. 'So, Mr Stone, I hoped you brought something to make me feel better.'

'I did,' I say.

'Hand it to me,' he says. 'How do I know you won't trick me with a chemical which will react against me?'

I look at him, seeing fear in his eyes. He doesn't like to lose control. And he doesn't understand chemistry. Not that many people do. And with the kind of formulas I've developed, there's probably only a handful of scientists in the world who would be able to appreciate the complexity of what I've created. 'You'll have to trust me,' I say.

'I repeat, hand the pill to me.' His hand is outstretched.

'Not so fast. The deal was that you would release the hostages.'

'Stanoski,' says Gunther, 'want me to beat it out of him?'

'No, no. Didn't you come across a pill box during your search?'

'No.'

Stanoski looks back at me. 'Gunther, bring him into the next room.'

Gunther pulls me up off the sofa then pushes me forward and together we follow Stanoski into another room, down the hall. Inside I see a man tied to a chair. He has a bloodied nose and bruises on his face. I also see he's been gagged. But what is disturbing is the finger lying on the floor and the make-shift bandage on his hand where his finger had been located before the cut.

'You see what can happen if you play games,' Stanoski says. Then he turns to Gunther, 'You can check on the others. I have my gun,' he says, pulling it out of his jacket pocket.

Gunther leaves and I'm facing Stanoski. I'm not keen on the gun as I know it could do me damage. Otherwise, I know I'm strong enough to overpower both men. I can see that Stanoski has aged since I last saw him. He's probably feeling miserable, too.

'Okay, smart man, where is the pill?'

'I brought it but it's not on me.'

'So where is it?'

'I buried it in the garden outside. And I will show you where once you release the hostages.'

Stanoski grins. 'You are here to do as you're told, not to negotiate. Do you understand?'

'I do. However, you should understand that if you kill me, you'll also die. I can see the pill working adversely on you. You will die a slow and painful death.' I watch while the message sinks in. I can sense he doesn't know what to do. He doesn't know whether to believe me or not.

'You're bluffing,' he says raising the gun level with my head.

'Think what you like. But you should know, the pill you took, as well as others I've created have been tested, as any new pharmaceutical product must be. I know what I'm talking about,' I say, sounding as convincing as I can. I'm beginning to get nervous. This is an unstable customer. He might shoot for the hell of it. And I don't know what would happen if he doesn't get the antidote. He's right, I'm bluffing, but I have no alternative. If he gets the pill, he has no reason to keep anyone alive.

~

STANOSKI IS IN a quandary. He doesn't know whether Stone is telling the truth, but he needs that pill. He's feeling worse again. The feeling of keeling over comes and goes. But he can't release the hostages. There's no knowing what they might do. Of course, they'll contact the police and he needs a head start to get away. He needs to think but his mind is unable to see reason. He wants to sit down. 'Go outside,' he says to Stone.

He follows Stone to the living roomand he has Gunther secure him to a chair. Gunther also uses a tough cloth to gag him. When Stanoski sees Stone has been properly secured and gagged, he walks with Gunther down the hall, then tells his assistant to go outside and inspect the garden for any recent digging. The garden is immense so it could take some time. Stanoski goes back to where the hostages, except for Thomas, are. He sits down, pleased he can rest. He puts the gun in his jacket pocket. He feels better. He needs some coffee but can't be bothered to get up and make it. Perhaps he can untie one of the women and get them to make coffee, but his eyes are closing. He feels extremely tired.

He shakes his head. He must not fall asleep.

~૭

I CAN SEE Stanoski fighting to keep his eyes open. The mental stress and physical activity are taking a toll on him. I glance at the other captives. They are not looking at him, or me, for that matter. They appear to be resigned to their situation, boredom their companion.

The rope holding my arms in place is bound tightly. Testing its strength again, I feel confident I could break the bonds easily and quickly. Would the snapping of them be quick enough so that I could charge Stanoski before he could take his gun from the table beside him? The success of this strategy is an unknown. But I'm conscious I can't wait too long. His mate, Gunther, might return any moment to report back on his search of the gardens. And Gunther also has a pistol.

I'm sitting at right angles to my fellow living-room captives: Sarah, Gina and Warren. I need them to not alert Stanoski. They can't make any sounds when I finally decide to act. I check them out again. Sarah is staring ahead, deep in thought, it would appear. Gina who is dressed entirely in her standard black outfit has her eyes closed. The sight of her dark form makes a stark contrast to the white leather sofa. Warren seems to be unfocused, eyelids downcast.

Apart from the occasional car driving past the house, silence reigns. I have to take a risk, otherwise we're all doomed. Stanoski is desperate but he won't leave anyone alive once he has the antidote.

I calculate the distance between Stanoski and my chair. Checking that he hasn't moved, I prepare myself. Just as I'm about to break free, Sarah begins to sob. Damn. Luckily, the gag muffles most of the sound. I look over at her and get her attention by moving my neck back and forth. She looks at me. I whisper, 'Quiet'. For a ghastly moment, I fear she's going to sob even louder but, thankfully, she stops.

Without further contemplation, I clench my fists, swell my chest and rise, snapping the rope like it was no more than a rubber band. Stanoski looks up and reaches for his pistol but he's distracted by the sound of a loudspeaker coming from outside. I jump at him pushing him off the chair. The gun flies off, across the carpet. When we're both on the ground I pin his arms.

'Pavle Stanoski, come out with your hands in the air. The house is surrounded, and your accomplice is in custody,' screams a voice outside through a loudspeaker.

I stand, pulling Stanoski up. My enhanced strength and his weakness combine to make it seem like I'm dealing with a ten-year-old child. I march him to the front door easily, despite him dragging his feet. I open it and push him outside. Cops swarm and two men grab him.

Activity is suddenly heightened. Men with guns stream into the house, telling me to raise my hands. I comply. The captives are untied, and they confirm I disarmed Stanoski and that only two armed men had taken the victims inside. They are also told about Denny Thomas who is rescued and helped to a waiting ambulance.

When I'm escorted outside, Kirstie runs up to me and gives me a hug. 'Thank God,' she says, 'I wasn't sure whether what I did, by telling my ex-colleagues about your meeting, would endanger you. I simply hoped you'd talk your way out of it.'

'Really?' I gave her a crushing bear-hug, then said, 'You know I hate guns. But I'm flattered you think I'm so persuasive.'

FORTY-FIVE:
Tuesday (April)

~

THE RAIN IS persistent. It hasn't stopped all day. Even now, at 9:20 p.m., the rain flows down the aircraft window. I fasten my seatbelt. Kirstie seems quite excited about our trip to Sydney. She knows the journey is long-haul but doesn't appear to mind. She's flicking through a magazine at present and I see that she's touched up her fingernails with a different shade of red than the one she normally uses. Not that I'm great at differentiating the various names for subtle changes in colour. To me she has red nails, not burgundy or magenta or names I can't get my head around.

The British Airways flight is due to depart at 21:35 and I'm not aware of any delay which means we'll have a meal just after take-off and then we'll be able to turn in for a long sleep. As we're in Business Class, we'll be able to stretch out in our seats which are comfortable. Our seats are wide and as long as a normal bed. Although Kirstie has flown around Europe before, she'd never experienced Business Class.

She turns to me. 'Are you looking forward to going home?'

'Yes, I am. I've emailed some friends in the last few days.'

'Will they be shocked by your youthful appearance?'

'Who knows? It depends if they even remember me.'

Kirstie smiles. 'Right. After a few years, they'll have no memory of you?'

'We'll see. Of course, after you called the police to surround Warren's house, I may have been killed and then I wouldn't be here now.'

'It seemed like you had matters in hand. You had subdued Stanoski and you then got hold of a gun to take care of the man outside, Gunther somebody.'

'That's true, but I always assume the worst.'

Flight attendants interrupt our conversation by asking all passengers to pay attention. They perform their safety demonstration, which I've seen many times. I watch the brunette doing her best to entertain, although I have little faith a yellow floatie would help if the plane dives into the ocean and smashes into multiple pieces.

After take-off, Kirstie tells me about the outcome of the raid to rescue the hostages. 'Apparently, Warren had a recording of the activities in the house. He and his associates have been arrested for carrying out a scheme to con people. He was the English head of the firm and apparently the American partner, Anton Jefferson, was shot dead by Pavle Stanoski.'

'So Stanoski was justified in carrying out punishment?'

Kirstie looks at me with a smirk on her face. 'Only if you believe in a vigilante kind of justice.'

I don't respond, simply take her hand and squeeze it. Of course, I do believe in revenge and I'm pleased Warren has been taken into custody. After a moment, I ask, 'What about Gina?'

'I don't know. She was taken to hospital for a check-up to see whether she's been unduly traumatised. As was Sarah, your colleague, right?'

'Yes. That was three days ago. They've probably been discharged. Gina may still be suffering, though.'

'Why are you more interested in Gina than Sarah?'

'I was curious to see whether she was also involved with Warren's crooked dealings,' I say as I see food trays being readied for passengers.

'Do you think she was involved?'

'I really don't know. But what I do know is that she and Warren were close, as was the old man, Derek.'

Kirstie lowers her tray. She is going to eat. I'm not. I'm going to order a beer. That will help me sleep.

Kirstie says, 'She may have been Warren's lover and nothing more.'

'No, they were just friends. Warren and Anne were a couple.'

'But Warren may have cheated on his girlfriend,' Kirstie persists.

'You're probably right. Besides, it's nothing to do with me.'

Kirstie chooses a chicken meal while I order a VB. Kirstie looks excited as she arranges the contents of her meal in an orderly fashion. As she pulls cutlery out from the paper cover, she says, 'Sounds to me that you'd like her to be part of the scheme and punished.'

I pour the contents of my beer into a glass. 'Of course not. I was just visualising Gina in orange clothing instead of her usual black. I think that would be punishment enough.' I laugh. Having said that to Kirstie, I examine my motive. Gina knew the architects of the fraud and I can't quite believe she is totally innocent. But I could be wrong. I've been wrong before.

But as the plane hums along, at an altitude of 35,000 feet, I visualise my favourite lady in black. Gina is actually quite attractive as a woman but the black obscures that fact. I wonder if it's deliberate.

∼୨

Thursday

I look past Kirstie out of the porthole and see the familiar view of Sydney under us. I'm not sure how I feel. I'm excited to be back to visit familiar spots. But I'm wary of meeting friends and, of course, my younger brother. They will see that I've changed, in appearance, and may press to understand what's happened. And if I reveal my invention, they'll probably push to get a pill themselves, prematurely.

Tests of my invention in the UK are being supervised by Heidi. I'd convinced my employer to carry out further tests with a view to gaining an upgraded contract with them. It was the only practical solution. Heidi and I discussed manufacturing the formula ourselves, but we found there were all sorts of obstacles. We weren't in a position to produce commercial quantities, nor would we receive sufficient funding by submitting our business plan to a bank. I had seen a few banks and was soon shown the door. The excuse was that the enterprise was improbable and hence too risky for them to commit funds.

GlaxoSmithKline were enthusiastic about the project. They felt with the right marketing, it could be a huge seller. But of course, the drug requires MHRA (Medicines and Healthcare products Regulatory Agency) approval. I'm aware it usually takes around ten years for a new medicine to complete the journey from discovery to market, but I've already done much to hasten the process. But I'm in no hurry. I'm young but then, thinking it through, I reconsider. Will I live longer, or will I simply look younger for longer and die at the usual age I would under normal conditions? I'll never know for certain. At least not before it happens. But looking younger is still an attractive proposition for most humans.

Kirstie is also getting a little enthused about it. She'd said during one of our discussions about it that, if it proves safe, she may be tempted to try a pill. After all she has nothing to lose.

The plane hits the tarmac with a slight thud and taxis towards the terminal, interrupting my speculation about our future. Kirstie says to nobody in particular, 'What lovely weather. And my phone shows the temperature is twenty-two degrees outside.' She's looking out of her window, oblivious to my presence.

The blue sky with a few white clouds scudding across reminds me of past Octobers in Sydney. I like to see Kirstie so happy. It occurs to me, when I witness her smiling face, influenced by the beautiful autumn sky so unlike the grey one we left behind, that she may not want to return to London. That would be problematic for my plans, but I'll tackle that issue when it emerges.

'Are you alright, sir?' says a passing flight attendant. She looks at me with horror.

'I'm fine, thanks,' I say, concerned. What has she seen?

The mature, wide-hipped flight attendant moves on. As a result of my interaction with the woman, Kirstie turns to me.

'Oh my God,' she says, 'you look like you've aged a decade. Your face has lines and your hair is greying.'

All the way through Customs and baggage collection, I worry. What has happened? I don't feel different but when I enter the men's facilities and view myself in the mirror, I can see why the flight attendant and Kirstie have reacted with shock. And I can't figure out why I've aged. I go back to the baggage carousel, next to Kirstie who peers at me grimly.

'Did you see what I'm talking about?' she asks.

'Yes,' I say watching the bags move along.

'What do you think happened? It's so sudden,' says Kirstie, more intent on looking at me than watching our bags.

'I don't know,' I say, genuinely bewildered. Has the pill worn off or did something spark this sudden reversal? I need to talk to Heidi to communicate this transformation. It occurs to me that a permanent change to a younger appearance may not be possible.

I sight our luggage and move closer to the carousel. Kirstie joins me and as soon as our navy-blue bags pass, we haul them off. I find my extra strength has disappeared as well. The whole episode is baffling and a dark mood envelopes me. I feel fearful of the outcome and the future. What if my invention cannot stabilise? Will I grow old and weak and perish sooner than my time, if left to natural elements?

Our taxi ride to the Four Seasons hotel in George Street, apart from advising the driver of our destination, is done in silence. Kirstie watches the passing traffic and buildings. I sit back, eyes closed, deep in thought, although I'd rather not think at all. Is this the time when people consider suicide? When everything is shattered? Dreams, plans: all gone up in smoke.

I own a property, a two-bedroom unit, in Chatswood which is rented out. But I don't care. I was going to make enquiries of the agent to understand how things were progressing but now I don't have the motivation.

After checking into the hotel in the CBD, I slip between the sheets on the king-size bed. Kirstie thinks I'm tired because she asks whether I want to join her for a walk, and I decline. I wave her off because I'm depressed, not tired.

~

I WAKE FROM a deep sleep, disoriented. I'm fully clothed except for my shoes which I must have kicked off. Where am I? After a moment, I realise I'm in a hotel room. Then it all comes back. I feel better, the cloud I was under has dissipated. I check the time. I'd been in Noddy land for four hours. Kirstie is not back yet. Some walk. Rather than speculate where she might be, I call her mobile with my Australian mobile, having left my UK one in London. The call doesn't work. Kirstie may not have bought a local SIM card yet. I'll have to wait for her to arrive.

An hour later and there's still no sign of Kirstie. I'd taken this time to unpack, enjoy a hot shower, brush my teeth and stretch. Now I'm beginning to get worried. There's no way she'd be away for five hours. Surely, she must have gotten lost. But we're in the Central Business District, close to the tourist spots in The Rocks and the Quay. And surely, she'd have the sense to obtain a SIM card compatible to Australian conditions.

I'd call the police, but they would laugh at me. Kirstie, an ex-cop, lost in Sydney. Lost in broad daylight or attacked and killed in broad daylight. It's so ridiculous, it's laughable. So, rather than waste more time wondering what's happened, I exit the hotel, pausing in the lobby to take in the sight of this luxurious hotel, the Four Seasons. I'm sure there's a logical explanation for Kirstie to be out. Perhaps she got carried away and ended up walking many kilometres. Perhaps she met someone from England, and they went out for lunch. Who knows?

The weather is superb, at least compared to what it was in London. The sun is blazing, and I feel warm, content in a T-shirt and jeans. As I cross over the street to witness the view of the harbour and the Opera House, nostalgia assails me. Crowds of tourists and everyday office workers and other locals wander about. I'm hungry and I'd like to share the first Australian meal with Kirstie, but I have no choice. I enter a nearby pub, The Ship Inn and order a beer and a steak sandwich. I've been here before with my Sydney work colleagues.

Waiting for my meal, I call my brother. The phone is engaged. I leave a message. After a satisfactory pub luncheon, I walk along Pitt Street to see what's changed. As I turn into Australia Square, my phone vibrates. Hoping it's Kirstie, I dig it out of my jeans.

'Hello,' I say.

'Ethan, it's Ryan, what's up?'

'Hi, little bro, are you at work?' The familiar voice of my brother calms me.

'I am. Missed your call before. In a meeting. Where are you calling from?'

'I'm here in Sydney. Wondering if we could catch up?'

'Great. Want to come over? Kim would love to see you too.'

We arrange a time and I continue walking. Conscious that time is getting on, I return to The Four Seasons, the 5-star luxury hotel which I've booked for two nights until we get our bearings and decide where to get cheaper accommodation. When I open the door to our room, I expect Kirstie to greet me. But I find the room empty. Now I'm seriously worried. I call the police.

Finally, I reach someone after a myriad of transfers. They seem confused, telling me my girlfriend will get back soon. I give up, lying on the bedcovers, irritated and frustrated.

An hour later, I hear a knock on the door. I'd fallen asleep again, so I wasn't roused until I hear the persistent banging.

I open the door, rubbing sleep from my eyes. Standing before me are two uniformed policemen.

FORTY-SIX:
(June)

~

'HERE, HAVE ONE of these,' says Ryan, handing me a glass with something which looks suspiciously like Scotch whisky. It's Friday around seven o'clock, minutes after arriving at Ryan's house in Forestville.

I take the glass and taste the liquid. The burning sensation is welcome.

I'm sitting on Ryan and Kim's sofa. Kim is in the kitchen finalising dinner while Ryan is attending to my grief the best way he can. Last night and most of today have been a blur. When the visitors to my hotel room asked me if I was Ethan Stone, I nodded. That's when they told me Kirstie was involved in a road accident. She'd died at the scene. While crossing the street, she'd been run over by the proverbial bus.

Ryan sits down on a comfortable armchair facing me. 'There's nothing you can do, bro, so just take it easy for a few days or weeks or for as long as you need.'

I take another sip of whisky. 'I know. But I feel miserable,' I say, actually feeling like I'd like to die myself. I've lost everything. Kirstie. I was going to propose to her during our visit here. I've also lost my youthful appearance and with it the opportunity to have a successful life. My formula will join all the failed pharmaceutical trials throughout history. And I've lost my flatmates in London, murdered by somebody in pursuit of my so-called miracle drug.

'Boys, dinner's ready,' calls Kim.

Ryan and I take our drinks into the dining room which is located between the lounge in which Ryan and I were relaxing and the kitchen. The dining room table is large enough to seat eight people with solid cushioned chairs placed around it. The room has a large top-to-bottom window at one end and three walls, adorned with a variety of landscape and cityscape prints.

Kim bounces in carrying trays of food. She's made a lamb roast accompanied by roast potatoes, broccoli, cauliflower, sweet potatoes and peas. She says, 'Sit down, guys, and serve yourselves. I'll get the garlic bread, then we're done.' She bounces out of the room again.

Ryan, who is stout and an inch shorter than I am, sits at the end of the table. A bottle of red wine is close to him. He pours wine into the three wine glasses. Kim returns with the garlic bread wrapped in foil and smiles at me. She is a slight, bubbly, energetic woman who seems to have great organisational skills.

Ryan and Kim have two sons, Andrew and Michael, both of whom remember little of me. They have soft drinks in front of them.

The food is superb, and I wonder why Kim, who is a talented cook, is so slim. But I imagine my brother does most of the eating while she does most of the cooking.

Ryan raises his glass and the three of us clink the wine glasses together. 'Here's to a rare guest,' he says.

'Ryan tells me you're only here for a holiday. Is that right?' Kim asks.

'Yes, a few weeks, that's all.'

'Don't you get tired of the weather there?' Kim continues.

Ryan pours mint sauce over his meat. 'Yeah, Ethan, aren't you sick of the rain and cold yet?'

I finish chewing the lamb in my mouth, then say, 'I'm employed by a large company which has been good enough to consider buying into one of my personal projects.'

'What kind of project?' Kim asks.

I don't know whether I should be candid but, given all that's happened, I'm beyond caring. 'I'm trialling an anti-ageing drug.'

Ryan laughs. 'Really. Why?'

'Thought it was a good idea,' I say.

'I guess it would be popular,' says Kim, 'If it worked, you'd get rich.'

'If you want to get rich, join the bank, like me,' Ryan says, munching on a slice of lamb.

'That wasn't the purpose,' I say, recalling all the drama I'd been through. With Kirstie gone, it just doesn't seem important anymore.

'How long before humans can try it?' Kim asks.

'I'm not sure. Tests on mice are being run currently,' I say. I daren't tell them I've tried some different pills, all of which have failed.

'How can you tell if the test pills will make the mice look any different?' Ryan asks, refilling his wine glass.

'Good question,' I say. Indeed, I don't think the test committee has thought their tests through. But maybe they have a plan. To change the topic, I ask, 'And what's new with you guys?'

'I'm pregnant,' Kim gushes.

'Congratulations,' I say. 'Ryan, why didn't you tell me?'

'Early days,' Ryan says. 'I'm not telling friends until Kim has progressed to three months safely.'

After the meal, we retire to the lounge and chat about changes to things in Australia since I went abroad. The two boys head off, probably to their rooms to play computer games, something Ryan has complained about.

When I get back to my hotel room, I check the time to see what time it is in London. Using the What's-App-app on my phone, I call Heidi. 'Hope you're out of bed.' I say when she responds.

'Yes, I am. Good to hear from you. How's everything?'

I don't tell her about Kirstie. It's still too painful to broach. Instead I say, 'Fine, just caught up with my brother who has a new house, a large three-bedroom one, and a pregnant wife.'

'Your little brother?'

'Correct, my phenomenally successful banker brother. But I'm calling to talk to you about the pill. This current one has worn off, too. So, I'm wondering whether what we're trying to achieve is simply too ambitious.'

A brief silence follows as Heidi seems to be whispering to somebody. 'Sorry to hear that. My pill is still working. I had a guy stay overnight. A young bloke so I guess I can still fool people.' She laughs. 'But he doesn't know about the pill and I probably won't see him again, so I won't bother clueing him in.'

'Good to hear you've benefitted by the invention. Maybe it's only ever going to be useful for brief periods.'

'Possibly. Do you think the changes you've encountered are due to cabin air pressures?'

'That's a thought. The tests should cover that. Perhaps you can arrange for appropriate simulation tests in addition to the other tests.'

'I will. I have to go. Chris is getting restless and I need to go to work.'

'Take care, Heidi,' I say then switch my phone off.

WHEN I RETURN to London, I don't feel much better. I'm still in a state of grief over Kirstie. But after two days at home, sleeping mostly, I snap out of my depression. I figure I need to focus on the future, not drown in the swamp that is the past.

I'm going to continue my work. It's Monday morning and I wake early, showering and dressing in fresh clothes. I feel better already.

Some of my colleagues are pleased to see me but comment on my haggard appearance, looking spent, some say. I think they mean I look older. They still don't know of my experimentation with my anti-ageing product. Self-testing drugs is frowned upon, so I haven't informed anyone of my work, except Heidi, of course. I find her in her cubicle and sit in the visitor's chair.

'You're looking great,' I say, 'I guess the pill still works for you.'

'Yes, I feel good, more energy and everything,' she says looking away from her computer screen. Then when she sees me properly, 'My God, you look terrible.'

'Thanks,' I say, 'Nice to know.'

'You know what I mean. It's just that I got used to seeing you so much younger looking.' She places her hand over mine. 'Don't take it personally.'

'I won't. How is the testing going?'

Heidi tells me of the various aspects of the testing programme, who's been involved and how the project has been quarantined so that it remains a secret. News of the pill leaking could be catastrophic for the company, the top brass believes. Then she informs me of the effect of cabin pressure on the brain and the negative impact on our chemical mixture.

'So, do you think the formula could be changed to fix it, I mean, make it viable for most conditions?' I ask.

'I feel positive about that idea but then I'm a positive soul, not a grumpy pessimist like you.'

'Thanks for that. What I needed --a reality check,' I say, scratching my chin.

'I'm joking. Come on, Ethan, it'll be fine. We've overcome obstacles before, haven't we?'

'Of course, we have,' I say, 'I won't take another pill until it's been thoroughly tested.'

Heidi peers at me thoughtfully. 'I understand. You have been through a lot. It might pay to take a break from the various changes your body has suffered.'

I smile. 'I better go do some work. Catch you later,' I say, getting up.

'Oh, there's one thing I need to tell you.'

I wait. 'Yes?'

'A woman called Gina has left messages for you.'

'Thanks.' I walk to my cubicle. I wonder what she could want. I dismiss it once I see all the emails awaiting me.

At lunch time, I walk outside to stretch my legs. The sun is making a half-hearted attempt to shine but soon it will be defeated by the dark, grey clouds moving across the sky. I miss Sydney but when I think of what happened, I dismiss the visit as an unhappy experience. On my way back, I remember Gina, my favourite woman in total black attire. At my desk, I call Gina.

'Hi Gina, it's Ethan, I understand you called,' I say when I eventually get her to pick up.

'Lovely to hear from you. I don't mean to bug you, but I'd like to see you.'

'Why? What's this all about?'

'Not over the phone. Could you come over?'

We agree on a time.

It's no surprise when Gina opens the door to her basement flat to see her in black boots, a black skirt and a tight black top, revealing an unexpected deep cleavage. She actually smiles as she invites me in. She gestures for me to sit in her living room and hands me a glass of beer. She has a glass of beer, too. She turns to me on the sofa on which we're both sat.

'Cheers,' she says.

'Cheers,' I say, wondering what this is all about.

'You're looking more mature than when I last saw you. But you look handsome.'

'Thanks,' I say, not sure whether to take her comments as flattery or a sinister way of saying I look old.

'You're wondering why I've asked you over, aren't you?'

I nod and pour a mouthful of beer down my throat.

'First, I want to apologise for pestering you to give me your pill. I had little choice.'

'Ok, I'm listening.'

Gina moves her right leg further back on the sofa so she can look directly into my eyes. 'Warren was paying me to look after Derek. Derek's health was deteriorating quickly, and Warren wanted to keep him alive as long as possible. So, when he found out about your invention, he needed to have it. For Derek.'

'I get that but why did he need Derek alive? Was he related?'

'No, Derek supplied him with contacts. He had access through his former role in government to lists of people who had money. And Warren needed this to satisfy his boss, Anton.'

'How did Warren and Derek's paths cross?'

'They were both members of a chess club. More than two decades ago when Derek could still move around.'

I sat back. It was all making sense. The scam could work on people who were greedy and generally people with money were those people, the people who wanted more and more money. Derek supplied names. Warren and his company cold called them and using a little market savvy and sales techniques, they probably hooked an acceptable percentage. It was a numbers game. So, when Warren tried it on me, it hadn't worked because I simply declined straight off the bat. 'And what was your role?'

'Apart from looking after Derek, my only form of income, nothing.'

'So how do you know everything about it?'

'The mad Serb got it out of Warren when we were being held hostage and Sarah and I overheard the conversation, or rather, confession.'

I finished my beer in silence. It was all over now. I could continue with my work, without having to look over my shoulder.

'How's Kirstie?'

I was taken aback by her concern. I say, 'She died in Australia, in a road accident.'

'Oh,' she says. Then she places her hand on my thigh. 'Poor you. I'm so sorry.'

'Yeah…' I feel a tear sliding down my cheek.

Gina moves closer and gives me a hug. Her body is curvy and soft, and I sink into it. Before I know it, we kiss. I break away.

'Sorry,' I say.

'That's all right.'

'I'd better go,' I say standing, 'Thanks for clearing things up for me.'

'That's okay. It's the least I could do, given the grief I've caused you.'

I'm not sure what I can say so I leave without another word.

FORTY-SEVEN:
(July)

~

SUNLIGHT STREAMS INTO the bedroom as I move the curtains aside with my remote control. It must be later than I thought. No alarm clock or other annoying phone signal to get me up. I'm on holiday, in Tahiti, at the Hotel Tahiti Nui, with my latest woman, taking a break from the Australian branch of a company set up between my English partner and myself to sell safe, appearance improving drugs. The business is booming and I'm comfortably off. But it's not the drug I'd originally designed. It doesn't reduce ageing by more than a decade, merely around ten to twelve years, depending on the individual's chemistry. It doesn't enhance strength either and side-effects are non-existent. But it's immensely popular with almost all demographics, except, of course, the young. The chief benefit of the drug is that surgery to smooth out facial and other worrying bits of flesh is not required as much as previously.

I check the digital clock on the dresser. 9:12 a.m. We had a late night so it's pleasant not to have to get up. I stretch my arms and squint. The sun is harsh, its power overwhelming, and I settle down and place my arms around the still-sleeping body beside me.

Gina stirs as I squeeze her right breast. She moves a little, then turns towards me and we cuddle. As she settles back to sleep, I reflect on aspects of my life which have led me here. When we return to Australia, to a penthouse apartment in one of Sydney's most prestigious Eastern suburbs: Watsons Bay, a place overlooking the water.

I recall that night when I met Gina again. It was a few weeks after visiting her flat in Camberwell. Outside the pub where I'd met Warren that first time, I was about to enter. It was eleven o'clock on a cool night. Gina, laughing at a comment, exited the noisy venue with a girlfriend and almost ran into me.

'Sorry,' she said, 'Oh, Ethan, I almost knocked you over. What are you doing here?'

'Hi Gina, I'm here for the same reason you are. For a drink.'

Gina turned to her friend, 'Jenny, this is an old friend, Ethan.'

Jenny nodded to me then said, 'I have to get going. See you on the weekend.'

'Sure,' said Gina who watched her friend trot off.

'She's in a hurry,' I said. 'Do you need to catch her up?'

'No, she has to meet somebody else. I was heading home.'

'Can I buy you a drink?' I asked.

'Why not? I know a quieter bar.'

We walked to another place where the atmosphere wasn't as hectic. It was a wine bar, a small place. I had no idea this establishment existed, and I felt certain I wouldn't be able to find it again, following Gina through a maze of back streets. Gina ordered a glass of chardonnay; I chose Scotch on ice.

Soft music wafted from loudspeakers which weren't very loud.

'I like this song,' said Gina.

'You like jazz?'

'Yes. You?'

'I do.'

We chatted about favourite artists. Al Jarreau, Van Morrison, Diana Krall and even Gary Barlow who was a pop artist but did some jazz too.

Then Gina talked about some wonderful Afro-American artists, which made me think about something else.

'Tell me, Gina, why do you always wear black? No offence but I'm sure you'd look good in other colours, too.'

'None taken. It's a long story.'

'I'm not going anywhere,' I said, relaxing in the comfortable chair I'd chosen.

Gina peered at me to check I was serious about hearing her story. Then over her next four glasses of white wine and my four Scotches she told me of her childhood in Northern England. She came from a poor family in Durham. It was always cold and dark, as she recalled it. Her mother neglected her because she was one of six children, the youngest. She never owned her own clothes, wore hand-me-downs from one of her three sisters. The boys were always on the streets, brawling with each other or fighting other kids when they joined local gangs.

Gina kept to herself most of the time. Her father forced her to do chores as her mother was often too drunk to be of any use. Her sisters were often out and about, too, when they didn't attend school.

Then one day almost the entire family piled into a van the father used for work. He'd brought the vehicle home one weekend, borrowed it to go to a fair in Scotland. The Highland Field and Sports Fair. All except Gina were loaded into the big black van. Gina was told to clean the place up while they were out. She was given no explanation why she wasn't to join the others.

On the way to the fair, on a wet, slippery road, the van crashed, smashing into a lorry head on. The collision was reported on the news as being one of the worst road accidents in County Durham's history. Gina's entire family perished. From that moment on, Gina only dressed in black, to grieve but also to mark her independence when she joined a group of Goths. She was fifteen years old. After a year, unable to get a job, she travelled to London. She got a job in a department store and went to school at night. Although she was no longer involved with Goths, she maintained the look. Dressed in black, the look became her signature, to emphasise her individuality.

I stir at the memory. Finally, we rub sleep from our eyes, as I too had fallen asleep again, and together we rise. We kiss then hit the shower together and luxuriate under the cool water. It's a hot day and I wonder what it holds for us. I'm not going to worry about planning; I'll take the day as it unfolds. The holiday goes all too quickly and soon we fly back to Sydney.

Walking through Sydney airport, we hold hands. I'm feel, for the first time in years, positive about the future. Gina, too, is smiling. She told me, on the flight from French Polynesia, that she was pleased to be out of the UK, a place which held so many bad memories for her.

As we taxi to our home, I ask Gina what she wants to do when we've settled back into our routines.

'I have an interview with Hilton hotels tomorrow.'

'Good, I'll need to catch up with Heidi in London first, then I'll check with Alistair on this quarter's sales figures.'

'I'm surprised you were able to relax in Tahiti without calling in to the company,' says Gina.

'Me too. I guess you made me think of us more than the business.'

At home, we unpack and get some rest before getting ready for the evening. We take a shower together and I still find it hard to observe how white Gina is, naked. Particularly after seeing her constantly in black clothing in England.

Towelled dry, I choose casual gear. I wear blue jeans and a black T-shirt. Gina slips into a sunflower dress. She doesn't wear black much anymore. I guess that phase of her life has ended.

Author's Bio

PETER STANKOVIC STARTED his career as a chartered accountant and over the years became an independent finance professional. Writing was something he did occasionally until he retired from his finance career. In 2012, he took up full-time writing and to date has had 9 books published. He lives in Sydney, Australia.

Acknowledgements

I WOULD LIKE TO thank the team from The Writers' Circle who provided useful feedback on parts which were read out to them. I would also like to thank Andrew Akratos for his guidance, personally, and through his instructive meetups.